Dark Muse

by David Simms

Edgar "Muddy" Brooks dug his fingers into the dirt and weeds to keep himself from shouting to his brother, Zack, who stood dead center in the crossroads, illuminated by moonbeams piercing the clouds on a starless night. The teen was caught up in a frenzy, entranced by the music he was playing. The eighteen-year-old stood his ground, tall and lean, muscles taut beneath his Led Zeppelin T-shirt, a stark contrast to Muddy, who was four years younger, five inches shorter, and rail thin.

Beneath his brother's caressing fingers, the Les Paul guitar screamed and howled. He played notes that whined, cried, and pleaded for resolution. Yet his brother kept pushing.

As Zack lost himself in his music, thunder boomed, and lightning illuminated the smile on his face. The sky colored the evening a violet hue, roiling in waves of deep clouds. No rain followed, but the air pressed down on them like a soaked woolen blanket. Each shaky breath Muddy took felt as if both lungs filled with thick water. Something sinister added to the weight of the air. He ached to shake his brother free from the music's hold but found himself fixed to the ground.

The earth beneath the teen trembled with the next smash of thunder.

A crescendo ended in a smash of thunder. An explosion of light began another flurry of notes and screaming bends. Zack fed off the storm, and maybe, just maybe, the storm was feeding off him.

Zack's[face broke into an even bigger expression of joy, yet tears streamed down his cheeks. The crossroads shimmered in the moonlight under his sneakers. Still, he played like his life depended on it.

Like the music was his life.

Acknowledgements

This book would not have been possible without the inspiration of my students, the many who have graced my life over the years. They have shown me what true magic is by overcoming odds which would cause many others to quit. The band in Dark Muse is based on many of those who have taught me about treasuring what I have instead of lamenting what I lack.

Thanks to all the bands that have fired up my muse. Without them, my guitar would have turned to dust in the closet. The magic from Led Zeppelin, Def Leppard, Queen, Aerosmith, Triumph, Ozzy, Queensryche, Metallica, and so many others opened the doors for the blues and classical music in my life and will ring forever in my ears.

For my parents, who have always kept my muse burning.

Chapter One

Edgar "Muddy" Brooks lay flush to the edge of the hill overlooking the train tracks, the wasteland of garbage, and the two narrow roads that met right in the middle of it all—the crossroads that existed long before the town of Carter Hills, New Jersey.

He dug his fingers into the dirt and weeds to keep himself from shouting to his brother, Zack, who stood dead center in the crossroads, illuminated by moonbeams piercing the clouds on a starless night. The teen was caught up in a frenzy, entranced by the music he was playing. The eighteen-year-old stood his ground, tall and lean, muscles taut beneath his Led Zeppelin T-shirt, a stark contrast to Muddy, who was four years younger, five inches shorter, and rail thin.

Beneath his brother's caressing fingers, the Les Paul guitar screamed and howled. He played notes that whined, cried, and pleaded for resolution. Yet his brother kept pushing.

And pushing.

What was he doing? Muddy opened his mouth to scream for Zack to stop, but couldn't make a sound.

As Zack lost himself in his music, thunder boomed, and lightning illuminated the smile on his face. The sky colored the evening a violet hue, roiling in waves of deep clouds. No rain followed, but the air pressed down on them like a soaked woolen blanket. Each shaky breath Muddy took felt as if both lungs filled with thick water. Something sinister added to the weight of the air. He ached to shake his brother free from the music's hold but found himself fixed to the ground.

The earth beneath the teen trembled with the next smash of thunder.

Down below, Zack kept playing, fingers dancing in mad passion along the frets, completely oblivious to what was happening around him. He was fading into the night, dissolving into the darkest song Muddy had ever heard.

Muddy didn't want to be there. He wanted to be home in bed, tucked in nice and warm, but earlier that night, he'd followed his brother out of their house, guitar in hand. By the time he'd reached the top of the hill and spied Zack below at the desolate crossroads, he was doused in sweat. The older boy simply started playing his prized guitar, dropping the case into the brush. He carried with him a tiny, portable amplifier powered by batteries. Leaning down, his fingers jacked the volume up to ten; the amp sounded much louder on this crazy night.

In the shattered moonlight, Muddy saw dark streaks of blood from the slices in his brother's fingers. They ran the tightropes of the strings down to the pickups where his right hand strummed and plucked and twisted out violent cries of emotion. The teen had thick calloused fingers so to break open the flesh had to bring some terrific effort.

A crescendo ended in a smash of thunder. An explosion of light began another flurry of notes and screaming bends. Zack fed off the storm, and maybe, just maybe, the storm was feeding off him.

With a tremor, the ground shook so much Muddy nearly slipped over the edge, tumbling down the hill. Muddy's fear of this bad section of town gave way to another, more pressing fear.

Zack's face broke into an even bigger expression of joy, yet tears streamed down his cheeks. The crossroads shimmered in the moonlight under his sneakers. Still, he played like his life depended on it. Like the music *was* his life.

Just before *it* happened, Muddy sensed a feeling of foreboding, like something bad was about to break through. Not from the ground. Not from the sky either. From somewhere else, somewhere he doubted either of them had ever imagined.

Finally, the night opened, like the thick velvet curtains hung in the vintage movie theater in town. It sucked Zack's music into whatever lay behind it. The air shimmered around him, nearly turning him invisible to his brother.

Muddy managed to stand on wobbly legs and was about to run down the hill to stop his brother, save him, but something obstructed Muddy before he could start, and he fell to the ground.

The curtains wrapped completely around his brother in an otherworldly embrace, taking the older boy and his music away.

When the moonlight returned moments later, the cross-roads stood deserted.

Chapter Two

School dragged by on Monday as though time insisted on becoming Muddy's newest enemy. From the moment he stepped through the yawning jaws of the building, minutes turned to molasses through an hourglass. He knew he wouldn't get a chance during the day to speak to his band "The Accidentals" about his brother's strange disappearance. The story would have to hold until practice. His anxiety boiled, his arms clenched tight to his sides as he walked the hallways. Of all the days that he needed things to glide by as his freaked-out mind scrambled to think, the elements of fate threw him a curveball whenever he turned around. Right as he headed to lunch, they smacked him right in the forehead with a doozy.

"Hey, loser!"

Great. The town's biggest tool is talking to me.

The moment froze as he turned to face the six-foot-two, ghost-like bully and his buddies. Muddy didn't take drugs and this guy knew it, but ever since their mother died, Zack sometimes wavered. His brother read that the stuff helped musicians "connect," just as Jimi Hendrix did, as some of the other greats supposedly did. Muddy knew that Zack ached for a realm most musicians only dreamt of, the feeling when melody, instrument and soul became one, when the barrier broke between worlds, dimensions and anything else life threw in your way. All musicians shot for it. Muddy had been close to the "zone" several times, but had only danced on its edges, had never plunged into its all-encompassing embrace.

But then he wasn't his brother. He wasn't the rock god in waiting.

"Yo," the slime said, this time even less friendly, if that was possible.

Ice frosted Muddy's spine as he turned to face the older boy. His fingertips tingled. Vince looked like an evil imp with sharp cheekbones and a pointy chin.

In Carter Hills, Emmett Middle and Morse High connected through a long, dingy hallway that students traversed for electives and special events.

"Yeah?" Muddy's voice shook the word into three syllables.

The bully's smile broke wide open. At the same time, he nudged his buddies, the guys who sold the drugs in school, so nothing could be traced back to him. Vince was a senior, probably headed to a good college the following year due to his dad being on the school board, but still a terror to anyone he disliked. He had the makings of a lawyer, Muddy often thought. Or a politician.

"Where's your brother?" Vince asked.

I wish I knew.

"No idea, Vince. He didn't come home last night."

"You do know he has business with me, right?"

Muddy didn't and wished he could punch his brother right then and there.

"He blew me off last night," Vince said.

If you only knew.

Vince tried to angle him into the locker but the bell for first period rang, saving his butt for another period or two.

"Tell him to watch out if he tries that again." The punch to the shoulder didn't hurt but rattled Muddy.

Sure thing, he thought. *If I ever find him.*

"Yo, man," Otis called, twirling a drumstick in one hand and folding a slice of pizza in the other. "You look like you spent a week in Metallica's bass drum." Muddy's best friend stood a good five-foot even but carried himself like someone twice that height.

One by one, the band members filed into the music room to eat their lunch together, the one place where they felt completely at home outside of the stage. They'd be in high school next year, formally, but it felt like eons away to Muddy. Middle school seemed like a chapter he hadn't visited in forever. The music program often combined students, giving even the outcasts a haven regardless of grade level. Music bonded people and stripped most of labels there.

He prayed that Bentley Chittum didn't appear. The stuck-up jerk lived in the only wealthy section of town and liked to remind everyone of it. Now officially a sophomore, he felt empowered to bully anyone who was poorer than him. The jerk's band also won the Battle of the Bands. Every single year. Thankfully, the boy wasn't present.

"Yeah," Corey said. "Did you fall into someone's locker again?" The complete opposite of Otis, this guy, originally from the poor side of town, towered over all of them at over six-two and wasn't anything like the brittle drummer.

"Funny." They had no idea what heck Muddy had stumbled into last night. Running on two or three hours of sleep, the nightmare continued to pull him deeper. "Where's Poe?"

"We thought she might be with you," Otis, the diminutive drummer said, smiling.

"Why the heck would she be with me?" Muddy snapped, now worried.

Everyone in the band knew about his silent crush on Polly, but he hoped she didn't—yet.

He shook his head. No. What mattered now was what happened last night.

"Sorry, man."

He plopped down into one of the padded chairs, already depressed. "We gotta talk, guys."

"You're breaking up with us?" Otis was always the first one to joke, alluding to his condition, which could turn deadly any day.

The others cut the tension with laughter, despite the ticked-off expression carved into Muddy's face. As they continued, the door edged open, allowing a tall, slender female with raven-colored, mid-length hair to enter. She never let on if she had an inkling of suspicion that Muddy thought anything of her. He didn't even know what he felt. With a name like Polly, she preferred the more goth-sounding "Poe." Obviously, "Edgar" and "Poe" would've sounded a little too cute—or not. Plus, there was the fact that *she* thought he wanted to date Chelsea, the ditzy cheerleader who once called him "Special Ed."

"Dude, what's wrong?" Otis asked, tossing a stick into the air, catching it with a skeletal hand. "You look like you've seen a ghost."

Muddy's lips moved, but a phantom force held the sounds within his throat. If they only knew how true it was—and that was only *half* of it!

"Are you okay?" Poe moved closer to him, close enough to tell that she could see his silhouette and not just a shape through severely damaged eyes. She wasn't totally blind, but in the legal sense, she qualified, and never let on that it bothered her. "Was it your mom again?" For a moment, he allowed himself to stare. He didn't like to since she wasn't aware, yet she always was. Her pale blue eyes appeared to gaze through people, to a place where maybe she would be happy. They shone bright but much older than her thirteen years should allow. However, when she smiled, as she usually did when singing, every fiber of her being lit up like a million candles at midnight through them. Smarter than most, she skipped a grade in elementary school, simply because she was a badass. She sat in the chair next to him, showing more grace than someone without sight should have, but this was just one more reason she rocked most people's worlds.

"Zack's gone," Muddy blurted, arms hung low and numbing at his seat. "I mean, really gone. *Gone.*"

They hit him with a barrage of questions, but the storm in his belly stopped Muddy from saying a word. Even just looking at his burger nearly caused him to vomit all over his friends. He ached to empty his guts, spilling the horrors he'd lived the previous night. Yet as much as they pried, and he tried, the words just wouldn't materialize.

Muddy waited, but knew the darkness he sensed was coming would greet them all too soon.

The four met again later in the music room for practice. The side rehearsal spot was smaller than most, but the school didn't have the funds for more. Painted plywood walls covered in band posters surrounded them. Amps, mic stands, and other equipment forced them into close quarters. Otis, the diminutive drummer, sauntered in, sticks-a-spinning, followed closely by a heaving Corey, hands full of skinny wooden reeds. "Am I last, again?" They often wondered how he fit comfortably, anywhere.

"As always," Poe cracked. The ham loved to entertain a full audience whenever possible.

Muddy felt the spotlight shine mercilessly on him, something he hated.

This time, he told them everything, from the suspicions that grew when his brother first began skipping rehearsals with his own band and locking himself in his darkened room, to the crackle and spit of the lightning at the crossroads.

Muddy's flesh turned to goose bumps as he recalled the music Zack played, the song that would haunt him 'til he felt his last breath decrescendo into oblivion.

Otis shook. "Man, that blows. But what the heck are the crossroads? I haven't heard that word since that Britney Spears movie bombed."

"Hey, cut the crap," Poe said. "No jokes. Not now."

"No, seriously," Otis replied, "this is stranger than that bubblegum moron's success story." He held his head in his hands as his eyes never fully closed.

Sometimes they forgot his fragilities, the vulnerable kid that hid behind his cool persona, a porcelain egg existing beneath a thin veneer of steel. His own story made Muddy's problems seem trivial.

"Isn't that a show on VH1?" Corey asked, sounding serious. "They have that country-rock thing happening there? I saw Taylor Swift and Def Leppard on there once."

Muddy felt his blood begin to pump liquid heat through his body, throbbing like an untuned bass drum. He couldn't unscramble his thoughts with everyone yapping like that.

"Just shut up!"

They did, shocked into silence. He *never* yelled, even during rehearsal, or when Poe's dad did…what he sometimes did. Muddy preferred to simmer, a seething kettle on the edge, but never blowing his lid.

He managed to get through describing last night and when he was done, they all just sat there in awe, staring. Whether it was due to his explosion, or the wild story, he didn't know, nor did he care. When he finished, he sat atop the bass amp, shaking.

Poe broke the silence first. "So, let's go find Zack and bring him back."

"From where?" Muddy's voice cracked with pain. "Where did he go? Where do we look? Who do we talk to? This is crazy; this is *all* we need at school."

Poe still had her hand on his arm. "Let's ask Satch," she said, referring to their music teacher by his nickname. "Satch has been all over the country. He's even been in that weird rock band, Turkey Legs, or something. He knows tons of weird stuff with music. I'd bet my left eye he's heard of the crossroads. And I'll bet the other one that he can help," she said with a wink.

"So, what do you want to do, Muddy?" Poe rarely used his nickname, the name Edgar preferred, instead of sticking with his given name. It meant she cared about his plight.

The sound of her voice brushed away the fog in his mind for a moment. He turned to her, formed the only thought he could think of and cleared his throat.

"We find Zack." It sounded simple falling from his lips.

But nothing was ever that easy.

Chapter Three

As the band sat in Mr. Satriani's music class, waiting for the bell to end the day, Muddy imagined what the others thought. He knew that at least one of them figured he was nuttier than a squirrel's butt in October. Hopefully, Poe wasn't the one.

Otis nudged him with his foot. "Are you sure he'll listen to us?" Whispering didn't happen in the band room, so neither teen cared about their voices carrying.

"Zack was his prize student," Muddy replied. *I hope that's enough.*

Mr. Satriani helped them survive the higher-level classes so far by giving the band a place to hang out, a place to escape the crap from the Bentleys and Vinces and ignorant teachers who thought the group stood a step below them on Darwin's ladder. During orientation, he let on that their middle school music teacher gave him the heads-up They loved Ms. Jett, the leather-loving trumpet player who had a thing for metal.

The group hadn't fit in well anywhere else, always labeled the "different" kids, the "special" ones, but in the music room, they were treated like family. Disabilities didn't matter there – only the songs did.

They waited, as patiently as possible, toes tapping and fingers drumming, until the rest of the class left the acoustically perfect room. It was a haven for anyone who loved music, either to perform, or to simply listen and enjoy peace from the chaos outside its door.

The bushy-haired man bustling behind the mass of piano, lyres, music stands, and at least three trees worth of sheet music was a true genius of disorganization. The music director of their high school, Mr. Satriani was always working on some symphony that never saw the light of day, and never ceased to be working on some creative endeavor. Sometimes that endeavor meant their little band, with whom he spent countless hours honing their skills and in the chaotic, cacophonic concoction that was Poe, Corey, Otis, an occasional bassist and him.

"Hey," Mr. Satriani crooned, dropping a few sheets of scribbled staves. "It's the next big illegal download superstars! How are "The Accidentals" doing? Need help with a new song?"

Muddy's mouth opened to speak, but only stale air burst from his lips.

Poe stepped up to the plate to save his butt, as always. "Nope, no new song. We need something a little more important." Her voice, always pitch perfect with harmonics flowing, could convince a deaf man to help.

"Well, I guess big brother's helping plenty on the musical end now. No need for this old guy to bring you to celebrity status. I was jamming with my friends Giddy and Jimmy last night. I think we might have something. Maybe? Maybe Zack's rubbed some of his wild mojo on you, gave you a smidge of his skills. Maybe—"

"Maybe he's friggin' missing!" Otis said. Okay, the silence was officially broken.

If the man heard correctly, he didn't show it. He didn't move a muscle, nor did his face register the slightest emotion.

"Satch," Poe yelled, calling Mr. Satriani by the nickname they'd given him. "Did you hear Muddy?"

Mr. Satriani simply picked up the papers and went about rearranging them on the piano. "I heard. Did you check the police station? Vince's shack? How about Iron?"

Muddy felt himself tense. Zack wasn't bad. He just wasn't handling things well.

"We checked everywhere," Poe said, saving Otis from a suspension. The boy was prone to outbursts that were Crayola colorful.

Mr. Satriani wrinkled his face. "He wouldn't..."

Muddy nodded. "I saw what happened."

The man knotted his brows, sat down on the stool and reached for an instrument that wasn't there.

"Well, Mr. Brooks. What *did* you see? Where did you *see* Zack go?" Sometimes Mr. Satriani suffered from verbal diarrhea. Many a time, someone in the band wanted to shove Imodium down his throat.

"I don't know," Muddy answered, feeling the choke of the first tear. "I have no idea."

After listening to the watered-down version of the previous night's events, minus the disappearing act behind the invisible curtain, their teacher and mentor, whom they counted on for guidance in most of life's endeavors, sat on the piano bench, dumbfounded.

"What do you think, Satch?" Poe asked Mr. Satriani. "There's gotta be a plausible reason for what happened, right?"

"I just don't know, honestly." Mr. Satriani looked sad, as though he understood, until they asked the key question.

"Just what *are* the crossroads? Last night I Googled it and found some legend about musicians selling their souls at a crossroads in Memphis."

No answer.

"Right?" Muddy tried to keep his voice from breaking.

He looked past Mr. Satriani, into the field beyond the windows.

They would've believed him if eye contact had been made, as Mr. Satriani was one of the few people who treated them as equals. He never even once mentioned the words "special ed learning disabled" or worse. But this time, he spoke *through* them, as if his cat sat before him begging for a treat. "So you don't know the stories?" Muddy knew he'd lost his teacher's attention, but for Zack, he persisted.

"No, I don't. I'm sorry." Mr. Satriani shoved some papers into his bag and grabbed his keys. He stared at everything but them. "I have to leave now. See you tomorrow."

"Lying mother…" Otis muttered. "Son of a friggin' traitor."

But the man simply ignored the accusation and moved for the door.

Poe shot out her arm and grabbed the teacher. "Satch, you *do* know about the crossroads. Look at me and lie to my face. Please."

Even though she was the only female in the group, Poe had the biggest pair of stones on her and often "out-manned" the rest in many situations. Muddy figured that when someone had survived her kind of life, one either learned to ride the monster waves or drown in the undertow.

The teacher gently pulled away, as if he had leprosy and didn't want to infect her.

"Please." Her pale, silvery eyes pleaded with him.

He walked to the door. "I'm sorry," he said as he walked out, his voice full of something other than bull. Was it fear or sympathy? "You're on your own this time." Then he was gone.

But that night, an email arrived from Satch. Three words in the subject line said it all.

I can help.

Chapter Four

Poe arrived first in the basement rehearsal room Muddy's dad had built for them between writing novels last year. She always arrived first, as she couldn't escape her father quickly enough. By the look on her face, the night had taken a negative turn. The clouds swimming in her beautiful gray eyes could never hide the truth from Muddy, no matter how much she tried.

"Bad night?" he asked, even though they both knew it was just small talk.

She clenched her eyes shut, as if those near-sightless orbs could blink out the awful life she endured day to day. "Corey walked me over, but had to run back for his special reeds."

A smile crept from her lips, and from Muddy's as well, over how the lanky kid who used to live in the dangerous neighborhood called Iron worried about how his lips hurt if he used the wrong gauge for his sax reeds. He felt even more protective of her than Muddy did. She needed little of it once she left her house, but it made them feel better to know they were watching out for her.

"I'm okay," she said, plopping her tall, svelte, but still awkward self on the worn sofa. The room had little furnishings other than a few bean bags and a trio of stools. "No different than yesterday." For someone who was visually impaired, she had seen way too much for her age.

The man drank too much and took it out on her and her mother. After her mom disappeared with someone Poe never knew, hell just became nonstop. Now it was just her to endure it all. Neither of them had a mother around anymore, another bond which bound them. Except that hers hadn't died. Poe's mother had abandoned the family instead of divorcing such a violent man. The band figured the police would believe a fellow officer, but Muddy couldn't comprehend how a parent could just leave a child. How one could abuse his own daughter baffled him even more. Calls to CPS never work. They never even bothered to send case workers anymore to even pretend to care.

"He didn't—"

"No," she replied, cutting Muddy off. "Otis is here." She could always hear someone way before anyone else could. They assumed her other senses took up the slack for her eyes.

If the man touched her again, he might just snap and go over there. What Muddy would do once he got there was beyond him, but his anger burned every time he thought of the man taking out his life's shortcomings on his daughter. If only he were more like Zack.

He almost voiced his intentions when Otis and Corey entered and sat in front of them. Once the door closed, the room became nearly soundproof. They knew her story, but never asked. Still, they'd back up Muddy with anything he chose to do.

Muddy forwarded the email to the other guys. None of them had thought Mr. Satriani would be able to help them find Zack. But now he sent them the equivalent of a map for buried treasure—of a sort.

Muddy,

I can't find your brother, nor do I know where he really is, but if there IS an answer, I know who has it. Go to the address below and be as open as your music. Don't go at night, please, but go soon.

Be careful. If this guy is real, if what I hear is true that he can do, you could be in more danger than you could ever dream of—but don't go alone. There's power in your group.

I wish I had some to give you.

Satch

"Well what are we gonna do?" the drummer asked. "Just sit here picking our thumb?"

Otis never pulled punches when he spoke. One of his

handicaps that landed him in the special ed classes at school was that his eyelids never closed fully, even when he slept. The kid always looked stoned and was a saline junkie. But never shutting his mouth?

Muddy's fist tightened on his phone as he tried to Google map the address his teacher had given them. According to three different websites, Sixty-One Mustang Drive simply didn't exist.

"Maybe you're spelling it wrong."

Wrong thing to say to a dyslexic kid, Muddy thought.

Muddy nearly broke the Android, but held back. This one and only clue had to be the answer.

"It's gotta be there," Poe said. "Satch wouldn't jerk us around. He actually cares."

Muddy sighed, relaxing his grip. He got up and paced the room. Part of him wished to bang out some metal on his guitar. The other half wanted to smash it. His gift from his mom. He treated it like gold. "I know. He's one of the few who does, at least for who we really are."

Corey finally said what they'd all thought but avoided, until now. "Do you know where Mustang Drive is? I do, kind of. It's smack dead in the black heart of Iron. Talk about scary."

"It's like Iraq, ghetto-style," Otis said.

"More like, Detroit, Baltimore, the Shore, and East L.A.—all rolled up into one—on acid," Poe added.

"The Shore?" Otis almost choked on his Coke. "There's mostly white trash and preppies there showing off their gym bods and spray tans."

"Exactly."

"Oh..."

"My old friends would kick my butt if they saw me on those streets," Corey said, shivering just a bit.

"So," Poe said, clasping her hands as she stood. "When do we go?"

"Tonight." Muddy had to show the strength his brother would need.

"Whoa," Corey said. "Love the hero mentality, but don't like the stupid part. We wait until morning."

Muddy stared at each of them, anger seething through his

eyes at first, but then he relaxed. He hated being wrong, but his friend knew better. Emotions ruled him right then.

Poe leaned in and touched his arm. "Six too early for you?"

They all took a collective breath. It would be early enough for sunlight, at least an hour and a half before sundown, but still hitting the danger zone.

Corey sighed and pocketed his reeds. "I really wanted to practice tonight."

Muddy shrugged, accepting the obvious. They would leave immediately. Zack's life could depend on it.

How does one prepare to travel into the worst part of town, somewhere that even the police tried to avoid?

Each house the band passed blinked at them, eyes hidden by the dark, but curious about the strangers who tread on their territory. The flickers of light in the windows scared the teens more than anything, mostly because the houses sat in eerie silence. Rows of streets dimmed as they traveled from their neighborhood to this one. Real families lived here. Real lives, just like theirs. Bad people too, but here, weapons and a gang or two. Monsters came in many forms. The band had faced them in school and at home. This was just one more type.

Muddy hoped that no one cared about the intrusion.

But of course, they did.

The band slunk down Terminal Avenue, walking cautiously along the street. To stay on the broken concrete of the sidewalks meant walking too close to the shadows that hid between the shops, both open and shut down, the jagged hedges of clapboard houses and crowded apartment buildings.

Up ahead, a group of gang bangers, maybe eight or nine, suddenly came out of nowhere and blocked the intersection. Forming a line under the shadowy glare of the streetlights, they appeared larger and more menacing than Muddy had ever faced down before.

Bullets of ice formed on his neck and spine. His anxiety finally had a reason for existing.

"Oh, crap." Otis practically hugged Corey. "We're dead."

Muddy wondered how many packed weapons. He never

knew a dealer in town who didn't carry at least a blade. Or worse.

One of them strode toward the band, hands deep in his pockets. When the light struck his face, Muddy's mind didn't know what to register, fear or relief.

"Brooks, that you?" Vinnie closed the gap between them. Muddy thought, *This could be really bad or really good.*

He tried to look into Vinnie's eyes, but the broken beams of light from the cracked streetlights above split the boy's face into weird prisms—some smiling, some touched with evil, some inhuman.

"What are *you* doing out here, little man? You have a death wish?" His posse laughed, mostly at the band.

"Is your deadbeat brother out here, too?" His gray eyes scoped the ragtag look of the band. "As much as I like the guy, he still owes me cash."

"We're looking for Zack and don't need any crap tonight." Otis never held back.

The dealer's eyes widened. "Oh, really," he said, crossing his arms instead of whipping out a knife. "And you think you'll find Zack here?" Muddy hoped that the bigger boy had a shred of compassion in his drug-addled veins and wouldn't snap Otis like a dried wishbone. "Because if he were here, I'd know about it."

Muddy took the break in the tension for a shot. "So you don't know where he is?"

"Nope again, little Brooks. Wish I did, seeing as we have some business to discuss, but he's a cool guy. I look out for him when I can, but he's changed—a lot. I'd go back home if I were you. Things get nasty around here when it gets dark."

Poe looked at him, then at Corey and Otis. "We need to find someone first." Her hand shook, holding the phone with the illuminated map containing the address Mr. Satriani had indicated they needed to find.

Vinnie's skinny, calloused hand reached out. "Lemme see that," he said, snatching it from her open hand. His beady eyes widened "I'll give it back. This is crap anyway."

He straightened up, returning to his tough image. "Your

funeral." He turned to walk away, a business deal likely in the vicinity.

"But, Brooks," he said, a little softer, "watch your step. Death walks around here and even scares away the shadows."

Within seconds, the band stood alone again. Furtive eyes played behind dusty windows.

Corey spoke up for the first time. "Guys? You still up for this?" They knew he was petrified.

"I can't see a problem," Poe quipped.

Otis and Muddy snickered softly, nerves jangling. The most vulnerable member of the band resorted to joking when they were walking through fire, possibly heading straight to the dragon. But how could they turn away now? The night grew darker and soon, the dangers that emerged in the moonlight would be creeping into their world.

Chapter Five

Mustang Drive did exist. Never mind that it was in an area where no one in their right mind would live willingly. Only a few of the buildings on the street remained intact. The rest had withered away into bad memories and dust. None could be called homes. How could *anyone* live there and call it home? Muddy felt terrible for judging but why didn't the town do something to help those people?

Corey pointed towards where their eyes already focused.

A ramshackle red house stood at the far end of the street, almost leaning, as if held up by wood and stones that had lost all will to possess any strength centuries ago. Two windows gazed out like bloodshot eyes, filthy and draped in shadow. Around the mouth, a decrepit porch yawned in a wood-warped smile that suggested it knew something they shouldn't. On the right side of the black door, a brass "61," tarnished and chipped, tangled on a rusty nail. A light within flickered, like a candle in a rotted jack-o-lantern.

"Ready, guys?" He shook as if a ghost blew a chilled breath across the back of his neck.

Poe held Muddy's hand in a vise-like grip. He knew she would need some help to walk through the landmines of junk littering the front yard, hidden beneath foot-tall weeds. Nobody would accuse her of flirting with him, not in this situation.

"Sure, let's kick it."

"I'm in," Corey said.

Muddy turned to Otis, who suddenly lost his jokes.

"What?" Otis said, his voice a little higher than usual. "I'm thinking. Okay, I'm in too. No way am I gonna wait outside this place while you guys play detective."

The quartet walked up the stairs, testing them one at a time. One by one, the planks groaned and cracked. They likely hadn't been stepped on for years. Muddy silently prayed that none of them would crash through a step and wind up captive in a dungeon filled with torture devices.

The wood held firmly. At the top, Poe reached forward to knock on the door before any of them could stop her. The moment her knuckles touched the black paint, something inside the house exploded in a frenzy of barks and howls. She yanked her hand back and screamed. By the looks on the faces of the others, Muddy guessed they'd nearly wet their pants. He knew he almost did.

"Who's there?" a deep voice bellowed from within, drowning out the animal.

The barking, from whatever beast lurked inside, added to the question.

"Holy crap!" Otis yelled. "Who's in there, Cujo?"

Corey stepped up to the front of the pack. His fingers found a cracked doorbell hiding in a mass of spider webs and splintered, flaking red wood. "Don't be a wuss, little man. You don't have a backbone here, you're dead."

Corey, a lanky tough kid who had spent most of his childhood ducking bullets in the projects, knew more about backbones than all of them combined. They'd all had their challenges, but their enemies came from within, from genetic demons. Muddy was dyslexic and motherless. Poe, well, Poe was legally blind and her father—Muddy clenched his hands so hard thinking about it his nails cut into his palms. And Otis, he was the worst of them with his brittle bones, tiny body, frizzy, colorless hair and a life expectancy that had expired five years ago. No wonder he was always so mad at the world. Corey had secrets he had yet to tell them.

Put all those things together and "The Accidentals" were quite a bunch. But they had friendship and music and that made most things feel okay. It was special in a good way when it came to their talent. When they played, no one made fun of them.

The doorbell rang. The beast inside the house barked louder and threw itself toward the door, the wood booming.

"What is that?" Poe whispered, her hand shaking in Muddy's. "What kinda dog is…"

Another slam.

Whatever it was, it threw all its weight against the brittle door again, this time sending a blizzard of paint chips and dust into everyone's hair and eyes. Muddy swore the wood buckled at least a couple of inches during the attack.

"My eyes!" Otis shrieked. His voice rose an octave. The rest of the band rubbed the flakes out with hands and tears, but tears were a luxury Otis didn't have. He shook his head and his white afro threw more dust into his face. There was no way they could get him home or to the ER if he started to bleed.

"Where's your saline?" Muddy asked, checking his pockets.

He shivered. "I…don't know." His hand danced around his face, not wanting to make anything worse, but writhing in agony.

Before Muddy realized what had happened, Corey had knocked him aside and leaned into Otis. In his hand, a small bottle shone in the red light. "Relax, lean back a little bit, and *shut up!*"

Corey, the gentle giant.

As the drummer complied, Corey squirted a stream of solution into both of his eyes, washing away the debris. Several blinks later, all was calm again. Except for the strangled dog cry. Muddy imagined it a beast gnawing on someone's femur.

"You okay, big guy?" Corey asked.

"Yeah. Thanks."

"I hate being ignored," Poe said as she pounded on the door. "Anyone alive in there? We need to talk to you! Mr. Satriani sent us!" she yelled over the animal's braying. "Can we talk, or what?" Her fist drummed against the wood. "Our friend went missing—at the crossroads."

"Shut the hell up, you ugly beast!" came the reply. Muddy thought the angry man was insulting Poe, but then realized the man was referring to his dog. It was a good thing, because Poe could be a real viper when she got mad.

They all feared her temper. Sweet as honey on the outside, but cross her, and even a rattlesnake would curl up and roll away. Muddy couldn't blame her though, not with the life she had.

"Excuse *him*?" she said.

Otis, fully recovered now, half-smiled. "I do think he means his dog."

A tense silence hung in the air for a few seconds, then stumbling noises sounded within the house.

"What the heck do you want? If you gang-banging little turds spray paint my house, I'll shoot a hole in your crack so big, you'll never have to sit down to move your bowels again!"

"Sounds convenient to him," Otis quipped.

Poe tapped the back of his head. "If you don't shut your mouth, I'll let that dog use you like a chew toy. Got it?"

From the look on his face, Otis got it. The rest sure did. None of them wanted to laugh.

Poe leaned toward the door. "Satriani told us to come here, and we're not leaving until you talk to us."

From inside the voice bellowed, "I don't know any Satch. Sounds like a half-wit, retread, no-talent hack to me. And I don't help anyone. Leave before I let Sally have at you."

"Sally?" Otis said. "That monster dog's name is Sally?"

"Hey!" the voice from inside boomed. "What's going on out there? I'm getting my gun now."

"Wait," Muddy's voice trembled. "We just need your help. Just a few minutes of your time. Please. We're not from here, we're a little—"

"I already told you, I don't know any Satch. Go away!"

"We never said 'Satch,'" Muddy called. "His name's Satriani. *You* called him Satch."

Poe squeezed his arm. "Good one, Edgar. Nailed the mean old creep."

All was quiet for a minute. Even the dog didn't budge.

"Please, we need help. We've heard that you know all about our problem."

"What problem? What are you talking about, boy?" This time, the voice sounded normal, without murderous overtones.

Muddy swallowed hard and steadied his voice.

"*The Crossroads*. I need to know all about them and how *they* work."

CLICK! It sounded like someone had cocked a gun. A big gun like in those lame cop shows.

"You sick sons of demons! Get off my porch and don't ever come back."

Otis and Corey began to run, but Poe stuck her ground. So did Muddy, even though he was scared so much his shoulders shook. She held both his hands and gave him strength.

"Sir, I *need* your help. My brother disappeared there last night. I saw *everything*. I *need* to know how to get Zack back. Please..."

The dog howled as objects smashed inside. It sounded like the guy was breaking everything in sight. A minute later, the front door creaked open.

The band stood there, not sure what to do.

"Well, are you going to stand there all day, or come inside? If you want to learn how to kill yourselves, come on in and I'll show you how."

Within the derelict house a shrine to blues music existed—everywhere. Pictures of Jimi Hendrix, B.B. King, Buddy Guy, Ella Fitzgerald, Albert King, all the greats, hung from the walls. The frames made the room seem almost homey, instead of homely. Almost. It smelled like something had died in there, long, long ago. The man who sat in the rocking chair in front of Muddy seemed familiar—very familiar. Then it dawned on him. This old guy was in every picture on the walls with the greats of the blues! Hugging Jimi, jamming with B.B., getting a kiss from Ella; the man knew all of them.

Geez. This guy, living in this broken-down shack, with his ugly dog over in the corner, half-growling, half-drooling, he knows, or knew all these famous people. And now, he lives in the worst part of town? Without a pot to pee in? Muddy's mind reeled.

At first, when they saw the man behind the door, Muddy almost laughed. The older guy looked anything but threatening.

Maybe thirty or forty years ago the man might have scared the group, but not now.

That mongrel that he'd originally thought to be a demon was only an old beagle. Yet when she howled in this old house, her little voice echoed through the walls, transforming the sounds into something deeper and darker.

Corey fed her doggie treats from a bowl on the table, but the dog kept glaring at him. Black eyes locked onto his even as she chewed away.

The black man ambled over to his rocker, motioning with a wrinkled hand for all of them to sit wherever they could find a spot. Piles of old newspapers and old vinyl records filled most of the space, but they managed to shove everything aside just enough to make the mess more chaotic. Poe snagged a ratty couch covered in beagle hair. *It was probably better*, Muddy mused, *that her vision wasn't so sharp.*

The guy looked about seventy, but with a hundred years of wear on the tires. Wearing a moth-eaten wool blazer and sky-blue pants, he looked like he could fit in any senior citizens home. He was a bald Morgan Freeman without all the smiling. When Muddy finally got a good look at his face, he winced.

The old man's eyes were mismatched. The right one was cocoa, but the left was silver. Not icy blue, or one of those colored contacts that Chelsea or the girls at school would probably wear to prom—it was shining silver where the color should be. The teen wondered if the old man could see out of it.

He looked deeper. Yes, those eyes had seen a lot. The hair stood up on his neck as he held the gaze.

"Seen too much," said the old man, jarring Muddy from his stare. "Way too much."

"What?"

"You in charge of this little posse?" Old Silver Eye asked him.

Again, Muddy swallowed. "I guess so. Yes, sir."

The old man chuckled to himself and coughed, then drank a swig of iced tea. "Yes, sir," he repeated and shook his head. "Most kids out this way are disrespectful little runts. They come and spray paint my house, kick my dog, shoot each other, whatever. I should've never come back." His head dropped a bit.

"From where, Memphis? Chicago? That where you're from?"

He shook his head, still dropped. "Nope, not what I meant at all, but you might find out if you're unlucky enough."

"What do you mean? I just want to find my brother. Where did he go?"

"Where do you think? You don't seem like an idiot to me. Are you?"

Poe, once again, jumped into battle for her friend. "Relax there, Mr. Music Man. Just because you know all these famous people," she gestured with her arms, "doesn't mean you can put us down. We're not stupid. We're just…different."

Muddy smiled at the angel of his life, *his* secret angel. Could she really see who was in the photos? No, he guessed, but she figured things out real fast.

"You don't say?" he asked, amused at her reaction. "I can tell. Easily."

The whole gang tensed up. They'd always had to deal with that stuff in school. They didn't need it here too, not with Zack missing. Something, or someone, was going to explode.

Corey stood. "What does *that* mean?"

More laughter erupted from the old guy. "Relax, relax." He waved at him to sit back down. "I didn't mean anything derogatory by it. Look, I just met you. I have no idea what you're about. All I meant were two things."

Muddy felt his muscles untangle a little. "Oh, yeah?" He still wondered where the old man had stashed the gun he'd heard click. "And what're those?"

The man downed the rest of his iced tea then called Sally over to sit by him. "First, some of you are going to be surprised at what the crossroads can do to a person. It ain't natural—at least to this world."

"What do you mean?" Corey asked. "There's no such thing as supernatural…stuff. And what do you mean by *some* of us? Why not *all* of us? Aren't we *different* enough?" Muddy knew his friend had spent his life labeled as different, just like all of them. Nothing got under his skin more.

Poe tried to diffuse the stress. "You said there were two things. What's the second?"

"Hmmm," the man replied. "You guys have no idea what music is *really* all about."

"You old dog!" Otis was never one to mince words.

"Otis!" Poe sounded disgusted. She turned to the man, who still had not introduced himself. "Who do you think you are to tell us what we know about music? Is it because we're not famous like those people you posed with on the wall? Because we're young? Not from the 'ghetto?' What?"

Otis drew back and leaned into Muddy. "Are you sure you like her?"

"Shut up," he whispered, hoping she'd missed Otis' comment.

The old man sat there, shaking his head. "No, ma'am. It ain't any of that. That there was 'Silver Eye Watkins' up there on the walls with those so-called famous musicians. *They* know what it means, what it takes to *be* the music. When ol' Silver Eye brought them over, their talent exploded from little seeds into whole fields of song. Unless you've been *over*, my beautiful little dear, you have *no* idea what music really is, or can do. Got it now?"

Poe's expression changed to something else, as though she'd just smelled Otis after leaving Taco Bell. "Umm… I have no idea what you're saying at all. What do you mean by *over*?"

She turned to the rest of them. They simply shrugged.

"Bottom line," he added. "If you want to find your brother, sit down and tell me what happened so you can go over there and get him back. But unless he's got *it*, he's probably dead by now."

After Muddy finished his story, sweating on the old cushions in the stuffy living room, nervous as all get out, the silence washed over the group like a swampy wave. His fingers drummed the coffee table, thoughts rolling through the possible options.

Would Silver Eye believe me? Would he laugh or think I'm nuts? What was up with that eye?

When the tension swelled in the room, Otis broke the taut line.

"Well? How do we get Zack back? Can you help us or are you just going to stare at Muddy there with that freaky silver eye?"

The old man's head came up, and instead of telling off the little drummer, he gazed around the room. "Who the heck is Muddy?"

Poe leaned toward her friend. "*Edgar* here likes that nickname. It goes well with his last name, Brooks. We're all big fans of the blues and classic rock."

The eruption of laughter from Silver Eye Watkins rattled the group. His eyes teared up and his one foot stomped the floor.

"Muddy Brooks? *Muddy Brooks*? You named that, kinda like Muddy *Waters*? Was 'Dirty Puddles' or 'Cruddy Creek' already taken? Come on, speak up, blues boy."

The boy burned with pure embarrassment. He'd always felt confident with the name, but now this old coot had stripped him of his armor in one fell swoop.

It started with Otis then Corey, and after a few seconds of those two giggling to themselves, even Poe fell apart. Suddenly, everyone cracked up, even Muddy.

"I like the name," Poe said. "I think it fits him."

The older bluesman gazed into Muddy's eyes. "Okay, *Edgar*."

More waves of laughter shook through the group.

"Please," the Muddy begged. Still, the laughter helped calm his anxiety.

"Okay, *boy*. You want that name you call yourself?"

Muddy stared right back at the old man, suddenly serious again. "Definitely."

"Then earn it."

I will, Muddy thought stubbornly to himself. *I will*.

"When do we start looking for Zack? I want to find him before something bad happens."

A deep breath vibrated through the old man. "Oh, but something bad has already happened if he's over there alone."

"Over *where*? Where's *over*?"

The rumbling started up again in the ranks of the group.

"I don't even know where he is. Where *is* he?"

"First," Silver Eye said. "You need to know, it's not a picnic. He went someplace many musicians and artists and writers went before, but not all have returned."

"So?"

"So," he said, staring at him with that one dark eye and one unblinking silver eye, "are you willing to take that risk?"

No doubt about it. He's my brother, Muddy thought, but the man's comment did scare him a little.

"I'm in."

"So am I," Poe added.

"Him too," Corey replied, pointing his big finger at the drummer.

"I don't have a date until this weekend, so why not?" Otis, always hiding behind his jokes. Thankfully, they had the old man with them.

Silver Eye shook his head. "Good, 'cept I've never crossed over with kids before."

"I'll try to leave my pacifier here if that makes you feel better, gramps," Corey said.

"Watch your mouth, boy." He slammed his fist into the arm of the chair. Muddy watched the thick veins on the wrinkled dark hands grow and shake. "You have no idea what you're dealing with over there." Fire burned in his one eye. "Take it seriously or go home and cry when your brother never comes back."

Why did the man seem so angry? What did he know about where they would go?

None of them still had any idea what "over there" meant and it was apparent the guy wasn't going to enlighten them just yet, but they figured he would show them the light—or lose them in darkness soon enough.

"What's the second thing?" Muddy asked.

Silver Eye kept his gaze on Muddy. "We leave tonight."

"But how? We have school tomorrow." Muddy's anxiety spiked once again.

"You chicken," Corey said. "It's your brother!"

"Yeah," Otis chimed in, "you're not scared, are you?"

The old man stomped his foot to get their attention. "You're *all* scared. Or should be. It's a messed-up world over there. I still get the shakes every time I go.

"Besides," Silver Eye continued. "Time doesn't listen to any of our rules over there. You might not even miss one of your arithmetic classes if you're lucky. If you're not, I hope who-ever manages to come back can spell the words right on your tombstone."

"What is *over there*?" Muddy asked, ignoring the taunt.

Poe jumped into the fray. "Is it beyond that landfill? Some isolated part where people don't go to anymore?"

The old man looked directly at Muddy. "You can't walk there. You know that, so why are you asking? It's not on a map. It's not past the landfill, but it is somewhere that people hardly visit anymore, at least from this area."

Otis smirked and added his two cents. "So...you're saying it's somewhere only *you* can take us, but it's not past the landfill and it's not across the river."

The old man went silent.

"So...are we gonna click our heels together like in the *Wizard of Oz* and float there?"

The old man suddenly stood. "Listen, you little... I don't need this crap. You don't believe me, fine. Let that boy die over there. It ain't my issue. You wanna cross over with him, fine, but don't go making me out to be no crazy idiot."

Damage control time. It always happened when Otis got riled up.

"Wait, Mr. Watkins," Muddy pleaded. "I need to get over there, wherever *there* is. I *know* it's something weird—I saw it with my own eyes. I believe you, but they don't. Can you tell them what this place is?"

"Nope," he said, shaking his head again. "You either believe and go with me or run home to mama and let *them* have at it with your kin." He stood, walked over to a closed door and leaned against it. "I shouldn't even be taking you there."

"Yes, you should," Poe insisted. "Whatever, wherever this

place is, we've gotta go there, for Zack's sake. Please."

A minute of silence ensued. Then his eye moved as his gaze slowly rolled over them. "You really think you're up for this? You're not too scared?"

"Of course we're scared," Corey said. "We're not stupid. The three of us haven't even seen the place yet."

"When's the last time you went there?" Poe asked Silver Eye.

"Never mind that. I know what I'm doing.

"But," he warned, "you can't go there unarmed. You go in there with empty arms, and you might as well be dead right now. You need instruments. Otherwise, you won't last a minute."

"But we didn't know," Muddy said. "All our band equipment is back home. Heck, I don't even have a guitar pick!"

The old man just smiled and pushed open a door in the back of the house. "Welcome to ol' Silver Eye's toy store." The door swung wide and a musty stench wafted out for all to choke on, but only until they saw what lay inside. The room loomed massive, yet it couldn't be—not inside a house as small as this.

"Now, come on back here and find something to play." He gestured to the back room where a bevy of assorted instruments lay scattered around as if a Hard Rock Café had exploded in there. "Pick one, something that you feel fits you. Calls to you."

"*Calls* to him?" Poe mused, as she ventured into the mess. "That makes it a little easier for him." Even though she primarily sang with the voice of a siren, she also tinkered on keyboards. "Wait. Some of these aren't normal."

"Where we're going is about as far from normal as you'll ever see, ma'am, so choose carefully!"

Otis wandered straight to the back corner where a jumbled stack of percussion lay. "Okay, I'm cool," he called out, picking up a set of ebony sticks and also something that resembled a small snare drum with a leather strap, but decorated in oddly striped colors with incomprehensible carvings of objects.

Corey rushed over to a tenor sax hanging on the wall. Hey, there's a fresh reed on it! And spares!" He removed it, reverently cradling the instrument.

"Wait," he said, obviously confused. "This isn't brass. Is it silver?"

The old man smiled. "You gonna complain or play?"

Corey played with the skill that life gave him.

"Aha! There you are." A glissando, quick, effortless flurry of notes rang out from where Poe stood. She held up something Muddy couldn't identify, something that resembled a xylophone, but smaller. A leather strap hung over her shoulder. "Very cool, whatever it is." Her long, smooth fingers danced over the slender metal keys, unleashing another pleasant flurry of notes one might expect from an angel's harp.

"Something tells me that the only thing you'll need is right inside your lungs," Silver Eye said, looking over her shoulder, "but go ahead and tinker."

Where's mine? Muddy thought. As usual, everyone else had their pick of and luck with the music. If Zack were here, a vintage Fender or Les Paul would probably leap out of a pile, straight into his arms. But Muddy? Nothing even remotely resembling a six-string lay anywhere.

He felt a tap on his shoulder.

Spinning around, he found Silver Eye standing there with a battered, natural wood-toned acoustic guitar. Dull brass tuners jutted out of the headstock like crooked teeth. The neck and body held more scratches and chips than his grandfather's 1972 Chevy. Stranger though, was the end of the neck. It curved into a horn, like an old Victrola record player.

The man held it out like a proud father. Muddy took it, but it felt more like cradling a nephew from the circus sideshow than a bundle of beautiful joy.

"Sweet, ain't she?" The old man offered this prize to Muddy with a smile.

"Uh...yeah." Muddy never could lie well. "Sweet."

"Know where this has been?"

Pulled out of the Jersey swamps? A member of the original landfill?

When the teen shrugged, the old man clapped his hands together and leaned against the wall.

He looked at the band when he spoke. "No one's sure *when* she was built, but let's just say she's been to the Memphis Delta, down to the bayous of Louisiana, even hit the Chicago strip."

"And then..." Muddy leaned forward.

"You took *this* thing over *there?*" Poe sounded incredulous.

"Son, this *thing* has saved more people than the number of guitar picks you've lost."

"That's lot. But how? That thing is a piece of crap!"

"Yeah, I know," he said, nodding at the condition of the instrument. "But strap it on and I guarantee it'll save your crack over there."

Muddy threw it over his shoulder and tightened the strap. The leather looked like it had jumped off an alligator a few eons ago.

Silver Eye tossed him an odd pick.

"What's this made of?"

Again, that mysterious smile. "Eventually, boy. Eventually."

He strummed a chord and then a quick rock riff. The "thing" sounded like nothing he had ever heard before, but where was the amp? The volume? It rocked like something Led Zeppelin might have jammed with.

Silver Eye called out as they tested their new toys. "Remember, things operate differently over there. Things *sound* different there. Amplification will be provided."

Corey's voice sounded from behind them. "What do we do with these? Are we going to play a concert where we're going?"

"More important than that," the old man said. "Much more important."

Otis let loose with a drum roll on his newly found toy. "Okay, enough with the hoodoo voodoo vibe. When do we hit it?"

Muddy checked his watch. Ten minutes to eight. Darkness would overtake the town within a half hour. How they would get home safely through this part of town at night, he had no clue.

He could swear that silver orb in the bluesman's eye-socket saw right through him at that moment. "We'll be there in no time. Let's go. Remember—different place, different rules."

Muddy wondered if they were following a crazy man to their graves, but realized they had no other choice.

Corey turned to Muddy and then Poe. "Wait a sec. You mentioned 'weapons.' We're not getting real ones, are we?"

The teen had vowed never to touch a gun or knife after his experiences in Iron with the gang.

Silver Eye softened his gaze, likely understanding what the boy was getting at. "Son, we've got all the firepower we need in those hands of yours."

Chapter Six

Within ten minutes, the band reached the crossroads. The walk instilled in Muddy a deep chill that eclipsed what he felt after watching his brother disappear. A cascade of oranges, reds, and much darker shades crept over the top of the landfill as they moved to the "X" cradled in the epicenter of the two roads. Bathed in light that seemed much too much like blood, Muddy shivered. Looking around at the others, he wondered if anyone else felt the dread that lay ahead of them. Poe appeared calm, spotlighted in an array of earth colors that accented her beautiful, but cloudy eyes. Corey and Otis jittered a little in the reds, obviously feeling the same. But Silver Eye simply stood there, eyes closed.

Was he meditating?

The two well-worn dirt paths crisscrossed at the dead center of the valley between the monster-tall mounds that buried at least fifty years of human trash. Rumor had it that the Jersey mobs often tossed their enemies there, but the police wouldn't bother to search the area.

Who'd want to?

At one time, each path might have been a dirt road leading to the water's edge, a path for a fishing boat before the pollution overtook the area. They leaned out as far as they could see. *Who'd ever fish there now?* Muddy wondered why the piers were boarded. Was it to protect the trespassers or mutated fish? Either way, he stood there amazed at the perfect perpendicular "X" that was born in the middle of a place no normal person would ever tread. One thought crossed his mind—*did they build the landfill* around *the crossroads, to hide it where its supposed secrets were obscured from the eyes and curiosity of the many?* He wondered how many townsfolk knew about them.

Corey seemed to be reading Muddy's mind. "Hey, did you notice that none of these paths have *any* junk on them? Does someone actually *clean* here?" True enough, not one bottle, bag, can, or paper littered the paths that crossed under their feet.

"Weird," Otis added.

"Welcome, my new friends." The bluesman spread his scrawny arms wide, the dying sun silhouetting him in shadows. "Welcome to the start of a brand-new life."

Corey spoke first. "Are you trying to scare us with some hoodoo again?"

The wide smile opened with a wink from the man's good eye. "Actually, yes I am." If you're not scared now, then you're more messed up than I was when I first stepped here so many years ago."

Was this guy serious, or just screwing with their heads?

"Mr. Edgar 'Muddy' Brooks!" he bellowed. "Are you afraid to step into this journey to find your long-lost brother?"

"I said, are you ready?" he repeated, this time a bit louder.

No, I'm so not ready. Definitely not ready to die.

He sucked in a deep, calming breath. "Sure thing. When do we go?"

Poe vocalized what she was thinking next. "Is this going to hurt?"

Corey added, "Has anybody ever died doing this?"

Of course, Otis had to add his two cents. "Is there any food there? All this being scared is making me hungry. How about women? Cute ones, not ones with glass eyes."

The bluesman continued staring as the teens babbled. They were scared out of their minds, whether they admitted it or not. After about thirty seconds of a pure tidal wave of talking, he'd had enough. "Will you please shut up?" he exploded. "You want to die over there? You want to get stuck over there like your dopehead brother?" he continued. "What the *heck* is wrong with you people?"

Muddy's mind spun. Nobody had ever talked to them like that. Most people treated the group like the label on them read "special" as in special education. Exceptional students. *Those* kids who tried so hard. Except for a few bullies, no one had mustered the guts to treat them as "regular" kids.

Somehow, Muddy didn't think Silver Eye gave a darn about what they were.

Still…

Poe wasn't having any of it. She strode right up to him and raised her gaze to his, burning a look into him where words would fail. Toe to toe, neither budged.

The old man raised one hand in mock defeat. "Okay, little lady, I give. But get your buddies' butts in gear so we can get moving."

Muddy hung his head while Poe softened her stance, just a little. "Sorry," she said. "I'm just a little scared."

As the bluesman dug a harmonica out of his jeans, he muttered to himself. "So am I. So am I." He turned to the band. "Now follow my lead."

A stream of blues scales bled from lips, hands, and tongues, sending echoes off the landfill's walls. After a few cascades of passionate blues, the old blues man settled into a simple shuffle that Muddy quickly figured out was in the key of G. His favorite, and that of many musicians, whether it be for the smooth sound or the ease in jumping into a zone that let a musician stretch out and lose himself.

Silver Eye winked at him then nodded over to Otis and Corey. Poe simply began swaying, feeling the beat thumping in the air. Drumsticks slapped the side of the ancient instrument and a deep groove was born. A simple two and four beat, the backbone to most blues, rock, hip-hop, funk, and dance songs in existence thundered, causing the dirt beneath their feet to shudder. Cory's saxophone added low bass tones to complete the framework before Muddy felt connected enough to join the fray.

The guitarist felt his fingers acting on their own accord, fretting a basic barre chord, followed by his pick hand-slicing into the rhythm, chunking out what now became a solid blues-rock groove. He knew he was light years behind his brother, but felt he had *something* in him. Both hands synced up with the coordination of two entities that were separated at birth but had now found each other. As the old man vamped on the twelve-bar blues, Muddy jumped off the basics and into the depths of more serpentine chord movements and fills that curled around his licks.

He almost asked if this would work but felt Silver Eye would rip him a new one if he made a sound.

As the group gelled, Poe's voice crept into the mix as she first hummed a simple melody that echoed Silver Eye's blistering blues. The voice of an angel, an angel with an attitude, she completed the group. Normally, when the band hit on all cylinders like this, an adrenaline rush washed over them, bathing the teens in a chill that was like no other feeling in the world.

But another sensation crept into the groove. Both tickling and shocking, like when someone gave another a static touch, it permeated the night air. The sensation blanketed his skin, soothing and stimulating simultaneously. As the music shifted a bit, Muddy could tell he wasn't the only one to feel it. The music didn't lose the rhythm, but the intensity took a hit.

Silver Eye ripped the harp from his lips. "Don't *STOP* playing!" Flames roiled in his one living eye.

Even though the man yelled the command at the group, Muddy knew most of the energy careened toward him. For a long moment, he was back home, back in the first grade, back in little league. All those people hollering at him for not holding up his end. Heck, he was so used to hearing it, the harshness of the man's words barely affected him. Still, it stung.

Instead of crumbling and walking away like at a baseball game, he swallowed it whole.

His gaze locked onto the old man's and dug harder into the rhythm. His fingers scurried up the neck in fiery cascades that ended in a screaming bend before falling back into the groove. The others followed suit and upped the tempo, and intensity.

After about a minute passed, it happened.

One moment, his gaze was pasted onto Silver Eye, matching

him lick for lick in the song. The next, the landfill began to quiver behind the old guy. Muddy's legs buckled as he attempted to focus his vision.

What happened to Zack was now happening to them.

The tingling intensified, as if a million tiny bugs dug into his skin and danced to some hyper speed song. It didn't hurt, but it didn't feel great, either.

Muddy glanced at each of his band mates to make sure it was happening and that no one was simply hallucinating. Then his gaze skittered back to the world around the crossroads.

As if some designer of the universe had wrapped them in a clear shower curtain, everything he saw shimmered. With each passing beat, the curtain wavered faster. Muddy nearly had to close his eyes as his stomach churned. The tickling didn't help, either. He wondered what would happen if he puked during the process.

Still, they played on.

Then the curtain shook so fast that everything beyond it lost clarity. One moment, the landfill and the paths leading to where they were looked normal. The next, he couldn't see a thing, even though the moon still illuminated the scene.

It shook, then shook some more and the tingling forced Muddy's eyes to shut. He shook so hard he dropped his pick. Afraid to see what it fell into, his fingers plucked the strings in its place. Even before he forced himself to look, he knew what they *wouldn't* see.

"We're here," announced Silver Eye Watkins.

And their lives changed in a heartbeat.

Chapter Seven

Muddy opened his eyes when he heard someone gasp. The curtain had parted. Act two of their lives, destinies, fates had just begun.

The band still stood on the crisscrossing paths, but that was the only similarity to the world they stood upon moments ago.

Gone was the landfill. Lush greenery exploded everywhere in a forest that bordered on jungle status. The wind whistled in an odd key. Trails ran off into the dark north, south, east, and west. Other than that, it looked like nobody had been there in ages.

"We're not in Jersey anymore," Otis muttered, unable to keep the fright out of his voice.

Poe lifted her head. "Definitely doesn't *smell* like New Jersey."

"All of you—shut your traps!" Silver Eye looked scared enough for all of them. Whether he was scared for himself or for the band, Muddy didn't know, but the expression on his face quieted them in an instant.

"You don't want to let *anything* know we're here."

The guitar nearly shook from Muddy's hands. "Who's here?"

"We don't need to worry about *whom* just yet," he said. "Right now, the *what* around this place can kill you before you tune that thing."

The what? We're in Jersey, aren't we? This area didn't have any wildlife that could harm us, at least not without guns.

"And yes," he continued. "The trip does screw up your guitar. Now tune that thing before you get us killed."

Just as Muddy twisted the first tuning peg, thunder roared all around them. This time, the ground did shake. He turned his gaze skyward and saw nothing but stars in the coming night.

"Hurry!" Silver Eye's fright burst out of his voice. Then he did a strange thing. He played a melody on the harp that sounded out of the norm. Blues, yes, but more methodical, more complicated in pattern.

"Why?" Muddy wondered aloud. "It's just a thunderstorm. Don't worry, I'll cover the guitar."

Silver Eye shook his hands while his neck craned left and right. "That *ain't* no storm. Lightning is *not* what you need to worry about tonight."

"Then, what is it?"

"Just tune the dang guitar," he said, placing a vise-like grip on the boy's arms. "Drummer, sax boy, get ready for my cue." As their mumblings began, he cut them short. "Quiet! When I yell, blow out the best low C you've got. Pound that skin as if your life depended on it."

Poe sidled up to the guitarist, scared out of her mind. "Eddie," she said, using a name she only called him when she was upset, "what's going on? What do *I* do? What's out there? I can't see anything—or sense it."

The bluesman answered for both of them. "Little girl, you just sit tight for this one. I'll be needing your golden voice soon, but it won't help much here. Just stay out of the way and don't mess with me."

Wrong thing to say, part two. Yet instead of flipping out and tearing out the guy's other eyeball, she bit her lip and turned to Muddy. "You're still a little flat."

Muddy knew that but looked up at her and forced a smile. "Thanks, Poe." Using her ears, they tuned the guitar to perfection within a minute. Trembling, he turned to the group. He went to move in closer, with Poe in tow.

Silver Eye's hands shot up like an armed rifle. "Don't move! Stay on the path. Do *NOT* step off the trail, definitely not at night."

Poe stared into the green blades. "The grass is alive!" It swayed in the night breeze, but against the wind in a rhythm all its own.

Before anyone could register her comment, the thunder roared again. And again. Then once more. What kind of storm was coming? Why did he say it wasn't one?

As if reading the teen's mind, the old man's voice filled in the space between the booms. "Son, this is much worse than any storm, hurricane, tsunami, or what-have-you." He motioned for all of them to pull tight and face outwards, away from each other and toward the forest.

Otis's hand turned white gripping his sticks. Corey's fingers tapped out a jittery rhythm on the sax's pearly keys. Poe sank into Muddy's side, whether to be comforted or to comfort, he had no idea. He needed it, and sensed she did too.

Above the thick carpet of grass, swaying in the wake of the thunder, walls of trees stood, surrounding the group in a claustrophobic embrace. Nearly black against the night, they rustled and shook arm-like boughs, tossing creepy shadows across the trails. If they wished to run, which direction would it be? Muddy heard the rumbling around them shook everything by whatever caused the thunder.

Another sonic boom shook the air, the ground, and their bones. The trees trembled at the edges of the pathways. The sound pained Muddy's ears as he strained to keep his eyes open and focused on the rumbling walls of green. Thunder never lasted this long, nor did it hurt.

A moment later, that thunder walked right through the trees.

At first, he thought the trees themselves came to life and decided to attack. Then he noticed the fur. The long arms. Trunk-like legs. And then, the face.

With a mouth as wide and round as a dinner plate, but blacker than the soul of a math teacher, the *thing* ambled toward the band, in *rhythm*! When the thing's feet hit the ground, it sounded like a rock song two and four beat. Loud. Boom – cha. Boom – cha. Just like the beat of a good song. Bass drum, snare drum, then a cymbal crashed with the vibration of a gong, shaking them off their feet. Muddy and the others dropped to their knees in agony. The sound pummeled them with high and low pitches, rattling teeth and vibrating bones.

"Holy cow..." Corey whispered, although even if he had screamed, they wouldn't have heard it. "Look," he said and pointed.

The cymbal didn't exude from a rock drum kit, Buddhist monastery, or marching band. When the lumbering, thundering *thing* slammed its mouth shut and then sprung it wide open again, Muddy imagined himself in the front row at the heaviest of metal concerts. It blew a gale force wind at them, knocking leaves and twigs from the trees, mussing their hair. The creature stood firm, those massive legs holding its stance steady, arms swung back for better projection, Muddy guessed. Then it lifted one of those limbs up and out, ready to beat on an imaginary drum. At the end of the arm grew not a hand, but a stubby lump, rounded with the girth of a volleyball.

Silver Eye raised his head and yelled for Otis to do something.

What did he expect Otis to do to that thing? Bite its ankles? Did it have *ankles?*

Otis waved at the man, signaling that he didn't understand.

The branches in the thick curtains of green parted again in a rolling wave of sonic pain. Two, three, four more behemoths of fur and massive mouths burst forth and lock-stepped their way to form a semi-circle. Just like a *bigger* mouth. Opened in their direction.

Silver Eye yelled again. Otis waved once more, but Muddy stopped in his tracks. The lead creature wore a guitar string around his neck with a shiny, silver triangle dangling from it. Could it be...?

Zack used a pick just like that.

He almost charged toward them to get a better look, but suddenly all five ogre-like creatures raised their arms, as if waiting for a drum major to commence a marching cadence.

Muddy could see the drummer's eyes dancing in fear and confusion, then saw him mouthing, "What? What do I do?" along with some other choice words.

The old man raised his hand and thumped the ground. Slowly at first, then his withered palms sped up into a full-fledged drum roll on the path. Otis nodded like a bobble head on speed and readied his sticks.

The first creature swung his mallet hand down in a power-ful arc, straight into the middle of a chest that resembled a swol-len kettle drum. Muddy felt the beat before it hit his eardrums. A fist of sound punched him, sending his body flying across the grass. He landed in a lump of pain about twenty feet away.

Immediately, he looked for Poe. The deep grass split to his right. Seconds later, a hand rose through the shaking blades. It was Corey.

"Get out of there, man!" Corey's hand swallowed Muddy's and yanked him back toward the path. The grass shivered and swayed. Something in there had been waiting for one of them to stray. Muddy booked it back to safety almost before Corey did. He kneeled on the trail shaking with deep breaths and scanned the scene for the others. Still on the path, but much farther back lay Otis and Silver Eye.

Where was she?

He couldn't stand to think of the possibilities of what might happen to her if one of those goons got a hold of her. Did one step on her? Could one swallow her in that cymbal-sized mouth?

As the echoes of that boom faded, whispers assaulted him from every direction. Muddy turned and found the others, not whispering, but screaming to each other. The old man furiously motioned to the band to grab their instruments and stand.

Still, where was she?

The other four things readied their arms, waiting to knock them into the dark of the forest.

Then they froze. At first, Muddy swore he heard an eagle's cry. Piercing, yet beautiful, it rose with the parting of the razor-like grass. From it sprouted Poe.

What the?

She sang like they'd never heard her sing before. Toward the creatures she strode, eyes wide open, as if she could see them clearly. Her voice rose in pitch, intensity and volume. She sounded like a cross between an angel and a ticked off eagle. The creatures remained still as the band took up their instru-ments and ran behind her.

"Watch it!" Muddy yelled to her as she came within a yard of the beasts, arms frozen in midair. "They're right—"

"I can *see* them."

"What?"

She stared straight ahead then turned to the band members. "I can see them." The excitement in her voice shook her skinny frame. "Look at their faces. Look at them. There's nothing past their mouths. Only blackness." When she stopped singing, the ice in their movements began to melt. "I can see here." She had lost her sight so long ago, when that monster back home had hurt her.

"Then dang it, girl," Silver Eye hollered, "don't stop singing!" He put his harmonica to his lips and motioned for the rest of them to start playing.

Start playing? Start playing what? Muddy's mind was still stuck on what he saw hanging from the lead creature's neck.

Yet Corey, after a few fearful squeaks, began echoing the old man's staccato bursts of blues. His tone grew more confident with each deepening breath.

Otis beat a simple blues rock pattern, lock-stepping with the others. Muddy knew his friend felt just as scared as he was, but when someone faced dying early every day like Otis did, fear was a bit easier to swallow.

Knowing his behavior to be cowardly if he remained frozen, Muddy picked a few notes in the pentatonic scale, the easiest scale there was for a rock guitarist. The best one. Silver Eye turned to him and winked, a signal that things would be fine. How, he had no idea. Yet it infused the guitarist with fire as he hit a few chord stabs here and there, weaving in and out of the beat, creating a weird syncopation.

An *off* the beat rhythm.

The creatures stood their ground, staying still until the biggest one slowly raised both of his hands. Despite the spell of the music, he'd broken free and set himself for a strike.

If the coming explosion knocked them hard enough, their instruments might break—or worse, their bodies themselves. Without the music that the band played, only a fool would believe they would survive the attack.

Silver Eye stopped his song and turned to the little drummer. "My man, rip it up. Shut those oafs *up*. Now!"

Otis looked as if he had just heard a war cry in Swahili,

but nodded, maybe in comprehension, maybe in resignation. He answered those doubts in the start of a twelve-bar pattern, something that rocked on its backbeat. He twirled his sticks then pointed them at the beasts. With a deep breath, he launched into the rhythm that caught the creatures off guard. Its offbeat nature, similar to what the greats, the drummers of Led Zeppelin, Aerosmith, Cream, Metallica, etc. played, countered the straight-ahead bass and snare rhythm heard in just about every popular song nowadays. The power of what Otis played rocked their insides hard. One creature took a step, tried to steady itself using the rhythm then tumbled. When it hit, its eyes glazed over and arms flailed in confusion. Its fall and inevitable crash shook the entire band off the ground at least a foot, but they kept the music going.

Otis intensified his drum retaliation. *He* became the thunder and shook all the creatures in their stances. One by one, the creatures attempted to rush the teens but encountered the same fate as the first one. Each stumbled, unable to lock onto the complicated, syncopated, off-the-beat rhythm. Their crashes turned the path and grass into a spongy springboard, sending each of the quintet into the air, back down, then up again. Yet somehow, they remained locked into the groove of whatever magic was created by the music. The harder the drumming, the harder they fell. Otis's thunder, their crashes. Together, they formed a backbeat that any self-respecting rocker would die for.

Once all the creatures were down, quivering and in obvious pain and confusion, Silver Eye conducted the song to an end.

Muddy saw his chance and before fear could take him, he ran right up to the fallen "thing" and lifted the guitar string over the creature's head with a shaking hand, freeing it.

"Nice job, boy," Silver Eye said, patting Otis on the head.

"Man, if this didn't just happen, with those things and that music, I'd pop you for that," Otis replied. "Nobody pets me."

The man retreated a bit. "I apologize, music man. After that show, no one should cross you; not if they want to stay on their feet."

Otis nodded. "No prob. That was awesome." He looked at his sticks. "How did I do that?"

Poe approached, slow and with arms spread as if the quaking might resume.

"I *saw* them," she said. "How?"

Silver Eye took her hands in his. "Girl, in this place, strange things happen. Not sure exactly why some of it does, but music *breathes* here. It's alive, part of everything. It changes things."

"But how? My eyes, things went from shapes in a deep fog to near crystal clear."

His own eye scanned the scene. "All in good time, my girl. But we've gotta move our cheeks outta here—now. Those things won't stay down long."

The group drew together again. "The way back?" Muddy asked.

"Same way we got here." He lifted his harp and began playing, thus ceasing further conversation.

Both scared and fascinated, the band simply followed. Once positioned at the "X," all of them repeated the same jam that brought them there. Only once did the old man gesture for them to pick up the tempo and power. Then the rolling began.

As they had experienced during the trip there, a "curtain" shimmered then parted.

All stepped through without moving and the images of the forest with the fallen creatures faded away.

Muddy shut his eyes as dizziness affected his vision. The music slowed then halted altogether. Curiosity compelled Muddy to open his eyes, only to find that the landfill and reeking air had returned.

Muddy felt he had just stepped off Six Flags' wildest rollercoasterThe music stopped, suddenly, probably due to the "wow" factor that they had just survived whatever they'd just traveled though. The silence struck a stronger chord than the drumming things they'd escaped. Deafening nothingness pressed on them, hard, causing them more than a little fright.

"What the heck is *wrong* with you people?" Silver Eye yelled.

His voice frightened Muddy so much he flung the guitar string into the air.

Otis stared at Silver Eye. "What?"

The old man waved his arms. "Were you kids raised in a dang barn?"

What?

"We haven't closed the *door* yet! You don't leave the door wide open at home, do you?"

But it wasn't a question. Muddy knew he was either mad or scared. Either one was bad. Very bad.

His old shoe stomped the ground sending a cloud of dirt and dust into the air. It gave Silver Eye a mystical aura that terrified Muddy. Then again, the whole night had scared the crap out of him.

Poe broke the silence. "What door? We're back safe. Aren't we?"

"No, we're *not*," Silver Eye replied, sounding cranky. "We need to *close* the door. You don't want something from over there to follow you home, do you?"

"What things?" Otis asked. "We kicked the crap out of those oafs...didn't we?"

The man walked up to Otis and stared deep into the kid's unblinking black eyes.

"Son, that's just the tip of the ugly iceberg that we saw over there. You have *no* idea what else is there, just itchin' to creep on through and wreak some havoc in our world."

His eye went a little crazy. His hands twitched. "Know how a few thousand people go missing each year? No bodies ever found?"

Otis nodded his head.

"Ever wonder what happens to them?"

Otis found his voice. "Serial killers?"

He turned toward Muddy. "He's been reading too many of your daddy's books. Or not enough."

"How'd you know about my father?"

Silver Eye belted out a laugh, melting the tension somewhat. "I ain't stupid. Or illiterate. I do know who's living in my town, good or bad." A half-smile crossed his face. "Smart dad you have there. Maybe one day you can ask him about where we went. He's got imagination and more."

Yeah, like Dad and I would ever...

Muddy had his music. Dad had his stories. Eye to eye, it just wasn't happening.

Hold on a second...

"Now, enough old lady talk." Silver Eye walked back to the center of the crossroads. "Pick up your guitar and follow me in D-flat. Shuffle, twelve bar blues."

"D-flat? What the...? Who plays in that key?"

"Yeah," Otis said. "We're not some jazz be-bop guys."

"Shut your yap," Silver Eye snapped. "*Any* self-respecting musician knows how to jam in *any* key. It ain't that hard if you've got a little soul in ya."

"Still," Corey added, "that's an odd key. I play piano..."

"Goodie for you, big windy," the old man retorted. "If you play the ivories, you should know D-flat is the opposite of G. Six steps away, three whole tones. A tri-tone," he said. "Can't get more opposite than that."

"But—" Looking at Muddy, he spoke in a serious tone. "Play."

The guitarist looked at his twitching fingers. All he could think of was the simple blues scale pattern a guitarist could use on any fret, any key. With the knowledge of what the man called for, it was akin to driving on the turnpike with a Schwinn.

"Play," came the stern voice, tinged with anger, maybe a little fear.

The teen chugged out a few power chords in a simple shuffle rhythm. A series of waves began like ripples in a pond, growing more intense each time.

Silver Eye joined in, switching to a new harmonica. Muddy looked at the old man's baggy pants and assumed he could've had a different one for each possible key. Or at least the ones that did something *over there*. Still, the boy felt no real comfort in the key.

Silver Eye nodded at Muddy, and something in the old man's eye broke the floodgates.

Muddy spun a lick, his right hand picking away like an angry hummingbird's wings, beating through the strings with speed, precision, and attitude. Then he coaxed a cry out of the guitar with a nasty bend. Pushing it a little more, it morphed into a scream.

He fell into the zone, that place where musicians lose themselves to the world. The music grew until it surrounded him in a cool, comforting blanket. Notes and melodies emanating from the Les Paul became who he was, all he thought, all he breathed.

Everything around him dissipated as he became the music.

Chapter Eight

The next thing Muddy knew, a strong hand shook him back to earth. Like waking from a sleep when sick, his world unfolded slowly into focus. Corey's voice penetrated the fog. "Dude, you okay?"

"Hey," someone else called.

"Muddy?" As usual, Poe dragged him back to earth.

"Yeah," he answered, not quite sure of where he was yet.

"What did you just play?" The voice sounded like Otis.

"I don't know." The last thing he remembered, he was launching into that bend, the one that erupted from the depths of his soul. "I have no clue." Poe grabbed his hand.

"What happened to him?" she asked Silver Eye. The bluesman stared at him with a look that he couldn't place. Muddy wasn't sure he wanted to know.

"The River."

The what?

Otis looked around. "Where? He isn't wet." He spun to give his black eyes the 360 degree view he needed with his damaged vision. "That dirty old toilet ain't a river. The Raritan has more sewage than water. You don't need to be Jacques Cousteau to figure out you could *walk* on that water it's got so much junk in it."

"It's not *that* river, you dolt," the old man said. "It's another dimension of creativity; genius, to be exact. Although, back in my day, it was an actual river. Anyway, even though it's not a real, water flowing river, you could get pulled under. In fact, I know of a bunch of folks who did sink so deep, they never came back out again. You'd probably know their names—Hendrix,

Morrison, Stevie Ray. Hendrix and Morrison didn't drown," he replied, "unless you consider their own vomit from overdosing as drowning. Amazing artists but drugged out of their minds. Stevie cleaned up his act but died in a plane crash."

He shook his head. "The River got to them. Too much swimming can kill you. There's never any excuse for the drugs, but people are human, and humans are weak. They got hooked on the River long before they found the ganga or the spoon. Heck, I even had my run-ins with them—addictions, both pharmaceutical *and* metaphysical—and look where it left me."

Muddy didn't understand. From the looks on the rest of the band's faces, he wasn't alone. "But you're a great musician."

"Without a pot to pee in. If I'd played it right, I'd be spinning out records like B.B. and Buddy and even McCartney. Incredible River, incredible obsession."

Muddy opened his mouth to delve further, but something in the old man's voice told him to zip his lip. "Hey," he managed to say. "Look at this."

In his hand he held a solid silver guitar pick—the one his brother used. It even had Zack's initials engraved in it, except this one had teeth marks, deep ones, through most of the letters.

"Zack's definitely there. We need to get back there before he winds up like that."

The old man whispered so that they barely heard him. "If he's not already."

They gathered their instruments and began the trek back to Silver Eye's home. No one spoke or made any noise. They showed no fear of walking through the worst part of town in the middle of the night with only an old man for guidance.

One feeling that did register with Muddy was a tingling of sorts, as if he had touched an electric outlet. Weird—he *vibrated*.

The empty streets glowed under the streetlights; litter fluttered and danced in the shadows, every dismal color jumped from wrappers, magazine strips, and plain old newspaper. Oil spots on the asphalt shimmered as though a pot of gold might await at one end. In the sky, beyond the smoggy clouds, stars shone through in elaborate constellations—something they noticed only in a blue moon.

He doubted he was the only one to notice the change by the silence that blanketed them. For now, they avoided each other as the space between them spread. Only the bluesman, who hadn't said a word since leaving the crossroads, had any spring to his step.

The night had scared them to their cores.

Muddy felt it had only begun.

Chapter Nine

Silver Eye Watkins sent them home with the instruments, despite their protests.

"Trust me, you'll need them," he said, without giving any explanation. "Practice on them. It's not like they're something you get at the store."

Like kids leaving an odd Santa Claus, they lumbered through the dark, somehow finding their way without encountering Vince or any other perils. One by one, they slunk away to their respective homes, dropping Poe off first, everyone gazing into her windows to make sure her dad wasn't home. If he happened to be home early from the bar or the police station, punches would likely be thrown, first by him, then by one of the band. The fact that he was a cop and could arrest them didn't matter. The man drank so much, chances were he wouldn't remember what the heck happened.

As usual, Muddy walked home alone. It partly made sense. His father wrote horror novels. He often guessed he should be afraid of his own shadow, but he knew all the monstrous creatures he invented came from his own mind. If someone saw enough scary movies, read enough frightening stories, sometimes the real world didn't seem as intimidating.

Then again, if someone had faced what he'd just encountered and went where he'd just gone, even a drug dealer or serial killer resolve would be preferable.

Howard Brooks sat on the living room sofa, laptop perched on a pillow, fingers dancing over the keys as he created images that would probably frighten readers all over the world. For a moment, a pang of jealousy ached within Muddy as he thought about how he could never enjoy those stories like millions of others did. Dyslexia sucked. Sure, Mrs. Berg had him hooked on that new reading program. She swore it would allow him to chew through a few pages at a time without his head spinning, without the letters swirling before his eyes. Okay, that was an exaggeration, maybe, but he knew the hell of being a successful writer's son who couldn't slog his way through even one of his father's novels. It really sucked. Irony at its best.

Maybe one day that would change.

"Hey, Edgar."

He knew his son hated his full name, but he loved to mess with the kid, anyway. Joking was one of the few things that kept them sane after Muddy's mom died. Still, being named after a horror writer should be cool, though, Stephen would've worked. Or Dean. Ray. Brian. Heck, even Ramsey had a cool ring to it. But no, Howard had conned his wife into naming him Edgar, the dark son of literary macabre.

"Hey, Dad." Howard was a cool guy, in father's terms, but ever since his mom died, a wall thicker than a math teacher's skull kept them from being how they used to be. His stories became darker; Muddy's songwriting became bluesier, more distant.

"Long practice?" His dad's fingers never stopped typing. He often had a half-dozen projects going at once, so giving his only son partial attention seemed normal to both of them. His mom had often suggested adult ADHD, but his dad simply laughed, stating his mind just never stopped chugging along. "Like a caffeinated locomotive," he often quipped.

Muddy headed straight toward the fridge, remembering he hadn't had dinner. After rummaging through a mess of takeout containers and his dad's leftovers from cooking experiments gone awry, he found two slices of pizza hiding in the back, probably afraid of the massive amounts of garlic the mad chef used in most of his concoctions.

"You guys play late tonight?" Howard asked, this time louder.

Not wanting to be rude, but not wishing to get into a

conversation either, the teen simply nodded. Part of his brain
had fried out from the trip; the rest normally retreated from
family talk. Zack was even worse.

Is worse, he chided himself.

"New guitar?"

Crap. Forgot all about that.

"Nope. Just something Otis's dad had lying around the
house. Just borrowing it."

Howard nodded, but the look in his eyes asked more. "Have
you heard from Zack today?"

Anxiety began to form within him. Muddy shook his head
as the pizza nearly slipped from his fingers.

"I know he didn't come home last night. Is he back with
that Rachel?" His dad had been attempting to rein in the older
brother for months now, to no avail. Punishing him only made
it worse, but as long as Zack didn't run around committing
crimes, his father decided to give him a bit of slack. Okay, a *lot*
of slack.

Nope, Zack couldn't stand that empty-headed, conceited
witch. Yet with Zack, there was always another female waiting
in the wings. He wondered if women surrounded Zack wherever he was now. Somehow, after that quick glimpse into the
nightmare at the crossroads, Muddy doubted it.

He gave his father what he hoped was a blank look, wondering how much of tonight was scribbled on his face. His dad created characters for a living and said his skills at reading people
gave him that talent. Rarely could Muddy or his brother hide
what they thought from him, which was why neither one spent
much time at home.

"Not going to heat that up?"

Muddy realized he'd started to carry the pizza, cold, out of
the kitchen.

"Doesn't matter to me," he muttered. "Sometimes it's better
if you take things as they are."

Father looked at his son as though he'd just spouted something from Plato. "You don't think that about Zack, do you?"

Muddy doubted his dad meant it as a question and not
about dinner, either.

"I sometimes worry he'll get himself into something he can't play his way out of," Howard said, "especially lately. The boy hasn't handled anything well since…"

Not finding the words to form a reply, Muddy trudged upstairs.

Like any of us have.

Chapter 10

Sleep found Muddy quickly that night, and without night-mares about his mother. Only one dream danced behind his eyes—the one about the crossroads. He stood at the epicenter, alone, or so he thought. A figure approached with the deliberateness of coming night. Muddy's hands scrambled for his guitar, only to find an empty strap instead. Fear gripped him.

The shape of a person loomed larger, but only in shadow. With the moon behind him, the person's face couldn't be seen. Muddy's feet were glued to the dirt trail; he could only stand and wait. His face burned, but ice rolled down his back.

Time crawled until the figure stood before him. Covered in a cloak of deep purple, its head pointed toward him, faceless under a hood. His fingers shook as he raised his arms to touch the thick material that masked the mysterious person. It felt coarse, dark and strangely warm as his thumb and fingers curled around it.

All the while, it simply stood there, unflinching.

After drawing a deep breath, Muddy did what he needed to do, what he dreaded. He yanked the hood back. And screamed himself awake.

Chapter Eleven

Muddy meandered through the following day, not taking notes or paying a speck of attention to the teachers, even the ones he liked. In between classes, he traveled the hallways in a fog, paying little attention to most of the conversation around him. Stress overload, the counselor would call it. Everything from the previous night's journey to Zack's disappearance and finally, to seeing that face in his nightmare, added up to a solid brain fry.

He spoke to no one until band practice, the last period of the day. During resource room, the period designed to help students with whatever ailed them, the other band members sat in uneasy silence. Muddy guessed, they shared his fears and doubted their own memories of the night. However, once the music flowed from their instruments, their real instruments, practicing a Mozart rip-off that some wannabe composer tossed off to the high schools as the next big fad, things opened up.

Otis broke the ice with the subtlety of a sledgehammer, as usual. "Hey, you swimming in the River there, Muddy?"

"Shut. Up." Muddy replied with more venom than he'd intended.

"Edgar," Poe snapped. "Relax. We're *all* on edge after last night."

So, it did really happen.

"Sorry, Otis. I just had a bad night."

Poe leaned in and whispered, "Dreams?"

"Bad one," he answered, not wanting to explain.

Her hand shook as it gripped his arm. "Me too."

"Make that three," Otis added.

"Four," came a shaky response from Corey.

After a minute of playing that awful song and tripping over the hackneyed, convoluted rhythms, Mr. Satriani eyeballed the foursome and signaled to them to break again. The friends regrouped and looked at each other, waiting for something to happen.

"Mine was just freaking scary," Poe said.

"Mine too," Corey replied. Otis and Muddy just nodded.

"I mean, it's normal to dream about those horrible crossroads after what happened, right?"

It hurt Muddy to see her so shaken, even if it was by something unreal.

"Yeah, of course," he said, but even as he spoke, the muscles in his shoulders pulled tight.

"And it's okay for me to be scared of something that seemed like it was from the *other* side, right?"

"Sure." His back became as taut as the strings on the guitar neck.

"So why did I dream of that freaky guy in the dark hood?"

"Holy..." breathed Corey.

"No way!" Otis started, but then simply shook a little.

Muddy felt paralyzed, glued to the metal chair.

Corey leaned in, letting the others hear his fear, even though their teacher tossed odd glances toward them from time to time. "Did you see? Did you see his face?"

"No." She shook her head. "Just that freaky hood. I think that was scarier. Did you?"

"Nope," the sax player replied.

"I didn't, either," Otis said, his fingers white on the drumsticks.

They waited for Muddy to speak up.

"I did. I saw his face."

Chapter Twelve

They left class shaken—no one more than Muddy—but things had to be done. Any plans they had to pursue the person in their shared dream had to be put on hold, at least for the moment. Set up and auditions for the *Battle of the Bands* was scheduled for right after school.

"How am I supposed to practice now with that image in my mind?" Otis swirled his sticks, but without the usual finesse.

All the bands were set up on the auditorium stage, many sharing amps and drum kits, much to the chagrin of the pickier musicians. Yet with only one PA system, they had to get along for this one day. Each group was allowed to play two songs. The Accidentals had yet to decide on which ones they were going to play.

Muddy shook his head, unwilling to meet anyone's gaze. "Just play. Pretend we're in the basement. Just focus."

"Okay," Otis replied. "Okay."

As they watched one lousy band after another, butchering cover songs to the point where even the student advisors couldn't decipher what they were hearing, the memories of the previous night faded enough so that the group could concentrate on the deal at hand.

Muddy thought back to their own genesis, when five misfits found each other in fourth grade, five kids who loved music yet had few friends. When Otis heard Muddy blasting "Crazy Train," he bounced over and began to tap out the beat on the other boy's shoulders. Poe howled the vocal screech and Greg, the bass player who held a standup, pumped out the rubbery intro. Within a week, the band had formed, and friendship had been cast in stone.

Until Greg's unfortunate accident.

At least the others bonded and survived. So far.

When it came time for Bentley's group to gear up, the butterflies in Muddy's stomach grew rusty barbs on their wings and spit fire through his insides. His guitar playing made him feel like a one-fingered, lobotomized accountant compared to his nemesis's speedy, fleet-fingered runs. True, not much soul existed in that guy's flashy playing, but no one seemed to care. The blonde sixteen-year old strode up to the stage in his white pants and expensive button-down shirt. The smirk on his face never departed. Muddy suspected the tool went to sleep wearing that smug expression. A good-looking guy playing fast guitar would usually win over the high school crowd, especially the girls. Plus, he could sing. Girls like Chelsea and Porshe fell for that every time. Muddy wondered if Poe ever would.

Even though six-stringing seemed to be embedded in his genes, his own vocal cords must've had some connection to the president of the Tone-Deaf Club. Thankfully, Poe's voice made up for any torture he inflicted on anyone's ears.

Bentley's singing fell way short of Poe's angelic style, but when you were popular, audiences forgave just about anything. He might as well have sung the theme song to Barney. Most of the student body would have still applauded.

They launched into an up-tempo version of a classic Van Halen song. Simple to pull off, technically, but with that band, it was never about technique, but about soul and rhythm.

As Bentley rambled toward the end of the song, the waiting foursome readied themselves. Muddy wondered if the others ever felt those same rusty butterflies.

"Hey, where's Aaron?" asked Corey.

He must have given Corey a dumb stare in return because Corey slapped the back of his head. "Our bassist du jour? Does he know the audition is today?"

Sighing, Muddy thought about their four-stringed situation. Most bands employed a full-time bass player, usually someone who couldn't handle guitar, a friend who'd do any-thing to be part of the band, or a singer who couldn't sing while playing. These days, few loved to play the instrument. Even fewer could play it well. Nobody wanted to be Flea from the Red Hot Chili Peppers anymore.

His dad called their problem the "Star Trek" situation. The teen had never watched the show, but the writer said that whenever the spaceship explored a strange new planet, they sent out a scout team to scour the area for life forms and omi-nous danger. In every single episode, one member never lasted for more than that one episode, always falling prey to what-ever terror lay in wait. He died within minutes of the show's opening, before anyone even learned his name or background.

The Accidentals' bass players lasted only a bit longer, thus adding another reason for their moniker. True, no aliens ever chomped down on their brief, four-stringed friends, but odd incidents usually befell them. Most of the time, a freak acci-dent took the blame. The other incidents weren't as colorful, but usually ended with stitches or at least an ice pack.

While anxiety readied its attack on Muddy with twitchy hands and a sweaty back, the auditorium doors burst open and in sauntered Leo Converse, a lanky goof who had close to zero musical skills. Slinging his vintage Fender P-bass over one shoulder, he approached the stage with a smile that sug-gested flatulence would soon follow.

"I'm here," he announced. Muddy knew the other was similar to the band in many respects, but he could hold his own, and that was all that mattered.

"Um," Muddy said, still anxious. "Where's Aaron?"

"You expected *him* to show up?" The towering bean pole nearly tripped over the PA. "Seriously? He got suspended yesterday for hacking into the school's computer system and putting a screensaver of Principal McIlveen in a bikini on the school's homepage."

They laughed, but time was tight. Muddy wondered if this guy could pull it off.

"All set to knock out some 'Sweet Emotion?'"

"Sure thing," the gawky teen replied, hooking up his

bass straight through the PA system, using only an EQ box to tweak his sound.

Muddy hoped Leo remembered the original. They loved the guy, often jammed with him when he was bored, but never considered him family. Loners will do that to a group. Still, he was likeable—and dependable.

As they entered the stage, the pompous leader of Silver Shadow *had* to toss in his two cents, of which Muddy was sure he thought was worth much more. "Good luck, Puddles." Bentley seemed to live for taunting the group, they had never fought back.

Inside, the teen's blood seethed, but Muddy kept cool, mostly from fear of retribution if he decided to give the guy dental work via a Les Paul. "It's Brooks, Chevy. Brooks."

He sneered as only a constipated-looking, anal-retentive snob could. "Brooks. Dirty Brooks," he said with a chuckle. "Is that like a special version of James Bond?"

"Hey, you," Corey said, "yeah, you—the proctologist's dream. Feel like chewing on a size fourteen boot today?" The band joked that Corey served their bodyguard, even though he'd called himself a mouse in a snake pit back in his old neighborhood. "Use that word again you might just taste leather." Nobody outside of the band knew that the sax player wouldn't fight anyone, but the big teddy bear thing worked.

"Oh, hey, Chambers," Bentley said, trying to remain calm, but his eyes sunk just a bit. "You still hangin' with these dorks? You should try out for a real band."

Corey moved to within a few inches of Bentley, giving him a hard stare. "I've got myself a real band, not like that soulless thing you put up on stage. And...you screw with my friends, you screw with me. Got it?"

The pale boy backed up, saluting him. "Got it, sir. Sad to see your talent go to waste, though."

"I'll give you one last chance. You mess with them, you mess with me." From the look in his eyes, one last ember of living in Carter Hill's hood still burned. Muddy, for one, didn't want to stoke that fire. It would be almost as fiery as his. Or Vinnie's. The teddy bear sat on what used to be, but the band knew that Corey, or any of them, would defend each other without hesitation.

Bentley grabbed his guitar and walked off the other side of the stage. The battle was over for now, but they knew the war would still rage on—at least until graduation, or until something from the "other side" ended his life. The way things happened in Muddy's life, either fate had a good chance of happening.

Poe laid her hand on his shoulder and the stress of the whole world went away. "Concentrate, Muddy. Remember, Chelsea will be out there watching."

Why did she have to say that? To set him off? To derail his anxiety? Did she even have an inkling that he wanted *her*? He might never have her. Why did so many people think he preferred Chelsea, a high-maintenance socialite who would never stoop to dating one of "his" kind? He'd need a miracle bigger than the crossroads to help him in that area.

They hit the stage and blasted through their three song audition: "Sweet Emotion,"

"Travelin' Band," and "Walkin' The Plank."

Not surprisingly, Muddy ambled through the set with his mind in another world, literally. When Otis crashed down on the cymbals to end their original song, the guitarist barely noticed.

"And that was 'The Accidental Muses,'" one of the judges said.

People rarely mentioned the band's name and they hardly ever used the second word. It had two meanings; one was musical, and one was demeaning, in a self-deprecating way. The first meaning was obvious. The second came from music theory, where a note out of a given key was added, usually a flat or sharp. It added character.

"You guys truly *are* accidents up there!" Bentley shouted as they powered down. He made eye contact with Muddy. "If I'd spawned one of you, I'd probably keel over and die too."

Son of a…

Muddy finally understood what "seeing red" meant at that moment. "I'll kill you, you stuck up—"

"Ooh," blubbered the smarmy prepster, waving his finger.

"A threat. They might lock you up for that, Puddles."

Corey had to hold Muddy back. He felt right then that if he swung, he wouldn't stop until blood hit the floor, even if it was his own. Then Leo grabbed Corey, as they all knew that if he took a swing, the golden boy's father would have the big boy from the bad side of town expelled on some false charges.

"Edgar!" Poe's voice cut through the throng of people and noise. That was all she had to say. The anger raged through him, but the magic in that voice bathed him in peaceful waves. "Edgar!" she repeated. "Don't. We'll be kicked out of the battle."

"Right," he grumbled. "Let me go, Corey."

When Corey realized Muddy wasn't going to race to his demise, he unclenched his fists, and Bentley slipped away, just like the loser he pretended not to be.

Rage nearly punched through the barrier of restraint. Muddy could tell Corey was about to blow as well. Instead, Corey likely let him go. Nearly tripping over the tangles of cords and cases, the guitarist must have kicked a dozen random items.

Kicking open the gym door, he tore into a sprint and didn't stop running until he hit the same street which changed his life the previous night. Standing breathless, he wished he had more athletic ability. Despite that fact, he'd managed to run about two miles without a hitch.

When he looked up, Muddy realized he stood in front of Silver Eye Watkins' red house. The old man would be waiting inside. Something within him assured him that the blues man knew his new protégé would be coming and knew much more about the days to come than Muddy ever would.

Chapter Thirteen

"Took you long enough."

"It's called school," Muddy said, pushing the door wide and nearly tripping over a gray cat. "They kinda get annoyed if you don't go. Wasn't this fur ball a *dog* last time I came here?"

Silver Eye waved the boy off. "Dog, cat—who cares? They come and go, just like my women, my friends, and my family. At least when I put out food, I know *they'll* be back." He snapped his fingers at the ball of charcoal-colored fur and it sauntered over to him, but not before hissing in Muddy's general direction. A far cry from Marshall, his Maine Coon, who would snuggle up to a serial killer.

"Whatever." Half of him still was choking back the tears of embarrassment and frustration of that afternoon, while the other half just was happy to be in a place far away from that soulless school building.

"What kinda critter skittered up your butt and died today?" Silver Eye asked with a crooked grin and a snicker.

Muddy's fist cracked against the door frame, causing more pain to shoot up his arm than paint chips to fly. "Don't mess with me, old man. Please. Not today."

"Well, don't go asking me for a hug or anything. I ain't no grandfather-type guy."

He felt his face scrunch up in disgust. "Don't worry about it. I wouldn't think of it."

The silence between the guitarist's words and the ones that he said next stretched into a long and tortuous moment. He just thought about the trip—and the guitar pick. Of course, Muddy had to be the one to break the silence.

"What happened last night? Is he still alive? When are we going back there to get him?" Anxiety ran his pulse into hyper drive, and he began to hyperventilate.

Finally, Silver Eye relented. Raising his hands in defense, he spoke. "Okay, I give. Just *relax*."

Muddy tried to speak normally, but his voice cracked instead "My brother might be dead in that weird place and you tell me to relax?" Why couldn't his hormones control themselves in times of crisis?

"Hold on," Silver Eye said gently. "I was gonna tell you everything, anyway. Ain't you ever seen *Star Wars*?"

"Which one?"

He shot Muddy an odd, quizzical look. "The one with the Force and those light sword thingies?"

"Yeah, I saw that one. There's nine of them now, you know," Muddy said. "Guess you haven't seen them all."

"What was your point?" Silver Eye kicked at the upright chair next to him and gestured to Muddy to park his butt in it. "This might take a while. You know how us old dogs like to reminisce about the good 'ol days."

Muddy parked it and within minutes, totally forgot his crappy day.

"Anyway, back to that *Star Wars* movie. You remember that whole 'Force' thing they talked about?"

Muddy nodded, wondering where this lecture was going. *Darth Vader with the blues?*

"The guy who thought that up knew there really *is* a force, or something like it. Has nothing to do with light sabers or Wookies or little furry creatures, either. Most of it has to do with music—and its power."

"So...the Death Star could've been a blues club?" Muddy couldn't resist. Humor was the best stress reliever he knew.

That one eye pierced Muddy like a switchblade. "Don't mess with me, kid. This is serious. Especially when we're talking about lives. Not just your brother's—yours too."

Muddy's icy blood froze over. "What're you talking about?"

"Promise to sit there and just listen now?"

"Gotcha." Muddy gripped the arms of the.

The old man grasped a beat-up coffee mug that the teen doubted held only coffee and brought it to his lips. "How do you write a song?"

"Huh?"

"How do you know when you're in that 'zone' when nothing you play is wrong? When all the notes are sweeter than honey?"

"I don't know. I just do it."

Silver Eye stared again. "You *do* know. You just don't realize it."

"*What*? Do you want to try English now?"

"You just do it. The ideas come from somewhere else, correct?"

Yeah, Muddy thought. When the guitarist simply played, ideas seemed to fall out of the sky. When he tried to compose something, he might as well have been yanking a brick through concrete with a strand of thread. But when he *didn't* think, when he just let it flow, that thread became a thick chain that snaked itself around him, pulling him into the song. Of course, dexterity, speed, and chord knowledge took endless hours of work, but when he was able to truly let go, bits of song rained down as he slid through a greased tunnel toward that…. River? Is that what Silver Eye called it?

"Yeah, man, the River." Silver Eye nodded as if he'd read the boy's thoughts.

"It's pure magic, but that's like card tricks compared to what you began to see last night." He rubbed his hands together in excitement like a kid on Christmas morning.

"*Harry Potter* magic," Muddy offered, knowing it would draw a stomp, but his mind was riddled with awe and tumbling thoughts.

"No!" Silver Eye downed the rest of his so-called coffee. "This is real." He slammed the cup down. "You need to hear this, need to understand this if you want to save your brother, if he's not already lost to—"

"To what?" Muddy really didn't want to hear the bad news but had to know. "Lost to whom?"

The man twirled a harmonica in his left hand. "In the River, in that world we went to last night, lives a figure that would send old Darth Vader, Freddy, Jason, and even Hitler back to their mamas needing a change of pants. You sink too low in that river and that's where his power awaits.

"We call him the 'Dark Muse.'"

"Who's we?" Muddy wondered aloud. His band? His family? His...whatever?

"All of us," he whispered. "Everyone who ever swam in those waters, tasted the music or other arts that mattered."

"What does this *muse* do? Inspire bad songs? That would explain what plays for music on today's radio." Muddy couldn't stand most current music, preferring to tune in to the classic rock stations on Spotify and YouTube.

Again, that one eye bored through him. "It. He. She. Who knows? All I know is it fuels what is wrong with that place, almost as much as the River does. Almost. You don't want to meet this thing. All I know is that everyone who's been in the River too long, who looked him in the eye wherever he resides, is buried. Along with their secrets."

"What do you mean, everyone?"

He huffed, staring at the walls, the myriad photos staring back at him.

"Son, this River's been flowing long before I came along. Long before man. I don't know who started it, or *if* anyone started it. Maybe it always was.

"But I do know *where* it began. And I do know *how* people like Plato, Mozart, Robert Johnson, Zeppelin, even cavemen brought music into this world."

"The other side?" Muddy guessed. "Where we went? But this is New Jersey. None of those guys were even *near* here."

Silver Eye stood and wandered around the room. "Yeah, I know. Jersey. No way Mozart or Johnson would ever soil their feet here, but you know the other names. Springsteen. Sinatra. Bon Jovi. Etc. Etc. Etc."

Oh, crap. "They all found the crossroads?"

Silver Eye nodded. "They found at least *one* of them."

"But—"

"Shh!!" he admonished, getting louder, irritated. "Just *listen*."

Silver Eye circled the room, setting off the cat, kicking the chair where the dog hid behind. The old creature howled and took off running. He mumbled an apology to both animals. "This is where it gets real. This is science, boy. At least, it starts there. I have no idea where it ends up."

"Wait," Muddy interrupted. "You're saying—"

"Yeah," he said, "there are *many* crossroads and they work both ways."

The look on Muddy's face must have said it all.

"I know you don't get it. And I hope you never do."

Chapter Fourteen

By the time Poe, Otis, and Corey arrived, Old Man Watkins and Muddy had immersed themselves in training. He barked out directions and the guitarist followed.

"Play a line in D pentatonic, first position."

"Bend that F up to a G, barely."

"Add some vibrato. No! Don't shake like you're carrying the smallest bladder in history. Use your body to move the note. Pretend like you have more rhythm than week-old roadkill."

And on it went.

When the bluesman finally took a break from wringing Muddy through the Jedi-like guitar boot camp, they noticed that the others had gathered round, watching them like a musical freak show. All sat around Silver Eye's sorry excuse for a living room, slack-jawed and ready to burst out laughing, but had enough respect for Watkins to hold off until he'd finished with their friend.

"Wow," Otis crowed. "Luke Skywalker rides the short bus to Bluesville."

Flames of embarrassment burned Muddy's cheeks, knowing even Poe couldn't keep from grinning ear to ear. So deep in the music, he must have seemed nuttier than a Texas president *without* the lobotomy to them.

"Shut it, Q-tip."

He only pulled that term of endearment out when the drummer really got to him, but his brain was flat-out fried. Otis sported a black frizzy mess of hair on his skinny head, skinnier neck, and slim frame. Once, when the band had been swimming, he'd toweled off and Muddy found himself cracking up with the image of a life-size Q-tip—*after* someone had cleaned their filthy ear with it. Thankfully, the joke had remained in their little group and his family, after his mom had overheard.

"Oooh," he said and whistled. "Now we know this is *serious* training."

Once again, the old man slammed his non-coffee cup. "Don't you kids take anything seriously?"

Poe, the voice of reason, spoke up. "Sir, no offense, but with all we deal with on a daily basis, if I didn't crack up or let these boneheads crack me up, my brain would have skipped town by now."

"Fair enough," he conceded, as most did when she spoke. "But if you aren't fully ready for what lies ahead in that place, you might as well get the nails ready for your own coffin."

She nodded and added, "I'll be as ready as possible for this, I promise you. However, I've also had those nails for a long time."

Muddy wondered if she could see the incredibly odd look he gave her at that moment, but somehow, he doubted she would be surprised at anyone's reaction to her words. At least, to anyone who knew her.

"So why did you guys come here? Was it that obvious where I'd go?" Muddy stared incredulously at his friends.

"Actually," Poe said, "we're kind of surprised you made it here alone safely."

The old man clapped his big hands. "Since we're all comfy and opening up like babbling babes, it might be a good idea to shut your yaps and get practicing. You're gonna need it."

Poe glared at him, but likely knew the old guy was only egging them on.

So they continued, playing alone, playing in pairs, playing in as many permutations as possible. Unlike the music on the "other side," no matter how they blazed or hooked into a groove, nothing magical happened.

"But, why?" Corey asked. "We're playing the same way as last night, even better sometimes. Does it only work over there?"

"And if it does only work over there," Otis chucked in his two cents, "why the heck are we practicing here when we can't see what it does?"

If that mug slammed one more time, Muddy expected shards to shatter into a cloud across the room.

"Better watch your mouth, little man. It might get you killed some day."

Of course, that only set the drummer off more. "You threatening me?" he asked, twirling a stick as he sauntered over to the man's chair. "Cause if you are, let me know now. I stopped taking crap a long time ago and stopped caring way before that."

The stare continued for a tense moment, then Silver Eye cracked a smile. Guttural laughter ensued, shaking the bluesman's entire body. "You guys are a little young to be such fatalists, don't you think? Personally, I think that if you saw what's *really* in charge over there, you'd pee on yourselves in a heartbeat and pray to whoever makes your world go 'round."

Corey stepped up, acting as the bodyguard again. "You don't scare me. So, I'll ask you only once, please show *us* a little respect. We don't see much of it, but after last night, I think we deserve it."

"Last night?" Silver Eye asked. "Are you kidding me? If you went there alone, you'd be in pieces right now."

"We kicked those things' butts!" Otis said. "Even you saw that."

"Such an ignorant fool, little drummer boy. Did you think you'd be alive right now if I hadn't shown you what to do?" His dark, wizened hand held up the mug. "Do you think you'd figure out how to whip those chest-beaters without my help?"

"Okay, Obi-Wan." Otis backed away, though he kept eye contact. "You made your point, but make sure you know we're not a bunch of wusses here."

"If you want respect, if you want me to take you seriously, finish your training here. Your brother," he said, pointed at Muddy, "if he's still alive, will still be kicking for another couple of days. You wouldn't go into Afghanistan without knowing how to drive a tank, shoot a machine gun, know who the enemy was, or even venture into the country's boundaries without a map, would you?"

"This isn't Afghanistan," Poe said. She had lost a cousin there, the only relative she'd truly gotten along with. "This is a forest with some goons stumbling around. Big difference."

"Girl," he said, leaning back in his recliner, face softening, though his gaze never wavered. "Whatever you know about the crossroads, it's *nothing* like the Middle East. It's *nothing* like *anything* on any map. What you experienced last night was just a tease of the real thing."

"I thought we were here to be trained like little Jedis, not listen to some mumbo-jumbo about your adventures."

Silver Eye just hung back, taking it all in, biding his time. "You kiddies done now? There's so much wine, but where's the cheese?"

If anyone else got the joke, they didn't show it. "My mom used to use that line on me. Took me a few years to get it." Muddy's almost grinned.

"Used to?" Silver Eye asked. "You finally stopped annoying her?"

"No, she died this past year." His heart hitched in his chest. Even joking didn't cut the pain. "Unless my prayers get a great long-distance plan, I don't think I'm bugging her anymore."

"Son, moms *always* hear. Don't matter where they are. I'm sure mine has wanted to use those angel wings to fly on down here and give me a whuppin' for so many of the things I've done in my life."

Muddy thought, *if only she knew what we were getting ourselves into...*

"Muddy," Otis said. "Your mom would kick yours if she found out about last night."

"Keep it up, Q-tip," Muddy replied, "and I'll let big Maggie in on what *you* do."

Otis's mom was a nice woman, but not easily fooled. Cross her once and you might only have to endure the "tongue of hellfire." Cross her twice and you'd likely end up with mental scars that would leave you drooling, trembling, and scared of your shadow for life.

"Anyway," Silver Eye continued, "getting back to un-reality here, you need to know a little story about the crossroads before we go any farther. If there's to be a journey, a funky trek deep into that other world where most humans have never returned to talk about, then you need to sit your tails down and listen to my little yarn from when I was younger."

"And had both eyes?" Otis just *had* to ask.

The mug missed the top of his head by inches.

"Okay," the drummer said, still ducking. "We're waiting."

Chapter Fifteen

Sucking in a deep breath, Silver Eye leaned forward and began his trip down memory lane. Muddy could swear that when he first spoke, the look in his eye seemed twenty years younger.

"Back in '45, right after they shipped my crack home from Germany."

Otis leaned in, staring. "Hold up the pooch here. You were in World War Two? But you look—"

Silver Eye waved him off. "The River does many things to many people, some good, some not so."

Muddy nodded at the others. World War Two vets tended to be about ninety. This guy couldn't be a day past sixty-five.

"Anyway," Silver Eye continued, seemingly disturbed by something in his memory, "the only thing I could find that would give me money to eat and live in a shack was music. Playing this harp, some guitar, singing, whatever. It got me through when this country said only white veterans were eligible for the pampered treatment.

"Anyway, I digress. So, there I was, pulling in the big nickels and dimes at night, slinging away at the blues in clubs that would have us. By us, I mean any group of musical misfits we could slap together into something that sounded good."

"But how'd *you* learn about the crossroads and that place?"

"Will you shut your trap already?"

The rest of them just sat and waited. Muddy knew something would spill from those old lips that would gear them up for Zack's rescue, and scare the heck out of them as well.

"The one steady band that rocked the pants off most of Jersey had this guitarist, Tommy Houston," Silver Eye began. "This dude, he burned the finish off the fretboard. When he took a header into the River, it was Olympic. With one foot in that deep blue and the other on the pulse of the rhythm section, that man balanced heaven and earth, good and evil, blue and the blackest black in his hands. His mind was a direct connection to the power source of the other side. Of course, that irritated whoever was in charge over there, but I'll get to that soon enough.

"I finally stopped him one night in the back alley. Asked him how he did it. True, he was talented, but heck, we all were. You had to be the cream on top of the cream just to get a gig back then. But one day, about six months before we spoke about *it*, everything changed. He went from everyday workman-type blues guitarist to slam-bam wunderkind. It's like he suddenly became a new person. We let it go long as we could then I broke."

"'What happened to you, man?' I said.

"'What 'chu talking 'bout, one eye?' He regarded me, not like a friend, but more of a child facing a wise old professor."

"It's Silver Eye, Houston," I said, "and you know what I'm talking about. You on something?'

"He just chuckled. Kinda like a kid who finds a hundred-dollar bill on the street every day. 'Yep, but not what you think. Ain't no wacky weed or snuff or voodoo queen. Found myself a new spring for my soul. My own little fountain of youth, but it juices my playing, like setting my muse on fire.'

"'You *must* be on something,' I said. 'If you're serious, *show* me, don't snow me.'

"He shook his head. 'Can't man, can't. This comes with a price, and it ain't one you pay off with cash. This can be bad.'

"'Man, you gotta bring me to this guy.'

"'Ain't no guy. It's a *place*. A *special* place.'

"I grabbed hold of him, thinking of my rumbling belly, empty pockets, and shoes with no sole. '*Tell me*,'" I said. 'I can't live like this no more. I play music for food. It was easier dodging grenades and tracer bullets than fending off rats at *American* restaurants and grocers. C'mon, man. *Tell me.*'

"He inhaled, deep as if he were about to sink to the bottom of some ocean—or if he was already there. Air or water, didn't seem to matter which filled his lungs at that point. Then he stared right through me as if he saw something far away, something that both amazed and frightened the crap out of him.

"He nodded and agreed to take me there but refused to talk about it until we reached the destination. We walked the same path you all did last night, he with his guitar and me with my harp in my pocket, right to where the trails crossed. Houston stopped a few steps short of where we played. Only one set of footprints marked the spot and I knew then and there that he was the only man who knew of its power—at least around here—at the time. Later, I learned that crossroads existed in several places, and all had the power to cross over, if you had the right stuff.

"'Watkins,' he said, 'I know this sounds wacky, but we're standing right there on that X and we're gonna play like our lives depend on it. Mine does and yours could.'

"Course, I figured he was either high or owed money to some mob guys who gave him the dope. But then when he stepped up to the plate with that look, I knew he believed in what he said. And that was good enough for me. I had nothing really to lose. Or so I thought.

"'Man, blues in B-flat. Keep it simple. Eight bar pattern. Real simple but let yourself go. Let it *all* go, that's the key—and this here spot where our feet are is the lock. Let it go like you never have before. Forget who you are, what ails you, and just *touch* the music'.

"'What are we trying to open?' I asked.

"'Don't *screw* with me,' he said. 'You might not live to regret it.'

"'Geez, man, I'm just askin',' I said. 'Relax.'"

"'No, *you* relax. *Close your eyes and just play. Now.*'

"So I did. Both of us did. We played tighter and yet looser than we ever did on stage. Soon the thoughts of confusion and doubt fell away. In a heartbeat, the ground beneath my feet just wasn't there anymore. I *fell*—just fell away and down into that place, that River that you swam in last night. I wanted to ask a million questions, but they melted just as fast as they formed in my mind. All that stuck was the music and yet, I didn't *try* to play. I just bled music. The current took me and swept me away with Houston, along with any words that tried to voice themselves. The most pleasant drowning sensation imaginable—you probably felt that last night—washed over me and filled every inch of me with its blue 'water.'

"I heard myself playing, but certainly wasn't thinking, wasn't attempting any lines, riffs, solos, or songs. It just happened, like someone, or *something* sliced me open at the soul and bled the music from me like a sieve. And I liked it. The waves kept pushing and rolling me in currents of sweet song until the tide swept back out to sea quicker than Lady Gaga changes her image and politicians lose IQ points.

"We found ourselves in that same spot as last night, probably feeling the same thing as you guys. And of course, within minutes, something came to greet us."

"'Holy mother of Ella Fitzgerald!' I said to him. 'Where are we, man?

"Houston just grinned and froze me. 'Science lesson 101, my man. Welcome to the crossroads highway.'

"*Where are we?*

"'Wherever the crossroads lead.'

"'Damn, man, are we in hell?' I said. 'Didn't Rob—'

"'Old Robert Johnson didn't meet no devil, at least not the one you'd expect. No deals here, but it's pretty damn easy to lose yourself here.'

"'How?'

"He just smiled and started walking away from me. 'Just wait…you'll see.'"

Chapter Sixteen

A heavy silence followed his story.

Silver Eye Watkins smiled that wicked smile as if he held the secrets to the universe behind it. "Go ahead. You can ask questions now."

Muddy thought they must have resembled the rejects from the *Dumb & Dumber* movies. He slapped the arms of the beat-up recliner and hacked a long, stuttered laugh.

"Something wrong with you?" Silver Eye asked. "I finally want your response and *now* you act like those idiots on the streets who act but don't speak?"

"They're called mimes, *Grandpa*." You couldn't shut up Otis for long, but even his rebuttal lacked spice.

Poe rarely lost her concentration, however. "You didn't finish the story," she said.

Silver Eye sighed, head hung low. "I went there with him a couple more times, but he got greedy."

"Where is he now?" Muddy asked, hands white on the guitar.

"Next topic, please."

Corey whistled to himself.

"If there's no 'selling of the soul to the devil,' then what harm is there in traveling? Besides those drummer apes, of course," Poe said.

Muddy had a feeling Poe's tongue was loose because she'd tasted sight for the first time since forever. She had to be aching to see again, even if it might kill her.

"Honey," Silver Eye cooed, "the devil would be chewed up and spit out if he took up residence over there. That little vignette you breezed through—"

"Breezed through?" Muddy sputtered. "Those oafs nearly killed us!"

"If you think they were tough, you've got another thing coming."

Corey tried looking cool, but his eyes told a different story. "Like what? Jumping thundersticks? Humongous hungry horns? Hordes of little people tooting flutophones?"

If one eye could pierce someone's soul, that bluesman accomplished just that as he stared back at their horn guy. "You wouldn't survive *one night* there, buddy."

"Who?"

Silver Eye waved them away. "Don't matter none. It ain't like you'll be getting that far, anyway. By the time you reached the real dangers, the ones you'd have to beat to get your brother back, I'd be able to find you by the trail of body parts the rest of that world's horrors left behind."

Muddy sighed, knowing the answer to his question. "You're not going to tell us, are you?"

"What would be the fun in that? Did Obi-wan tell Luke Skywalker about the trials he'd face in all the *Star Wars* movies? No, he let the kid fumble and tumble through those Jedi thingamabobs. Did Dumbledore tell Harry how to do all those wacky magic tricks? Nope, he let him fall flat on his face until he was ready."

The band sat there, allowing it all to sink in, brains brewing, but silent. Of course, the absence of sound could only avoid the vacuum that was Otis for so long.

"So, does this magic work in this world? Or just in the land of the hairy drums? You going to let us in on that secret or what?"

"Your mama ever whup you? Recently?"

The little drummer shivered. "Um…"

"I thought so," Silver Eye said, a knowing glint shimmering in his eye. "Maybe if she kept it up, you might learn to think before your lips flap."

The others giggled, knowing that Otis's mom was the one person in this world who could zip those lips. Muddy often wondered if something existed in that other world that rivaled the thunder that torched their ears every time she got ticked.

"And the answer is?" Corey asked, hands conducting in the air.

The old man grumbled to himself and tapped out a rhythm on his thighs.

"Umm..."

"Yes?

"Tomorrow's Friday. Come here after school. We'll train more, and then I'll answer your questions."

A cacophony of mumbled curses drowned out whatever he said next. Why would they have to wait another day just for an answer?

Obviously, Silver Eye knew this was coming. "If you're serious about this, you'll have no problem with tomorrow. Luke, Harry, Neo, and Frodo didn't become heroes overnight."

"But—" Muddy tried to step in.

"Yeah, I know. He's your brother. He's over there, I understand that. However, you remember what happened when Luke rushed to fight Vader? Or how Vader became Vader?"

Of course they did. Everyone knew *Star Wars*. The group might wind up losing more than a hand over there if Silver Eye wasn't bluffing.

"The bottom line is, you need to wait. Got it?"

A few mumbled, frustrated but dealing with it.

"You gonna listen to me? Speak up!"

Grumbling a disjointed "yes," they nodded in defeat.

Poe stood up, but instead of heading toward the door, she ran her fingers over the odd keyboard-ish thing the old man gave her. "So, what's the agenda?"

"What?"

"You said we're not ready yet. Fine. I can deal with that. But tell me what we have to do to get to Zack. You say we haven't hit the tip of the scary iceberg that comprises that little "crossroads" world of yours. If that's really true, you're missing the main point."

"Which is? Tell me, little angel."

Even with those cloudy eyes, the fire that sparked in them couldn't be missed. "Don't call me that, old man," she said and tossed the instrument back to him. "I'm not your angel or anyone else's."

Silver Eye raised his hands in mock defeat. "My apologies, Miss Poe. So do tell, what am I missing here?"

"He's been there for nearly forty-eight hours and *if* you're not shoving a pile through those lips of yours and *if* scarier things exist than what we've seen over there, then there's a good chance—"

"Don't," Muddy whispered, his mind already forming images of what could be.

"You're thinking the same thing, so grow up and deal with it, Edgar."

He couldn't believe she'd just said that.

Otis mouthed the "D" word to him, attempting to lessen the blow. Muddy did understand, but the lash from her tongue still stung. She knew how his mom's passing had affected him. "He's not dead."

"He might be, and you have to prepare yourself for that," she said.

"So then why do you want to go?" He usually held back, even with his friends, but now lashed out in anger. "Want to check out a dead body? You never liked him, anyway. Might be a thrill ride. Right?" Muddy immediately regretted his outburst, but instead of snapping back at him, Poe executed the worst retaliation of all.

She stared right through him, a sheen of salty liquid coating her clouded lenses of blue. Oh crap. Nothing else needed to be said. He'd stepped in it, rolled around in it and had submerged his head until both ears were clogged. He would pay for this. Didn't know when or where, but it would come.

Silver Eye whistled a dire tune. "Boy, you've a lot to learn about women."

Despite any intended comebacks storming within his head, he knew the battle was pointless. "I want all of us there when we go," the guitarist managed. "Without the whole group, it won't work, anyway. I really—"

"Shut up," Poe said, wrapping her arms tightly around herself. "I'm going. The band needs me, and I don't let people down." She refused to make eye contact, which was just fine with him for the moment. "When do we go?" She looked right at Silver Eye, the tears already burned away.

There it began, the would-be woman who normally reeked of sunshine, was now showing the first signs of a crack in her armor. Whether it would help or hurt her would reveal itself soon enough. Muddy hoped that when it did, they'd be there to help her.

"The lady asked, 'When do we go?'" Otis sometimes wavered in his bravado, but never his straightforwardness. "I think we've got ourselves a mission."

The old man stared at the group for a tense moment then spoke. "In time."

"What? We just agreed that Zack might be, well, he's not going to last long there on his own. You've made that clear."

"You're not ready. I said that already. You go there now and people will die."

Corey's head shot up. "You don't know that. If we *don't* go there, someone *will* definitely die."

Silver Eye shook his head slowly. "You're not going. Said and done. Remember the 'respect your elders' thing? You need training. I'm not about to sacrifice four pains in the butt just because they want to go, go, go. This ain't some videogame where you can read a book of tricks and beat the thing! Even people who know what they're doing sometimes don't come back." His gaze hit the floor.

"Houston's still there, isn't he," Muddy asked. "That's what you believe, isn't it?"

The old man waved his hand in the air. "Probably nothing left of him now. Stupid greedy fool. He *had* to go. The place is magnetic—it pulls you in—you'll see."

"When did you last see him?"

Muddy swore a tear formed in that one eye. "In nineteen-sixty-nine. He desperately wanted to do Woodstock and blow the place wide open."

"Like Hendrix did," Corey added.

"Yep, like Hendrix."

"But he never returned."

Sighing, Silver Eye continued. "Nope, and people here

thought he'd just picked up and headed for Chicago or New Orleans or some blues capital. I knew the truth."

"What happened to him? Was it the Dark Muse?"

The others turned to him, a million questions in their eyes.

"You think he's still alive? Him or the muse?"

Silver Eye's head turned toward the wall of photos. "The Dark Muse…it ain't always the same. I think the River—and what rules the other side wears them out from time to time."

Muddy felt worry wash over him. "They grow evil of that magnitude there?"

"Doesn't every world? When Hitler died, we got a whole slew of new demons, no shortage of them. Did it stop when Bin Laden got killed?"

"There's darkness everywhere," Muddy said, understanding.

"You got it, boy. Sometimes people even go looking for it."

"What do *you* think happened to him?"

That eye, the silver one, seemed to come alive and bore straight into him. "Probably the same thing that'll happen to you if you head over there before you're ready."

"Okay," the boy replied, even though he didn't know to what he was replying.

"You'll complete your training with me?"

He answered before his brain registered the question. "Of course."

Chapter Seventeen

The moment they left the house and crossed the street, Otis spoke. "When do we leave?"

Muddy didn't hesitate. "First thing tomorrow morning. Pack your gear."

"We're skipping school?" Otis sounded giddy at the thought.

Muddy grinned. "No one will notice. Besides, remember what Silver Eye said? Time acts different there. We could be gone a week and still make math class."

"Let's not."

"Still," Poe said. "You don't know that for sure. I can't deal with a suspension."

"Trust me, we'll be back in time. Why do you think Silver Eye looks so young?"

Corey put a big hand on his friend's chest. "I've got a bad feeling about this."

"Stop quoting movies." Muddy's focused stare rivaled Silver Eye's. "Even he wouldn't turn down this adventure."

"But we're not heroes. We're the 'The Accidentals.'"

Morning came without incident, but also with little sleep. No strange sounds. No mud-caked shoes. Yet Muddy would have liked to have encountered his mother, real or the dream version, one last time. Their little group of misfits was about to embark on a journey without permission into a land, or world, that none of them understood. In a few hours, he, Poe, Otis, and Corey would disappear at the crossroads—to hopefully return—and not alone.

Muddy and his dad exchanged morning grumbles, typical

of a weekend. He headed for the cereal and coffee, hoping to get through the meal with little or no conversation. Despite the friction between them, he couldn't bring himself to lie to the man who never failed him. Whenever Muddy did, it hurt, and as his father often told him, guilt sprouted in neon letters all over his face. Great writers understood characters and everything that went along with it. Reading his expressions must have been akin to flipping through those "See Dick Run" books.

"How's the prepping for the big battle going?" his father asked, reading the news on his laptop.

Muddy nearly launched his coffee mug into the ceiling. *Nerves will kill me one day.* Thankfully, he thought before freaking out. That was hard to accomplish with his anxiety running rampant.

"Uh...yep," he replied in a voice he hoped sounded normal. "Just one more rehearsal before the shindig tonight."

Crap! he thought, realizing that before they'd decided to save his brother's life, or attempt to, that they'd auditioned and had to perform at eight o'clock that night! The order of the bands wouldn't be determined until the lottery before the show. Hopefully, they'd get a later slot. Just in case one of them had to be replaced.

Bad joke, he thought, chiding himself. *Don't even think that.*

"Ed? Edgar? You there? I asked if you were ready."

"For what? Oh, yeah. The battle. We'll be set to kick serious butt tonight."

What did Silver Eye say about time behaving differently over there? Oh yeah, he didn't. They'd assumed and hoped they wouldn't return to a world which had aged centuries without them.

Then his father flashed a knowing smile, which always worried the boy.

"Who's the victim tonight?"

"*What?*" Shards of ice rained down his neck.

His father threw his hands up in the air. "The bassist who's enemies with fate and good luck. Did you find anyone brave enough to pull duty who's not worried about electrocution, impaling themselves on a string, or drowning in the crowd surf?"

A laugh escaped Muddy's lips. One thing about his father,

no matter how scary his stories were, he could always get people to laugh. Most horror writers could. He often stated that being scared and laughing your butt off were two sides of the same coin.

"Yep. Leo offered. Not the most amazing player."

"He's the only one left?"

"Just about."

He shot Muddy his best evil eye. "Better stop killing off the four-stringers."

The laughter came as a release, even though Muddy couldn't shake the bad feeling brewing inside him.

"Now hurry up and eat. You're gonna be late for school."

Man, he hated lying to his father. "Hopefully not," he replied, crossing his fingers that his words would be partially true. They had made a pact to be open with each other. Muddy felt a fist crushing into his chest knowing he was breaking it, but had to if he could save Zack. It wasn't like his dad or the police could help.

The rest of the meal ensued without discussion. His dad checked his writers' social media sites, whining and moaning about sales, the classics, and other stuff he usually did before he sat down to write in his "zone."

Muddy wondered if writers ever went over or was it just for musicians. Words could be just as magical as music, in a way, but he couldn't wrap his mind around how the curtain would part for a story. Weird. Too bad one of Dad's conferences wasn't soon. He'd bet money that if a passage were possible, one of the serious writers already found it.

Grabbing the strange guitar Silver Eye gave him two nights ago, he headed toward the door, half wishing his father would have asked where he really was going and forced him to stay home. His hands shook so hard he nearly dropped the case.

Chapter Eighteen

The group met at the corner of Muddy's street with quiet excitement, three of them bouncing on their heels. Even Otis remained relatively mum that morning. Muddy figured that fear had found its way into everyone's heart sooner or later. Only Poe appeared gung-ho, but after a fifteen-plus-year sentence in her home, not much *would* scare her. Hopefully, that would stay true, at least for today.

He wondered how they'd managed to avoid the school bus. Otis insisted on hitching a ride with Muddy instead of riding in his mom's convertible. Poe always walked and had Corey as a bodyguard.

"Leo?"

The tall player in the role of karmic misfortune smiled. Somehow, they had all doubted he'd go along with the idea, but he'd showed up anyway. "Hey bud. Heard you needed a hand. Since you didn't have an actual bass yet, I borrowed Poe's whatchamacallit thing. I can lay down a mean low line on that for you."

How Otis got Leo to come, Muddy would never know. He probably didn't believe much, if any, of the story, yet by the strained look on his face, something had clicked in his brain—something he'd sensed wasn't right.

But... what if something happened? The curse was all in their heads, right?

"Thanks, Leo. Trust me, we appreciate any extra hands we can get."

The journey took only a fraction of the time it did the other night, or so it seemed. In the daylight, shadows still existed in the Iron section of town, but didn't pose as much of a threat. In no time at all, The Accidentals found themselves out of their neighborhood and scaling the hump of the landfill, peering over the top as if a tiger or some other beast waited on the other side, because the real dangers lie behind the barrier they couldn't see. But reality ceased to exist over there. That was the problem.

The group walked the path to the crossroads as though they were simply following a well-traveled trail. Under the protection of the sunlight, the "X" of the passing lines seemed to be as imposing as an intersection in the middle of nowhere. Long grass streaked down each of the four lanes but lay trodden to the ground and devoid of any natural color. Wind failed to reach inside the amphitheater of waste and forgotten land, lending a silence to the setting that coaxed the fear back into Muddy's veins. Sometimes, the absence of a threat frightened a person much worse than when it was shoved right into your face; especially when that fear had seen your face and many more lurked behind its own.

Forming a cross, they unslung their instruments and gazed at each other, waiting for the word.

"Well," Corey said, "are we just going to stand here like idiots or are we going to play to get our butts over there?"

"Well, what do you suggest we play, sax man?" Otis chimed in, possibly feeling a little more brazen. "We don't know how the old man got the ball rolling the other night. Once it rolled, it was pretty easy to join in, but how do we start?"

"Muddy?" Corey turned to the guitarist. "You really turned it on with him and sent us over. Can you do it again?"

"Do what?" Leo asked. No one answered him.

Truth was, Muddy had no idea what Silver Eye did last time. He'd just followed the old man's lead until the music flowed from his veins. "Umm...."

"I know," Poe said, sounding impatient. "While you three were jacking around with ol' one eye, I paid attention to the music. It's pretty simple—in theory."

"Theory?" Otis squawked in a high-pitched whine.

Poe raised her hands in mock surrender. "Listen, if you're too—"

"Don't you *dare* say the word."

She smiled as though she could see his pained expression. "Okay, I'll shut up, but we've gotta get going here."

"Otis, give me the rhythm."

He opened his mouth to inquire which rhythm, but then zipped his lips and took hold of the sticks. Gripping them tight, he twirled them once, loosening his wrists and fingers slightly before rapping on the top of the drum skin. In a matter of seconds, a boogie-like, two-four beat echoed through the garbage canyon. His eyes closed and he hung his head back, drowning in the pattern.

A deep foghorn bellowed beside Muddy. He turned to see Corey sound a low D and hold it over the drummer's syncopation. The bigger teen inhaled, almost in a sonorous tone like what emanated from his sax. He sank—deep—into that zone, even with a dearth of notes. The way he played said it all. The sax became a voice that invited them to join.

Even Leo, the bassist du jour, hopped in on the fun and laid down a serpentine line that shook the dirt upon which they stood.

Muddy shivered.

They all seemed so focused. So determined. So...brave.

And where was he?

No matter how much he missed Zack, no matter how much he wanted to be the next Rambo, the Skywalker, even Harry Potter, he hadn't been born with a lightning scar on his forehead or Jedi blood coursing through his veins, so he was definitely out of luck in that department. He wondered if Poe knew what lie ahead. Or what lay hidden in his own heart.

She hummed, loud enough to cut through the others' noise, the voice of an angel who'd seen way too much hell in her short life. He wished he could tell her all, tell her how he felt, but his mom, her dad, both their lives' baggage—it served as an easy out. Maybe one day he'd have the strength to knock down those walls.

Sucking it up, Muddy gripped the neck until his fingers hurt and slipped a pick into place. Taking a deep breath, his thumb and forefinger plucked the first magical note. He thought it was magical, but knew there had to be some rational, scientific reason for what happened in the next couple of minutes.

The bends which rode Otis's rhythm slithered around Corey's sax line and answered Poe's call, wafted from the strings as they vibrated. Muddy spun a web of blue that made the antiquated oddity of the guitar seem like a vintage Les Paul. How Silver Eye got his hands on that musical contraption that no guitar luthier had ever imagined was beyond him, but none of that mattered now.

Chapter Nineteen

As the waves of melody and rhythm grew, the curtain once again parted.

He tried his hardest to keep his eyes open, to see what lay behind this reality and the one they'd visited—and were headed to again. Yet, whatever power controlled the front stage of life to the back lowered the drapes on his lids. He saw something that he would never, ever forget, but then it dissipated, just like the images of his friends traveling next to him. The last picture his open eyes saw was the peaceful, closed ones of the band.

Fear reared its head again as they came to, the other reality now theirs.

"Where the heck are we?" Leo began to freak out a bit. "I didn't sign up for this. Otis! What did you do to me?"

Poe gave her death stare to the little guy. "You didn't tell him?"

He shrugged. "He's a big boy. Besides, I didn't think we'd get back here to tell you the truth. Sorry, Leo."

The bassist continued his freak out. "Sorry for what? For where?"

"Guys, be careful. We don't know what's lurking around this place."

Leo's issues were suddenly forgotten. In all the turmoil, nobody had even bothered to check if those ape/oaf-like things were nearby. Everyone swung their heads back and forth, checking for the creatures that had nearly crushed them with their percussive bodies the first time. Ears cocked, the band listened, looked, even felt the ground.

Nothing.

But no one had warned Leo about the dangers here. If they had, he probably wouldn't have come. Muddy knew he wouldn't have believed anything they said, so leaving out a few key details was not the worst thing they could do. Unless... something happened.

But this wasn't the stage. It wasn't *Star Trek*. He wasn't just an add-on who was destined to bite the big one the moment the team landed, was he?

"Okay, I'm gonna go with the idea that I'm dreaming here, even though I'm probably not. I didn't need this today. I'm skipping a science test, so there's that, but still. Geez!"

Corey put a hand on his shoulder. "Dude, it's cool. This is nuts, but if you just hang with us, we'll get you back home, no problem."

The bassist's eyes darted so fast, Muddy thought they'd shoot right out of their sockets. But after a minute, he calmed down, taking in the adventure. Then again, he hadn't witnessed the dark side yet.

"Look, this path leads somewhere," Leo said. "There's a marking. I found something. He might be down this way!"

Then it happened. Muddy doubted Leo even saw it coming.

Chapter Twenty

One moment, the bass player skipped along the path, side-stepping long plants and weeds jutting into his way, giddy with the excitement of finding a clue. The next moment, something exploded out of nowhere. Leo screamed, more out of fright than in pain, but it still sent sheets of ice down Muddy's back. From the looks on the rest of the band's faces, they felt the freeze, too.

"Oh, crap—" Corey whispered.

Poe covered her eyes. "Not another one. Please, not another."

As Leo stepped off the path to the "sign" he'd believed would help, the entire ground leapt to life. The long, thick blades of grass took shape in the form of things that looked like a massive smorgasbord of linguini. Really thick, long, green linguini.

It sprang at his legs and spun around them, very much *al dente*. The green and yellow tendril-noodles slapped his flesh in a resounding thump due to his loose jeans. His scream echoed through the clearing, recalling classic Led Zeppelin howls. The three strands squeezed the circulation and blood from his limbs. Leo wind-milled his arms to counteract the grass linguini's pulling which made him appear a trapped duck, complete with sound effects. Then two more blades of the stuff recoiled and aimed higher, much higher.

To his credit, his spastic nature and lack of coordination probably saved his life. Only a moment after the pasta-like things clamped around his jean-clad legs, he panicked and fell backwards, straight onto the path.

The others surged forward, expecting the worst, when Otis

drew his oddly-notched sticks and slammed a one-two-three-four that shook the entire floor of land. Muddy, Poe, and Corey somehow managed to remain standing, but Leo vibrated free. The living linguini slunk back into the mass of grass, if any of it really *was* grass. Not knowing if it reacted due to fear or the vibrations, no one acted like they wished to find out. A collection of hands replaced the grass and pulled him clear.

"Did *pasta* just attack me?" Leo sat still. He breathed heavy but stayed on the path.

"Let's go that way!" Poe yelled, and the band simply nodded. All five headed west without question.

After about fifty feet, the edge of the clearing appeared. As usual, Poe saw the obvious more easily than anyone else did. It was amazing how her senses were enhanced not only when one was taken away, but because she'd learned to focus on the now, which was all she believed she had. But how? He wondered what went through her mind, the ability to see suddenly available to her after all these years.

Muddy half-expected the trees that engulfed them to swallow them whole. They didn't but fear still stoked his anxiety and the feeling that the behemoths above could do business with them if they felt the need. So instead of stopping to check on Leo's injuries under the cover of the canopy, the foursome continued to drag him to where the sun shone at the edge of the tree line. The clearing was only another fifty feet or so, but with their adrenaline fading, dragging the seventeen-year-old began to feel like they were pushing a full manure truck with no wheels.

Otis complained the entire way, as usual, which fit his personality, but also showed his fortitude. Any extreme stress on his brittle bones could cause a break, possibly compound, which in this situation could kill him. But his only concern right now was for a member of the band they barely knew.

Then there was Muddy. Getting beaten around by schoolmates for years, made fun of by them, even cousins, teachers, etc. had done its damage. It gave birth to anxiety, already festering in him from problems in the classroom. The fear of not being able to handle life as it was dealt disgusted him. Otis, who was diagnosed with a lifespan of less than eighteen years never faltered, at least in public, and treated the world as his stage. Muddy acted as though he was the world's opening band reject, caught behind the curtains, chained by his own demons.

The sun lashed through the last remaining branches above them, stripping away the heavy shadows that further weighed upon their backs. The group crashed to the ground and spread out on an open field, with grass—real, short, non-moving grass.

For a moment, a jolt of anxiety raced through Muddy's veins before he realized they had cleared the obstacle. It shook him out of his funk and onto his knees to check on their wounded friend.

"Is he okay?" Poe asked, putting her hands on his shoulder, propping up his head.

"Yeah," Otis echoed. "He okay? I don't think I ever pulled that much dead weight before in my life!"

Leo stirred. "Just tell me—am I okay? What *was* that back there? No one told me there'd be noodles masquerading as grass trying to kill me here!"

"Actually, it was more like thin spaghetti."

"The word's linguini," Poe added, "but green and brown, like the fancy kind."

Otis spun to her. "Who told you linguini was that color? I sure hope they didn't feed you that!"

"Guys," Corey said, shoving Leo back a little. "Instead of fussin' and whining, check out what that Chef Boy-R-Dee reject thing did to him."

Thankfully, the unlucky bassist had been wearing jeans. The living pasta grass had left them in tatters. Corey and Muddy carefully stripped away the remaining threads which were covered in sweat, blood, and—*goo*?

"Eww," Corey said, shrinking back. "What is that stuff?" he asked, rubbing it off his fingers onto the real grass.

"What's what?" Leo shivered beneath them.

Muddy swallowed with revulsion. He hated blood. Great disposition to have as a son of a horror writer, but his dad hated blood, too.

"I don't know," he said. "Plant spit? Digestive juices?"

"Poison?" Poe added, as they shrank back, staring at their hands.

"I sure hope not," Muddy replied. "If it is, then we're all screwed. We'll need a whole new band this time."

"Instead of worrying about yourselves," Leo whined, "can you please just tell me how bad it is?"

Nodding shamefully, Muddy went back to peeling away the last bits of denim that stuck to his friend's legs. What he saw underneath sent his stomach into spin cycle and he lost it. Swinging his head to the side, everyone cleared in time. He vomited all over the clean, non-deadly grass.

"Dude," Otis said, still backing away. "You okay?"

He spat out whatever remained in his mouth, gagging as he attempted to speak. "Yeah, I think so. Look at him," he whispered, not wanting to alarm Leo.

"Uh-oh," came the collective response.

Leo dropped his head to the ground. "I heard that. I'm dying, aren't I?

The band members stared silently at each other as each hoped to find the answer in someone else.

"Of course not," Poe said in her best reassuring voice. "It's just a flesh wound."

His fists smacked the soft grass. "This is no time for movie quotes!"

"Okay, okay, let's take a good look," Muddy said dryly. Humor seemed to be everyone's defense mechanism lately.

Once his system seemed bile-free, Muddy examined the wound. As Poe dabbed up the blood in some tissues she must have had in her pocket, what the pasta grass did became clear.

Inch long "bites" traveled up and down his leg, from ankle to upper thigh. The grass had to have some sort of "teeth" or else just whipped and constricted so hard it bit into the skin. But that wasn't the worst part. Each slice in his skin pulsated, as if something was pretty angry about being in there. Muddy prayed it was only Leo's system fighting a likely infection, but something in him knew better.

"What the heck?" Corey said, leaning in closer.

The paling flesh rose and fell as if a spastic heart lay beneath each open bloody slit. As each wound rose, it threatened to poke through and show what it actually was but stopped just short. As everyone gaped at his legs, an image came to mind of the bugs Muddy usually felt beneath his skin. But his never seemed to have a wild beat. Heck, these seemed to be having their own little circus.

"So, am I okay? Am I dying?" Leo asked, more panic in his once-deep voice.

They looked at each other, then at Poe, who usually equalized the group. She just stared, as if she could see his grim future. "Sure," she said, without an ounce of conviction. "We'll make sure you're fine."

"But what do we do? Drag him back through that stuff and try to cross back over?" Corey stood, and began to pace.

"I don't know, but we need to do something."

Muddy gazed back at the forest and remembered what lay beyond. "If we have to, so be it. But there's got to be another way."

"There is, but you'll have to come with me."

He turned to Poe, who shook her head mouthing, "that wasn't me."

Chapter Twenty-One

"I said it, and you'll have to come back with me if you want your friend to be healed in time."

They turned to the voice and discovered that The Accidentals weren't the only people on this side.

The girl seemed to be about their age. Not as striking as Poe, but seemingly familiar, especially in the eyes. About five-foot-three, long, licorice-colored hair hanging without a trace of curl, she stood nonchalantly watching the group as if she met five misfits from another dimension all the time. But those eyes... who did she remind him of?

"Um...hi," Muddy managed to say.

"Who are you?" Poe asked. "And can you please help us? He's hurt." She pointed to Leo's leg.

The stranger tilted her head as if to gauge the bassist's condition then back at Muddy. "I'm Lyra," she said in a voice that sent shivers down his back, so smooth and lilting, like waves of silk. "I think we can help your friend, but we'll need to get him to the town. He was bitten by the grass?"

Otis turned to the guitarist and whispered, "We just crossed over into some parallel world with tons of weird crap and they don't even have a name for that stuff that attacked Leo?"

"Why should we speak differently?" she asked, her tone staying the same. "Where are you from? Obviously, not from around here." This time a slight grin cracked her expression.

"She knows?" Corey whispered. "How? Wait a minute." He leaned in closer and squinted at her. "Man, she looks so much like..."

This time she giggled a little but remained far enough from

them. "It's been awhile, but we're used to visitors. I'm surprised you got this far. Most don't. Either you're pretty skilled or just very lucky."

"I think it's a little of both," Poe replied. "We had a little help."

"I know," Lyra answered, her expression unchanged.

But how? Muddy wondered. *Was she watching when we came with Silver Eye?*

"No, I didn't," she said.

"Didn't what?" Poe asked.

"Didn't watch you when you came here with Silver Eye."

What the…?

Otis hopped to his spindly, short legs. "You spying on us? Did you sic those big goons on us?"

She just gazed with an unchanging pair of alluring eyes. "No. What lives out here have knocked off plenty of our people in town. I stay clear of them. You should too."

"What do you mean knocked off? Killed?" Corey asked.

She averted her gaze.

"A lot?"

"Corey," Poe chided, slapping at his arm. "Get a clue!"

"We need to get him some help," Lyra said, pointing at their bassist.

Muddy's body trembled as he sought his voice. "Is he going to be okay?

She looked right into his soul and he swore he heard, "*He will die if the poison reaches his heart. Many do not make it with bites like that, but I have hope.*"

The rest of the group did not react.

Did they hear what she said?

"*You know they didn't,*" she answered, and he realized the voice had bypassed his ears, straight into his head.

Holy cow…

"*They'll hear if I want them to. Right now, I need you to understand and not worry them.*" Her eyes told him not to ask the details of her skill.

"Come with me," she said aloud. "We need to get him to the city—now."

Chapter Twenty-Two

She led them about two miles along the winding path.

As they passed the final grove of trees, a city appeared. Resembling something from pioneer times, houses built of logs and wood planks stood everywhere. Towers rose in the four corners of the development, which reached as far as their eyes could see. It must have been at least a mile or so across and possibly twice as long. Why people always imagined a city in an unknown land to be medieval, he had no idea. Maybe it was because of all those fantasy novels and movies. It seemed as though most movie makers couldn't imagine that any other civilization could exist as anything *but* something out of King Arthur. Were people so ignorant that they couldn't imagine another culture was capable of building a society to rival their own?

Yet there it was, something straight out of the late 1800s, not the age of *The Sword in the Stone* or *Merlin*. Within the quartet of towers lay a scene straight out of the Old West. Buildings a few stories high reached into the clear blue sky above, nestled in between the huddles of small houses and log cabins. Busy, but not crowded, a small market bustled in the town square. Colors bloomed outward in the shades of the basic spectrum—blue, green, red, orange, yellow, purple—some white, but very little black.

She halted before she reached the throng of citizens. "I think it's best if no one sees us."

"Why?" Muddy wondered if more monsters lived there, ones in human skins.

She looked around. "Let's just say that people in this town

don't look too kindly on your folk. They blame you for the shape we're in now."

"And what shape is that?"

"You don't want to know, but we once had music here. Now, if one is caught even humming a tune from someone who visited here, they… Well, they're not here anymore."

Muddy froze and knew the others felt the same chill.

They looked down at the instruments they carried. "Crap," he muttered.

People, more humans, strolled through the mini-streets and congregated in the city's heart, clad in outfits of those seven colors, mixed and matched in different fashions. Men, women, and kids carried various wares and baskets. Muddy felt as though a rainbow had exploded in front of his eyes and burst into life. Most of whom he could see strode in peaceful strides, some smiling, but more in slow, steady gaits that suggested something less than happiness lie underneath.

"What is that?" Corey asked, pointing at an odd-shaped, prism-type thing sitting in the center of the town square. People revolved around it like fearful moons, drawn to it but never daring to orbit too close.

The band stared, waiting for Lyra to explain, but she simply kept walking. They turned to Muddy instead. Why, he had no idea. If they only knew the fear he hid in his heart…

"Don't look at me, I suck at geometry." Something about it scared the living hell out of him. It looked innocuous, but somehow, its presence felt much like the tip of an iceberg. What lay beneath, he had no clue, but the feeling that seemed to reach out like invisible fingers nearly froze him in his steps.

Why aren't you telling us about that…prism thing? He reached out, hoping her apparent telepathy was on the way one more time.

She didn't even gaze his way.

Atop an ebony platform which stood about two meters tall in a series of decreasing squares, the crystalline pyramid of hexagonal sides, balanced itself—inverted. From his vantage point, the glass-like object appeared to be hovering an inch or so above the platform. Was it wires? An invisible magnetic field like the one he saw in the science center? Something about it freaked him out, but no one seemed to notice it even existed there, completely juxtaposed into the middle of their odd little world.

"Lyra?"

"Just follow me," she answered, ignoring Poe. "We need to get your friend to care, now. I know someone who will help, discreetly."

"But..."

"*Now.* You don't know the power of the poison." Muddy knew where the tension in her voice originated. Not much in that world could compete with what she dealt with back home.

He could tell both wanted to talk about the strange object and the things it suggested, but neither said a word. He prayed they would have time to discuss it later before anything else happened.

A young couple stood inside the house when they arrived. Greetings were exchanged, but not names. Both parties regarded each other with cautious looks. Muddy could swear he recognized something in their faces. Did everyone here look like they were related to someone famous back home?

The young man spoke. "You know Silver Eye Watkins?"

"Yes," Muddy replied. "Silver Eye trained us, but we're here to find my brother. He came over two nights ago."

The couple shared an odd look.

"Just bring in your friend. I take care of the healing in town."

"Will he be okay?"

"He'll be fine. We know how to cure the ills the forest brings as long as the poison hasn't reached the heart. He won't feel any more pain in a few minutes."

Didn't that exist as a cheesy line in so many horror and mob movies?

The band waited in the front room while the couple disappeared with Leo. Soon, Muddy felt himself dozing off, but before he fell asleep, he noticed the others were already zonked out as well.

A loud noise awoke him some time later.

"I'm sorry," the man said.

Anxiety flooded Muddy. "What do you mean? Sorry for what?"

"I sent my wife out for supplies and someone followed her back. I guess someone somewhere here knew you'd crossed over. You weren't exactly quiet."

"What does that mean for us?" Corey grabbed his horn.

Lyra shared a pale look with her friends. "Nothing, if we can get you back in time."

Poe stood, sneaking a gaze out the window. "And if we don't?"

"Then you'll find out what happens when the music dies around here."

They pushed open the front door and gasped at what lie before them. Men, women, and kids crowded the streets, all wearing the same expressions.

"They're not going to let us out of here," Muddy said. The guitar shook in his hands, sounding weird notes.

"What, no torches and pitchforks?" Otis quipped.

"Shut up. Just let me think about this for a second."

Yet the crowd advanced. They seemed wary, but intent on reaching the boys.

"They don't seem to be armed. We can run for it," Otis offered.

They looked behind them at the road to the forest's edge where the path began. It was maybe a hundred feet to a different kind of danger, but also a long way home.

"We gotta try it, Muddy." Otis knew his friend only felt confident when called by his nickname. Music gave them all a boost of self-esteem. "Let's go for it."

Muddy, confident as he was in his own sprinting ability, knew Otis wouldn't make it and everyone else knew it as well. If the drummer hit a hole or rock, an ankle might snap in a heartbeat.

"Okay, you go first. In the meantime, I'm gonna give them a little entertainment," he said, unslinging his odd guitar and swinging it into position.

"No."

But Muddy turned to the crowd, pick twirling in his hands. "Get. Out. Of. Here."

Something in Muddy's voice resonated with Otis and he ambled backwards toward the forest. The mob of townsfolk advanced with each step. He gripped both sticks and tapped them nervously.

I hope these guys like Ozzy. Off the rails?

Muddy's fingers went into motion and the famous riff roiled out in the crowd's direction. The low, train-sounding melody boomed, the leaves of the trees brushed back by the low pitches. Suddenly people halted as he finished the two-bar part and repeated it.

"Hey!" He called to the drummer. "I think it's work—"

The throng of people began moving again, this time with an angry purpose to their steps, though no one uttered a word.

"*Run, Muddy!*" The voice came from within, and he felt an urge to head to toward the forest.

Not one to argue with reason, Muddy did what the voice told him. He pumped his legs as hard as he could and reached the beginning of the trail where he saw Otis and slid to a stop.

"Duck!" A new voice rang in his ears.

Something sailed through the air from the left side of the woods, through the trees and over the crowd.

It struck the prism hard, sending a shower of sparks into the villagers. The softball-sized rock careened off it and knocked out one of the guards. Vibrant colors filled the sky over the village and the ground shook beneath them. If they weren't already on the forest floor, the percussion would have knocked them head over heels.

"What?" Muddy clung tight to the grass. "Who? Did they break that thing?"

Lyra looked at both boys, smiling.

"I had help. Not all of us here follow the rules. Some of us were born after the change."

Otis looked back at her. "Before I ask or seem to care about whatever you're talking about, can you get us back to the crossroads? Leo's hurt, and Corey can't maneuver both Poe and him through that killer linguini stuff."

Again, that smile. Why did females always shut him up with a great smile?

"Already done. I headed them off and made sure they navigated safely to the cross-trails."

"It's called the crossroads," Otis corrected.

"Whatever," she waved him off. "Regardless, they won't be safe forever in that forest. Get your butts in motion and play your song to get back home."

"But—"

"Now!"

"We can't leave until you tell us what happened back there, what's going on in your town."

"Next time."

Otis laughed an uneasy laugh. "Girl we ain't coming back here."

Muddy slapped his chest. "Zack's still here, somewhere. We'll be back," he replied to Lyra.

"I know. I knew that before you even got here."

"But, why did they want us? At least tell me that."

Her face turned to stone. "They believe you bring the Dark Muse. Your friend once did." She turned and pushed him away. "They're coming. Both of us will be here to help you next time."

"Both?"

As much as Muddy wanted to interrogate the annoying, enigmatic girl, he knew he had to get home ASAP. They followed her nymph-like movements through the trails, careful to step where she stepped. They saw glimpses of figures in the trees, in the grasses and bush.

Around them, they heard a rising wave of *things* coming that didn't sound happy. Hungry maybe, but not happy. Were they those drummer trolls? Or worse?

"Muddy," Poe pulled Muddy out of la-la-land. "I think you should play now."

"Yeah," Otis chipped in. "I don't want to be something's finger food here."

Corey's big hand landed on Muddy's shoulder. "Send us home, man. Please?"

Someone below him grunted and moaned. Leo. Muddy gazed down and was afraid of what he saw. "Sorry, bud. First stop is the ER." The unlucky bassist du jour looked horrible.

The second would be to visit someone and apologize for their stupid mistake.

Muddy began the song; the same one they'd played when Silver Eye helped them leave the first time. The others joined in once the scene began to shimmer. All at once, Lyra disappeared into the underbrush, and the drummer beasts burst through, as well as something else that would haunt the band for many nightmares to come.

Muddy forced the vision out of his mind and played until he felt the familiar pull of home.

Chapter Twenty-Four

The journey back took less time than the first.

"Is that all?" Corey asked. "Seems like something's missing."

"Like a wasted trip."

Muddy stood firm. "No. We learned that we could cross over by ourselves. When we rest up, we plan this out. Now we have an ally over there. Maybe she can help lead us to Zack."

Corey whistled. "Silver Eye's gonna be mad."

Muddy shot him a sharp look. "Who's going to tell him?" He knew they screwed up. He had to make it right. The old man had a reason for delaying them, but the band didn't know it.

Poe wrapped herself up in her arms. "It does feel weird, Muddy."

"Aren't we back?" he asked. "And safe?" He looked down at the wilting bassist. "Okay, almost totally safe." No one complained. It had been a harrowing experience, but they'd made it back in one piece and made a new friend. Or two?

Otis fetched the backpack with their stuff.

"You're not going to believe this. It's only five minutes after eight."

Classes began at 8:30 A.M. every morning.

"Then it's all gravy. Let's get Leo to the hospital and then meet during fourth period to debrief."

But he knew the song would not remain the same.

Muddy floated through the school day on an air of confidence. After surviving the morning, he was charged up and ready to return to the Crossroads to save his brother. Before first period, they had called 911. Otis had volunteered to stay with Leo, assuring the band that he'd make up a story about a dog attack. The rest of them managed to make the late bell with no one suspecting a thing. Nothing that any of the bullies or moron teachers did in periods one through three could burst Muddy's bubble.

Then he stepped through the door of Room 201 and everything changed. The group sat waiting for him, faces tight with stress. Otis had his phone in his hand, shaking.

"What," he said. "Is it Leo? He's not..."

Poe gripped the edge of the table and sighed. "No, Edgar."

She called me Edgar. Why?

"He's still alive," Otis said. "He managed to avoid the weird questions the doctors asked, but he'll probably never have the nerve to play bass again."

Like he would want to after our trip?

Poe looked him in the eye. "Corey rode his bike to see Silver Eye before school today."

"Uh-oh."

Corey shivered in his seat, a sight Muddy had never witnessed before.

Poe's knuckles turned white with tension. "Besides being PO'd at us for being stupid and arrogant, he sat quietly for a long time before asking Corey one simple question. A question that he already knew the answer to."

"Which was?" Muddy wanted to end this mystery, now.

"You—"

Otis broke in, his face whiter than normal. "You forgot to close the door."

Chapter Twenty-Five

"What did you say?"

"Dude," Otis said seriously, "you forgot to *close* the crossroads when we came back."

A waterfall of ice chased Muddy's blood up his arms and down his back.

Close the crossroads?

"But we played the same song as the first time. I made sure of it." Yet his voice lacked the strength he'd built through the morning.

Corey stood up. "Man, you screwed up. We all did. None of us should've gone there without the old man."

More ice slid down his back. His face burned with fear. "What did we *forget* to do?"

The sax player sat back down. "So simple, but so elusive. A blues scale in reverse, ending in a *true* blue note. Remember now?"

Darkness rained over the guitarist. He'd been labeled for years as the screwup when he wasn't but now, today, he wore the crown.

"Oh, no," Muddy said to no one. "I'm the *king* of accidentals."

Poe looked at him dead on and said, "Silver Eye said one thing to Corey. Just one."

"Which was? Please. Tell me."

She caught a shaky breath. She looked pretty scared, not an easy feat after what she dealt with at home. "He said, 'imagine what would happen when you left the door open if your house sat in the heart of a jungle. What would come inside?'"

Oh, crap. What did I do?

But what came out of his mouth was, "What's the worst that can happen?"

Before the period ended, the screams outside began.

"What the heck?" Otis tumbled out of his seat and slammed into the window. "I can't see anything."

Muddy sidled up next to him and peered out the wide, multi-paned glass. "All that construction stuff is blocking our view. So much for making the front courtyard pretty for us." His hands shook the frame.

"Let me in," Poe said. Despite her disability, she could hear a mouse fart a block away. Students learned not to whisper and gossip in her classes. If they were foolish enough to talk about someone she knew well, she retaliated online. She turned her left ear to the glass before Corey reached over them and lifted the window open.

"That better?" he asked.

"Thanks," she replied, leaning outside.

Then her face darkened. "Oh, no."

"What?"

Mrs. Berg crowded in with them and craned her neck for a glance over the mess of wood and metal that littered the grounds as far as the eye could see. "They were supposed to be done six months ago. I knew someone would get hurt out there. That darn superintendent."

"What is it, Poe?" Muddy needed to know.

The second scream rang much louder. It actually *sang*, he thought.

With a massive backup band.

Rumblings of music followed the female voice. Not a school band sound, nor a rock band sound. It was...different.

"What the heck is that?" Mrs. Berg's voice shook. "Did something blow up?"

"No," Poe replied. "It's worse." She turned to Muddy with a knowing look.

"You didn't close the door."

He was so distracted he didn't even recognize who'd said

it. The dread that poured over him like wet concrete made him feel two hundred pounds heavier.

I didn't play that song. The one that closed the door. But I didn't... know.

Oh, but he did. He simply forgot, caught up in the moment.

All of them gazed at him, save for their teacher. They all knew.

Corey sighed. "All of it's our fault, not just yours. We decided to go there alone. None of us knew."

Poe placed her hand on Muddy's shoulder. "And I don't know about you, but I was so scared, I couldn't remember anything." She gazed back out the window. "Silver Eye should've been with us."

Their teacher screwed up her face. She usually did when the band started in on one of their weird talks. "Silver Eye? Close the door? Did someone forget to give me a clue?"

"Well," Otis said, tapping his fingers as he always did when trying to talk his way out of something, "you see—"

"Oh, crap. I'd better go out there and make sure our principal doesn't do anything stupid—again." She hurried to the door but stopped before pushing through it. "I'm going to hear this whole story of yours later, right? I don't like being kept in the dark. I have a feeling about this one."

Didn't they all? Muddy thought nervously as he watched her run to the scene of the screaming.

"Shouldn't we go?" Corey didn't like to wait. "I have a feeling—"

"That it's something due to what we did? Or didn't do?" Poe knew each of them too well. "Okay. Guys, grab your gear and let's go."

Muddy flinched. "The real instruments or the ones we used over there?"

"How would I know?" Corey asked. "Both, I guess. Better to be safe."

"But they're all at Muddy's," Otis said.

Corey looked at him. "And your point is?"

At Muddy's house, the quartet gathered up Muddy's acoustic

guitar, Otis's marching band snare drum and Corey's sax. They also strapped the odd instruments from the "other world" to their backs. The school seemed miles away despite the brisk pace all of them set during the four-block jaunt from the rehearsal basement.

"Do you think this will work?" Corey asked. "Normal instruments here?"

"Does it matter?" Poe began their march toward school. "It's not like we have a choice—especially when it's our fault."

They broke into a full-out run when they heard the chorus of screams.

Within seconds, they turned the corner and saw what caused those screams.

Corey stared. "What did we *do*?"

Chapter Twenty-Six

The most frightening song imaginable echoed down the street in front of the school. A snake, or something like it but much bigger, slithered down Carteret Avenue. The biggest street in the entire town appeared to be a mere sidewalk under the beast.

"Dang," Otis said. "It must be a half-block long."

Scared out of his mind, Muddy stared, transfixed by the sight.

I know where you came from because I let you in. What did I do?

It wriggled on the blacktop with rhythm.

"Is that thing throwing down a beat?"

It was tossing around a syncopated groove that left the people on the street hypnotized, paralyzed. Onlookers stuck like glue to where they were with expressions of fear and confusion frozen on their faces. The more the thing moved, the crazier the rhythm became. Its undulating body shook most people out of their minds, transfixing them. When the band crept closer, hiding between a pair of school vans, it became clear that the creature was anything but the garden variety of basic giant anaconda-type serpent. Like one of those cheap toys a crazy aunt buys at a dollar store, it was constructed of several connected segments. When those segments rubbed against each other, the sound resembled maracas that island dancers shook. But this didn't inspire people to get up and shake their butts; instead, they became frozen where they stood. The serpentine thing was massive. Muddy thought they couldn't be more afraid – until he saw its mouth.

"Corey!" Muddy called, but the big teen simply stood there, eyes glazed over.

"Poe?" This time his voice rose to a pitch that sounded before puberty. She remained silent and glued to where she stood.

"Otis?"

The drummer stared ahead for a long moment. "Right here with you, man. That thing is wicked! I wish I could play that."

"Otis!" Muddy slapped his friend's shoulder, immediately regretting the action.

"Sorry," they said in unison.

"Look," Muddy said, pointing at the others. "They're not moving."

Otis poked Corey and almost touched Poe before he appeared to think better of it. "Wow, that thing has them stuck like that. I wonder why?"

"Predators do weird stuff to their prey."

The smaller boy shook and dropped one of his sticks. "Prey? You mean, like, it's going to eat somebody?"

Muddy shook his head. "Look, it's not the body. It's the fangs."

Jutting from the snake's refrigerator-sized mouth was a pair of long teeth that extended then clashed together. The noise rang out in an odd, exotic-sounding chord in high-pitched tones that were both metallic and organic at the same time.

"It's just like the tuning forks that Satch uses in class," Otis said. "Except, we usually ignore those."

"It must be hypnotizing everyone around here. Man, I hope this thing is gone before they let school out." "It'd turn this street into a buffet!"

"Oh, no." Poe sensed what she could not see. The thing slithered right into the path of a group of pedestrians huddled on the corner. With a few shakes of its head, the spot emptied.

"What happened to them?" Corey squinted, hoping to find a survivor. "Did it roll over them?"

"No," she replied. "They became brunch."

A numbness Muddy hadn't felt since his mom's funeral filled him inside. His fingers tingled with pins and needles. Just a moment ago, people had been there. Now they were inside that…thing. He looked at the others standing on either side of it, oblivious to it all.

Muddy's face twisted at the thought. "But how come we're not like them? We can move and talk."

"Well, simple. I'm a drummer. I'm immune to it. I get lost in my own rhythms but focus too much on others to let myself go. It sucks."

"Well, why isn't it freezing *me* up?" Muddy shivered.

Otis just gave him that deep, open-eyed stare that sometimes scared the heck out of him. "Man, I don't know. Maybe something happened to you over there. Or maybe it's something else. Worse, I mean. Different."

Ice ran down Muddy's back. Why didn't it affect him?

"Maybe something *did* happen to us over there," Poe said. "I still can't see, but the blurs mean something now."

Otis brought them back to focus on the problem. "We've gotta kill it. I think I know how."

"But Silver Eye said the instruments didn't work that way on this side."

The drummer smiled. "They don't need to. I've got this one."

He slung the drum in front and twirled his sticks of bone. Both ran out to face the adversary as it slunk toward them. It hesitated for a moment, lifted its head, swung it back and forth then did something that sealed the deal for the group.

It sped up and charged.

"It came for *us*, Muddy." Yet Otis didn't waver.

"All because I forgot to close the door."

He held the sticks at the ready, an odd grin forming on his face. "Dude, we screwed up. It's time to set things right."

Nodding, he framed the snake before him, swung down as hard as his arms could and shook the world with thunder. From Otis's feet to the creature's tail, the vibration of the street drum raced, cracking a line in the road and smashing right into the behemoth. The other-worldly sounds echoed and shook it. The beast lost its beat. Both teens left the ground as the serpent slammed itself into the street.

Muddy smacked Otis lightly on the back. "More! Don't stop."

Otis found his footing and began to roll out a rhythm that would shame most of the great rockers in history. The snake swung around, knocking a school security cart and sending it flying into the building.

"Uh-oh," Muddy muttered. "There goes the budget for next year."

With a swift shake of its tail, the serpent began the maraca-type sounds once more. With each undulation, it moved closer to the other band members, nearly knocking over several students who remained frozen in place.

"Poe?" He began to run, then stopped. This wasn't his game. He turned to his drummer. "Otis?" His voice sounded strange, even to himself.

"Gotcha, buddy," Otis said, not missing a beat. "I see her. Now shut up and stand back."

The snake and drummer began a battle of percussion in a match of musical chess. For each line the snake slithered out, Bones countered with one that altered the rhythm, first going along with it then changing it slightly.

He's drawing the thing in, suckering it. Beautiful! Just hope we survive the song!

Muddy began to feel his eyes glaze over as the snake began a more hypnotic rhythm. Maybe if he started playing?

"Don't," the drummer replied, possibly sensing his friend's intention. "I've got him." He played along with the creature, adding more and more to the beat while Muddy felt himself stiffen up from head to toe.

It was overpowering, whatever came over the other side.

Its progress stopped right before the two of them, almost within snapping distance. The man-length teeth slammed into the street, rendering Muddy deaf and petrified, glued to where he stood. Fear rippled through him, thoughts racing, praying Otis could win out, but his mouth failed when he tried to cheer on his friend.

Rattle. Dissonance. Jangle of alien chords.

Counter rhythms. Double beats. Trebly rim shot.

The two danced musically while the snake's jaws yawned precariously over the drummer's head. Whether Otis felt no fear, or he was entranced with his own beat, he showed no reaction.

On and on it went until…Otis stopped.

The snake attempted to halt its swaying, jangling, beating body, but it couldn't.

Otis smiled then launched into the exact opposite of what both had played.

The creature froze then stumbled then flopped onto its belly, shrieking. The concussion caused the cars on the street to flip, students to fly onto the sidewalk.

The drummer intensified his new beat, stepping right up to the massive jaws.

Don't, Otis. Don't.

But he did. He began to play on the serpent's pipe-like teeth. He beat a wild rhythm on each massive fang.

With a cry Muddy would hear for months in his sleep, the creature howled and spun away. Its body swung and slithered as if on ice, back in the direction it came.

It bolted away from them and as it moved, its song became a disjointed mess.

"Dang," the drummer said. "It doesn't die?"

"Maybe back there, but not here. I have no clue. More importantly," Muddy said, beginning to feel again, "where's it going now?"

They knew, though.

The crossroads. Like a beaten dog, it meant to head home with its tail between its legs.

"Do you think Silver Eye knows?"

"Are you kidding? He knows all about what goes in and comes out of that thing."

Corey stared at his friend. "Then why isn't he here? Why didn't he come to help? Why didn't he *know*?"

The world suddenly morphed from color to black and white as a thought cut like a razor through Muddy.

They began to run toward the landfill, toward the portal where they left the door wide open when Muddy stopped short.

"Look."

"What? Is that Bentley?"

Their nemesis, the cocky musician, stood frozen before them.

Otis shook his head. "Forget it, man. He probably didn't even see us."

"He didn't have to," Muddy replied.

The teen held a cell phone in the air. "He recorded it?"

"I guess."

"Well, don't be an idiot. Grab the phone and delete the video."

Muddy tried to wrestle the skinny phone from the boy's big hands, but Bentley's frozen hand clutched it too tightly. "I can't get it out! What do we do?"

Corey stepped in and wrenched it from the steel grip of the paralysis. The kid would never know what happened to it.

"Hope that it's gone," said Otis. "We have to make sure it's gone."

A thought scurried through Muddy's mind again. "Got to close the door. Silver Eye said so."

They ran off to their bikes and sped off to the trail leading to the crossroads.

As they arrived, the creature had just finished slinking back through the portal.

"What's that on the ground?" Otis' voice shook.

"No. *No.*" Muddy's heart broke as he realized the full gravity of his mistake.

"It's Silver Eye."

"Crap."

"Is he...?"

"No, but he seems close. Very close."

When Poe and Corey showed up half an hour later, Muddy figured out that Silver Eye was in fact alive, but barely.

"Hold on, buddy." Corey cradled the old man's head.

"What you talkin' about, little man?" Silver Eye replied. "I'm fine. Just get me to where I'm supposed to go next."

By then, Poe's eyes had brimmed with tears.

"It's my fault. It's all my fault!" Muddy cried and yelled into the ground as he hung his head. "We were so stupid. So dumb—just like they always said we were, especially me. We should've waited for you, but we didn't."

Silver Eye gurgled, his wounds visible to the group for the

first time. A pair of long fang marks had punctured his chest, dark fluid oozing out in thin rivulets. "No, I did the same thing when I was your age," he said and wheezed.

"You killed your friend?" Corey hugged the old man closer. He must have felt the kinship he'd abandoned when he moved from Iron. "You were an arrogant jerk who left the door open and let something crazy in to kill someone you cared about?"

The bluesman smiled, blood welling up at his lips. Clouds began to fill his good eye. "Something like that. There's a reason I live where I do, why my only friends are a beastly beagle and scraggly old cat."

Poe cried harder. "We're your friends! You have all those celebrities who looked like they love you in those photos."

He sighed, deflating just a bit. "Maybe they did one day. Maybe they did. But then I got cocky and she—" He coughed up some blood.

"Don't talk," Poe said, stroking his forehead. "The ambulance is almost here."

Something inside of Muddy told him that it wouldn't matter, that only one place could save him now. From the color of Silver Eye's skin, he knew the snake had some serious venom in its bite and had been seeking out the man all along. It had likely smelled him, sensed him—sent by someone over there.

First it aimed for him. And then for the band.

When it got scared, it headed for the door. But the old man had been there to greet it.

"She was special," Silver Eye continued. "Someone I wanted to bring over, to impress and teach, to be my partner, in music and in love." He gazed up at Poe. "Grab it while you can, missy. It don't come around often." Then he turned his head, to Muddy. "Even if the other fears what will happen."

"Who was she?" Poe's tears streamed down her shirt.

He managed to lift a hand, if only to wave them off. "Doesn't matter now. I'll be seeing her soon enough and we'll see if she forgives me for what I did." He pulled at Muddy. "Don't you dare. Don't you ever, ever betray her and turn your back on your world."

"I wouldn't," Muddy cried. "I did this! If it wasn't for me and this idiotic plan, you'd still be relaxing in your house."

"And dying slower," the man finished. "Who wants to fade away? You know the song. I've heard it myself. The lyrics came from ages ago. It's better to burn out than fade away."

He coughed again as he gripped Corey and Muddy's hand. "Find him. Make things right if you can. Just don't give up. Don't let the Dark Muse turn the blues to black."

The guitarist sobbed, not caring how he looked in front of Poe or the rest of the band. "First, my mother. Now you. I can't do this."

As his eyes closed, he said, "Muddy." The boy leaned in close. "Yes, you can. You have something in you that your brother never did. That, my boy, will give you the best chance. Now bring me over."

While Corey and Muddy helped Poe staunch the blood flow, Otis pulled out his cell and made a call. Five minutes later, an Explorer screeched to the curb.

"Satch?" Muddy shot an expression of both surprise and relief at the sight of their music teacher.

"I came as soon as Otis called me."

"How?" Then he remembered his friend had received music therapy lessons during one of his bouts with death a few years ago. The family had made a friend for life. "Thanks for believing in us." His words tasted both bitter and relieved.

"I had a feeling this crossroads thing was real all along. I wish I had the guts you kids do." He bent over the bluesman. "I'd always hoped to meet you. Tell me how to help."

"Did you run over any strange snakes while driving here?" The old guy managed to sputter.

"No," Satch smiled, "but when a golf cart flew into my band room, I figured I'd better do something. There aren't many reasons a reject from a Syfy movie would be traipsing down Carteret Avenue during a school day."

"Enough!" Muddy stomped his heel to punctuate his point. "We do this now. He'll be trapped here if we don't. The crossroads—now."

No one said another word as they loaded him up with care in the back of the Explorer and piled in. Tires pealed as they sped toward the crossing. Within minutes, they arrived at the zone where one world met the next.

The group laid Silver Eye at the center of the crossroads.

"Want me to come?" Satch helped unload the SUV and turned to his students, a confused expression on his face.

The guitarist looked at his teacher. "Thank you, but no. This isn't your fight and without an instrument over there, you'd be dead weight, literally. No offense."

He regarded Muddy with a tear in his eye. "Muddy," he said, his voice unsteady. "Are you sure about this?"

Muddy looked back into the eyes of his teacher and friend, thinking about what lay ahead. The fight. Finding Zack. The creatures already encountered and those yet to be faced. To trust Lyra and the stranger with her or not. Dying, like his friend here who was dying because of his impulses.

"I have no idea, but we're not coming back until we get Silver Eye to safety and find my brother."

"May the blues be with you," the teacher spoke with a smile, repeating the cheesy line he often ending class with. "Just come back."

Chapter Twenty-Seven

Muddy turned to his band and counted to four. The most heartfelt song he'd ever imagined poured from him as he felt blue in every inch of his body. Poe, Corey, and Otis joined in as their fading friend held on, breathing through one of his harps, sounding the softest note, but one which carried enormous power. The strings vibrated under his fingers, coming alive in both hands. Each wire he struck, each note he fingered shook his being into that place where he needed to be. He felt all of himself become the song he played.

The curtain not only shimmered but dropped on the band just as Satch dove out of the way. With a splash, Muddy left the others behind as he tumbled headlong into the River. He realized with no regret that the place was an actual River, flowing with a substance he knew nothing of and knowing he might not live to surface again. He grabbed hold of Silver Eye's hand and prayed he had what it took to deliver him safely to where he could heal.

The blues entered his skin, flowed into his blood and circulated up and down his arms, his legs vibrating with harmonics he barely heard, but felt. It smacked into his brain and heart as though his guitar's strings were connected to the battery of the world's biggest truck.

Silver Eye! his mind screamed. He felt like he was drowning but couldn't stop playing. Something called to him. It begged his fingers to keep playing to squeeze the soul out of each note. *I'm so sorry.*

Don't stop. Keep in the blue. Ride the River.

It pulled at his will power. Muddy felt himself sinking further, the strong current tugging at every inch of him, down, further away from his friends and the crossroads. Like an ocean, the pressure built up at his ears, but instead of pain, it yielded a high beyond anything he'd ever experienced before. Better than his first kiss. Better than the Hulk rollercoaster at Universal. Better than the first time playing onstage. Better than when he met Poe. The more he played, the more intoxicating the feeling.

The harder he played, the deeper he sank.

The faster the riff, the wider the vibrato, the further down, he went.

In the back of his mind, he knew it wasn't good, nothing feeling like this could be good, but the calling overpowered his common sense. Each time he inhaled, a cool blue flow of something filled him up and he cared less about rising to the surface, to his friends.

He was probably drowning—and didn't care.

"Muddy."

The voice sounded from below him. The sound of his name broke up into waves. He swore his imagination was screwing with him.

"Muddy." Louder this time. Still wavy but heavier.

"Yeah?" He opened his mouth to call back, but the blue coolness flowed inside, squashing his voice into a whisper. Would he really drown here? Silver Eye was, but then again, the bluesman acted like dying here wasn't such a bad thing.

He looked down and through a kaleidoscopic view, his eyes focused on the old man just floating out of reach. His eyes uncrossed and drew the old man into focus. The man stared at him through an eye that was no longer glassy. Its power nearly parted the blue between teacher and student.

"Boy," the voice spoke. "Take my hand. Now."

Muddy shook the blue substance from his head and stretched down with his left hand letting the guitar loose. It almost reached, but not quite. He extended himself further, throwing his shoulder and hip into it, and turned more than expected. Without something to ground him, his body was at the mercy of the River. Fingers touched fingers and the old man encircled his. A sudden warmth washed over his body and it dawned upon him that sinking was *wrong*.

His arms and legs kicked like a swimmer struggling against a rip tide. *Relax,* spoke a strong thought from outside his head.

The hand held like iron, and visions flooded his mind. Sounds and images of their impending mission branded themselves on his psyche. Now he *knew* what the group had to do in order to save Zack.

But instead of comforting him, it scared the heck out of him, bringing back the chill of the blue surrounding him. It would take all of them, some together and some separate, to survive the trials of the Triton and save his brother from the Dark Muse.

"Muddy," Silver Eye said. "Do you understand?"

He nodded but the images ran cloudy.

"Then let me go and get your butt out of here." Muddy looked at the source of the voice and saw a man growing younger by the moment.

No! he screamed in his head. He couldn't let the man drown down here.

But, Silver Eye said, the smallest of smiles curling his lip. *"Don't you realize? This is where I'm supposed to be. I'm home now."*

Muddy still held firm but felt strong hands reach under him and yank hard. The connection broke. The blue River's current washed stronger, as the image of Silver Eye faded away.

As he rose, he heard the old man say, *I'll be with you all the way, a part of you, just like the pick in your hand.*

Chapter Twenty-Eight

The sunlight broke through the darkness, blinding him. Corey, Otis, and Poe dropped him onto the path. "What the...?"

She looked at him. "Are you okay? We couldn't find you for a while."

"But," Muddy replied, confused, "you didn't play the song. How'd you get through?" Then he looked around them. The landfill was gone. The tide had carried them to the other side.

Otis patted him on the shoulder. "Man, you're a lot stronger than we thought. You surfed that River and told it who was boss." But even Muddy knew the truth. Both nearly died in there.

Yet neither did. He knew that now.

"How'd we get here?"

"Your song's more powerful than you know. I guess you really wanted to save him."

Panic struck him from all sides. Where was he? "We have to pull him out! He's too weak to do it himself."

Corey wrapped an arm around him. "Muddy, he ain't down there. Maybe this was his plan all along. Look around. The River isn't something we can get to now. We have live people to save. Zack, remember?"

"But we have to do something." Muddy looked down and sighed.

They stared at the river flowing between the crossroads. It had been fading, draining from a deep, dark current to what it remained now; a slow trickle that dried up right before their eyes.

Otis clawed the dirt. "Where'd he go?"

Muddy stood up and grabbed his guitar. "He'll be with us every step of the way."

When he opened his right hand, a silver pick lay in his palm.

They looked down the trail that lead to the town and then at the unknown path. "We need Lyra. We need a guide to get us to the mountain." Muddy slipped the pick into his pocket, right next to the one he'd retrieved from the creature. Silver Eye's and Zack's. He prayed it would give him the confidence he knew he would need.

"What mountain?" Poe squinted, her eyes adjusting to full sight once again.

"Where the Tritons have my brother. Where the Dark Muse is waiting for us."

"The what?"

Muddy shook his head. The images and revelations thrown before him in the River cleared up plenty for him but left him with more questions. Visions of his brother and his captors remained fuzzy.

"Don't ask – I can't explain. Yet."

Besides, the images of those people who were in the creature's belly stabbed at him. They might be dead, because of him. If only they could return home before it all began that day, maybe he could change everything, except he knew he couldn't save his friend.

"Do you guys always make such an entrance?" Lyra stood behind one of the non-living trees.

"What?"

"Whenever someone's stupid enough to go into the River, it pretty much feels like an earthquake here. Now you might understand why the elders here fear your group so much."

Otis looked at her and winked. "So, hot stuff, what does that mean?"

She swatted his head. "We'll go first thing in the morning. Now you need to rest. Some of us might not see another sunset."

Poe nodded at a male version of Lyra. "Sure, but first, who's he?"

"Hi, I'm Luke," the boy said. He looked about their age, which meant almost nothing in this world. "My sister told me you need some navigational help."

"I saved you," Lyra said. "My people trust no one anymore. I'm sorry. Ever since they built that *thing* and the music died in our villages, nobody's trusted outsiders."

"How do we know you're not baiting us?" Corey hadn't trusted many people lately, other than his band and family. "We could wake up chained to something or fed to one of those things out there." He waved his monstrous arms in an arc. The band understood that much more existed in this world than they knew.

"You don't," she said, sighing. "Most of the younger ones fight the change. The eye in the center of town, watching us, is listening for those like you."

The pyramid? Could he trust them?

"The last few who crossed over didn't fare so well," she continued.

"They were killed?" Poe bore into her. "Musicians? Like us?"

The other girl stared off into the direction of her town. "Some, but some were once welcomed here with open arms. They wrote songs that could appease even those that threatened their lives. Legends," she said. "I'm sure they were in your world too."

"Are they dead?

Her brother finally spoke up. "Nobody's sure. Those idiots in town captured some and let the Tritons take them away. Others simply went the way you're headed now." He bowed his head. "They might still be there. Or they're dead, if they're lucky."

"What do you mean lucky?" Otis yelled. "Dead isn't lucky!"

The twins locked gazes. "You're sure you want to go there?"

Muddy felt himself getting angry. "Isn't that where your people took my brother?"

The boy threw his hands in the air. "Hold on. First, I don't know who your brother is. Second, many walked right into the lion's den."

"Describe him to me," Lyra said.

Muddy did, as the image from the night his brother disappeared would be forever tattooed in his memory. He noted the teen's hair, eyes, height, clothing, and of course, his guitar.

The teens stared at each other again.

Muddy felt his stomach slowly snake into a knot. "What? You've seen him?"

Lyra didn't speak. Luke turned to him. "If it was him, he arrived and bypassed the village completely, as if he knew something the others didn't."

"Where'd he go?" The knot constricted.

The boy pointed at the peak in the middle of the distant mountain range. "Right into the lion's den, without saying a word."

Luke led the band to an outcropping on the eastern edge of the town, outside of the influence of the pyramid. "No one will know we're here," he said. "Even that thing won't sense us. Trust me."

"Why are you so sure?" Muddy felt no trust on this side. The sensation of being drugged, locked up, and chased down were all too fresh in his memory.

Lyra laughed. "Well, for one, your little stunt has them scared out of their gourds. They're convinced you're working with the Dark Muse and the Tritons."

"What stunt? Who are the Tritons?"

"Crossing over like you just did. Most choose the quiet way."

She paused. "As for the others, you'll find out on your own. Hopefully not, but they already sense you."

Muddy fell into a soft bedroll within the tent the twins pitched for them. "I just hope everyone else is fooled as easily. Again, who are the Tritons?"

"They're the ones who probably have your brother. They run everything. Everyone. Decide who survives."

Moments later he passed out, dead to the world and unable to tell the others what he'd learned the night he spent in the River.

Chapter Twenty-Nine

As the morning began, the sun blasted through the opening in the tent and shut out the nightmares of the River from the previous day. Silver Eye, their mentor, spoke to Muddy through the darkness, from deep within wherever he was now. Luckily, the message arrived right before his air ran out.

A scream pierced Muddy's lips but a hand doused it quickly. When his eyes shot open, he saw Poe bending over him. "Shh! You'll bring them running."

"Who?" His pulse already thumped through his skin.

She leaned in and whispered. "Everyone. And everything."

After the swim in the River, both real and in his nightmares, those creatures he met didn't seem so horrible anymore. "Something tells me this is going to be one long trip."

Outside the tent, Muddy watched as a quiet comedy of musical errors played.

Lyra stood in the middle of the group while Otis and Corey danced with the grass across from the safe zone where they camped. The same pasta grass which nearly had Leo for lunch a day earlier now swayed like soccer moms at a Bon Jovi concert. Their long fronds moved with a breeze that gave them the appearance of dancing.

Corey blew a soft stream of blues-tinged notes, aimed at the green ground surrounding the camping area. The bell of his sax-shaped horn sung to the murderous blades that waved back and forth, some sliding over his sneakers.

Was he nuts?

Muddy shook his head, astonished at his friends' actions.

The tiny drummer sat cross-legged on the ground before them, silently beating a rhythm into the earth. That must have propelled whatever it was, tide or wind, to make the grass wave. Otis turned and gave Muddy a sly grin that only he could give. He nodded, his John Lennon sunglasses blocking out the world.

Where was Poe? Muddy almost yelled her name when Lyra grabbed his hand and squeezed hard. Her gaze pointed to the most obvious place, the middle of the grass.

There she stood, the queen of the ball, all her suitors dancing around her. The blades cleared a spot for her, and she held her palms out, as if conducting them. She hummed a melody in sync with Otis and Corey, all of them holding court.

Wow. She's amazing.

He didn't care if she saw him staring this time. He hated the other guys in school ogling her, especially because he knew he would lose out to them every time. She could, and should, be a model with those eyes and that beautiful smile, but with *her* father, it would never happen.

Muddy wanted to run into the mass of green and pull her away. Just yesterday the green mixed with crimson as it nearly killed Leo. He might still wind up dead from their poison; another casualty of the bass player curse. However, Lyra held him firmly in place.

"Just watch." He did, but his anxiety reared up big-time and he fought hard to keep it at bay. He needed to be strong for Silver Eye and Zack. He couldn't afford to screw it up now. The band counted on him. Even Lyra did.

He took some deep breaths, forcing himself to take in the scene and marvel at its craziness and beauty. Everything around him seemed alive. The ground below him vibrated, lulling him into a peace almost like he'd experienced in the River. His senses heightened as if he grew into the environment. Then his nose took in the strongest sensation.

"What's that smell?"

"Wasn't me," chimed Otis, still tapping away.

Corey and Poe smirked, but kept up their antics.

"It smells like green," she sang. And it did with the typical bitter fruitiness of cut grass, but this had an added ingredient.

"Shrek?" Corey asked between notes.

"Kermit the frog?" Otis rolled as he drummed.

Muddy smiled at Lyra, who explained, "When the plants are charmed, like a snake they emit something like pheromones."

"So those bozos are putting that killer linguini in the mood?"

Lyra elbowed him, smiling. "Something like that. It helps them pollinate and communicate with other plants. Would you rather they get angry?"

He remembered the blood and his screaming friend. "I'll live with this."

"Guys," he said in rhythm with the band, "we need to go. Remember what we came here for."

Poe sauntered out of the grass, the fronds parting like the Red Sea for her. Within a minute, the song concluded, and the blades lay still.

Before Muddy informed the group of their next step, Corey stepped up to him.

"You know, he believed in all of us. He gave every one of us something that we can use to save Zack. You're not the savior here; we all are."

The words hurt. They also rang true. Muddy had figured all along that since it was his brother, he would be in charge. But just like in the band, no one was more important than another. They risked their lives to complete this mission as much as he did.

"I'm sorry," he said. "I'm just afraid we won't get there in time. Silver Eye talked to me in a dream last night." Tears formed in his eyes. His fault. Silver Eye and those people. He would have to live with the mistake, despite what the old man told him.

Corey put his big hand on Muddy's shoulder. "He came to me, too Otis and Poe. All of us. That's how we figured out how to calm the grass like that. Did you think we just suddenly went bonkers?"

"No, I know you're not that psycho," he replied with a smile, a little more at ease. He looked at Lyra, waiting for her to save him from whatever danger he got himself into next. She simply shrugged. He was on his own again. His dad would remind him that he needed to own up to his actions and words. "I think we do need to go, though, like now."

"We know," Poe said. "To the ocean, right?"

How did she know? Then he remembered. Silver Eye had trained them all.

"Which way?"

Lyra pointed due east. "Luke will meet us there. He needed to run back to the village for something."

Muddy felt his anxiety rise again. "Why is he coming? He doesn't need to risk his life for us. Neither do you."

She winked at him with those light eyes. "You need a guide. Our people can't live without music forever."

"But I thought your town outlawed it."

She shook her head, eyes shut as if remembering something awful. "No, *they* did, the same monsters who took your brother, the Tritons. It's about time someone put an end to our pain. Who could live without music all their lives?"

"How long?" Muddy's confusion only grew. In a world where music seemed to inhabit every living thing, how could someone outlaw people from enjoying it, performing it?

Again, she hung her head. "It's a long story. Maybe I'll tell you one day." She shuddered. "Let's get to the ocean and find out how bad your dreams really were."

"Are we going the way the others did?" Muddy pointed toward a slew of high peaks in the distance as they cleared the edge of the forest.

She didn't turn. "Only if you want to wind up like them. There's always another way."

The group gathered up their instruments. The packs of food that Lyra had prepared for them were in a knapsack slung across her shoulders. The southeastern path headed to an ocean, one which would likely amaze and frighten them as much as the forest.

Otis walked behind Lyra, checking her out, being obvious as usual. Muddy guided Poe, and Corey brought up the rear.

"So, beautiful," the drummer said. "Your brother? He has a

talent too? Can't wait to see what his is."

Their guide stared ahead and smiled. "He's amazing. He'll fit right in with you guys."

"Oh, yeah? What does he do?"

"Before the Tritons outlawed music, he once played a mean bass."

No one spoke for the next hour.

After a few hours they rested against some flat rocks, all except Luke, who had recently joined them. He kept watch for any unwelcome guests.

Muddy bolted upright, hearing one of his favorite riffs of all time. Suddenly, their need for a guide on the way to the castle lessened. The song kept repeating in his head and he knew right away that Silver Eye was behind it. *He* would be the guide they truly depended on. Lyra's brother would have to settle for the role of bassist. Maybe this time it wouldn't be a lethal job. "I know where to go!"

The others halted their play and gathered their instruments. Corey nearly dropped his horn in a deep crevice.

"Careful," Otis warned. "If you break it, I think we bought it and no receipt will get us back home."

"Yeah," Muddy added, "I doubt there's a Guitar Center anywhere nearby with replacement parts." Thoughts crossed his mind about a straw and a camel's back. He wondered if he could handle the stress.

Poe remained silent. That always worried Muddy. "What? Do you hear something?"

"No," she replied. "Just thinking. If you break or lose that guitar, are we stuck here?"

Great. Another worry to think about. The camel's back was creaking.

"Well, don't go breaking a string now," Otis added.

The whole group groaned a little. Hopefully, fate wouldn't depend on a wire .09 of an inch thick. The band knew of Muddy's penchant for bending the strings too much. Might not be a good idea this time around.

The camel's leg just buckled a bit in his mind.

The band began their journey along the western path. Muddy guessed that if this world reflected theirs in any way, west would take them to the water. Luke didn't try to correct him as they co-led the way. Nobody else did, either. Maybe for once, they saw him as bandleader instead of Zack's little brother, the lesser Brooks boy.

"Where are we headed, exactly?

" Poe asked.

Luke and Lyra shared a look.

"To find your brother," she replied. "I thought we all knew that."

Muddy shook his head. "Yeah, but where is he?"

Again, the shared look. "Straight up. No lie. If he's still breathing, he's in their fortress."

"The Tritons?"

They nodded.

Muddy's mouth went dry. All the questions he had wanted to ask disappeared. *Later,* he thought. He couldn't let the fear overcome him now. Zack was alive. He knew it in his bones.

The path soon led them out of the forest. The world of green disintegrated into a world exploding in soft blues and cool breezes.

The ocean.

As the edge of the forest approached, the band and the twins found themselves looking down a steep slope that led down to a beach with pure white sand and crashing blue waves.

Again, he heard the riff in his head. The familiar thundering, simple riff every guitarist cut his or her teeth on when starting out.

"Wow, we sure ain't in Jersey anymore. I don't see high hair, steroid bodies, or green water."

Otis spun around to Corey, who'd uttered the words. "Man, you trying to be funny? Finally?"

The bigger boy grinned. "I *am* funny, when something isn't trying to kill me."

Poe inhaled deeply. "And no pizza or funnel cakes, either, Otis. I think we took a wrong turn somewhere."

"Funny," Muddy said, although he worried about never again seeing the tainted shore they all loved. "We need to move, and quick."

"Why?"

He pointed toward the water on the horizon.

"Oh, my," Corey exclaimed. "Is that what I think it is?" They gazed across the calm, blue water and saw a thick smoke hovering about a football field's length away. "No freaking way."

"If it is, it can't be good. It wasn't good news in the song, but it does mean we're at the right place," the guitarist smiled. "Now let's go find ourselves a ride."

Poe inhaled. "Is something burning on the water? It looks like the water is on fire somehow; or is there something on top of the water that's feeding the flames?"

No one answered. After what they'd witnessed so far, no one wished to venture a guess as to what danger they'd face next.

The way down the slope consisted of snakelike switchbacks which made the descent easier. On either side lay rounded rocks of all sizes.

"Are these going to attack us?" Otis turned to Lyra, who in turn looked at her brother.

Luke shrugged. "I don't think so, but we've never been this far before. Neither of us have."

Lyra shot him a glance. "Just by leaving the city, they could kill us—the Tritons *or* our own leaders. Luke risked his life to scout out this little trip for you guys."

Otis spoke first. "Wow. We really aren't worthy to cause anyone's death. Why'd you do this for us?"

Luke kicked one of the stones, sending it rolling downhill. "I didn't," he replied and kicked another. "I did it for my family. We're sick of being told what to do, where not to go, never having that music to listen to anymore. Do you know what it's like to have people from your side come over here with such fantastic skills, only to have it disappear for good when they leave?"

"I'd go nuts," Otis said, twirling a stick on his fingers. "One day without my iPod and I'm a mess."

"Yeah, well imagine hearing something amazing,

experiencing how good it feels and then being punished for it. It's all we had left once they took power. You don't know pain like that."

"*What*?" Poe missed something, which was definitely unlike her.

Luke stared at her deep, translucent green eyes and his voice eased. "What I meant was, *you* survived. Most don't. We get maybe twenty or so musicians here a year."

"How many make it back?"

The group watched him skitter a rock across the water. It sailed through the air, splashing as it danced into the distance then disappeared into the deep. It didn't swim back and bite anyone. Muddy took that to be a good sign.

"You'll be the first I know. I hope."

They walked carefully along the beach path, nervously waiting for something to reach out and pull them beneath the sand. With each step they tread, yet no giant worm devoured them nor did any of them fall into spider webs spun from guitar strings.

As they reached the surf, Poe scampered like a nymph into the water. She splashed around, apparently thrilled to be off the path and facing seemingly innocent water. "I love the water!" she squealed. The waves crashed lightly as the tide rolled in.

Muddy ran to the edge of the foam and nearly skidded into the surf. He loved the water too, boogey-boarding and snorkeling for shells in water, when his family used to hit the shore. Used to.

However, he knew this wouldn't be typical beach water. The fear of the unknown paralyzed him as he attempted to scream at Poe. If anything happened to her, a part of him would be lost forever.

The other four jumped in, apparently not worried one bit. Well, he'd wait for them right there, just in case. He had a feeling if he dipped his toes, he might be tempting whatever might lurk beneath the surface.

After Lyra and Luke explained that they had never seen the ocean before, that they shared Muddy's fear of the unknown, his longing for frolicking back home ebbed. The concept of something unseen dragging one of them under the water for good was enough to kill the mood.

"I got carried away," Poe said. "After everything we've been through, I couldn't help myself, calling back to the band."

Muddy felt his guilt rise. "I'm sorry. I just couldn't live with myself if something happened to you."

"Ever see *Jaws*?" Otis poked the twin.

Luke gave him an "are you serious" look before he pointed north. They all gawked at the massive darkness swirling over the water just past the breakers. From black to light gray, it churned, roiling like flames licking just below the surface of the ocean. Muddy strained to see through the black clouds, to find the source of the smoke. A ship? *No*, he thought. *If it were, no sailors could have survived such a disaster.*

Was the smoke itself alive? No, it couldn't be.

They followed the shore northbound another hundred yards and Muddy felt paranoia creeping inside him.

"Call me crazy," Corey said, "and you know I don't spook easily, but is the smoke following us? I mean, the breeze is blowing *out* to sea, not inbound, right?"

Luke stopped. Everyone followed his lead. After a few minutes, they realized that the cloud of smoke did appear to be moving with them. Or was it just an optical illusion? "Walk faster," he said.

"No problem there," Corey agreed. "By the way, where are we headed? We're not walking all the way to the fortress, are we?"

The blond teen grinned a bit, though his eyes still showed fear. "We're supposed to pick up a ride sometime soon."

"Ride?" Muddy began to worry even more. "From whom?"

"Yeah," Otis chimed, "isn't this a bad place to be hitchhiking?"

Luke pointed to the bend up ahead where a black jetty stabbed into the sea.

"Right there, I think."

Chapter Thirty

"Is that what I think it is?" Muddy asked, his voice unsteady, not caring who heard.

"The heck with that. Are *they* what I think they are?" Otis smiled through his question.

The two locals, however, didn't smile as they hopped up on the jetty and speed-walked as though it would be their last mile.

"Guys, I think it's time to be afraid again. Let's go," Luke said.

Muddy didn't like seeing their guide turn white. He could tell that Luke had expected something different, maybe something human. "Do you think they really are what I think they are?"

Poe stared hard, tapping into the special vision she was still getting used to. "I'm not sure what they're supposed to be like, look like, or what they really like to eat. We read the Odyssey last year."

Muddy grasped her hand in his. "It's okay. I'm a little scared too." He squeezed. "But we'll be fine. I know it. Silver Eye wouldn't send us off to die."

Otis kept walking, still smiling. "Who cares? Oh, our guru did say we might not make it back, so that argument is shot."

"Otis!" Corey snapped. "We're supposed to make ourselves feel better, not scare the crap out of each other." He too, placed a hand on Poe, even though his own trembled.

"Sorry, man, but we've got to embrace the fear," Otis said. "Some of us face stuff like this every day. Suck it up, already."

Corey pointed, his finger shaking. "*You* face stuff like that every day?"

"Well," the drummer said, shrugging. "I'm allowed to be a touch dramatic, okay?"

Muddy looked at his friend. Too many times they forgot about his fragility and that each day might be his last. Maybe that was the way to view life, instead of worrying.

"Sorry, bud. You're right. Let's go ride that siren cruise."

As they neared the end of the jetty, a few of the creatures turned to stare at them. Fear raced through Muddy's veins. He hated feeling so anxious, hoping it wouldn't cripple him when he needed strength most.

Remember, he told himself, *Zack needs me. I can't let him die here.*

The alluring siren sitting on the bow of the ship spoke first. "Need a ride? We can take you anywhere you want. Just hop in and grab a seat." Her voice purred like a kitten yet carried a tinge of a hawk's cry.

"Hey, gorgeous," Otis said, stepping up to the ship's landing. "Just when I thought only ugly creatures lived here." Lyra slapped at his arm. "Oops," he said. "No offense. I only meant non-human ugly."

They gazed at the female who spoke. Her raven hair covered most of her body, nearly dipping into the ocean's waves. The thick tresses framed large eyes that drew Muddy in, despite his reservations. He now knew why they were the downfall of so many sailors in mythology.

But here, they were real. He should have felt scared but only found himself moving closer. He couldn't tell what she wore under the hair, if anything, but noticed the arch of black wings peeking out from the tops of her shoulders.

Luke stepped up and held out a bag. "Don't go thinking you'll get the meal you're used to, harpy. We need to be somewhere, and we know you can get us there quickest and safest."

She smiled with the look of another creature, perhaps a wolf. "But of course. Meal? We're not even hungry. What's in the bag?"

"What you really want. Seeds of new songs. Ones that no one will be able to resist."

"Why would you want to give us something? We do not need anything to help us sing for our food."

"Okay," he said, putting it back in his sack. "If you don't care about it, fine, but I gathered them from the banks of the River myself."

The others with her drew nearer. "How?"

Seeds? Silver Eye had never mentioned that to Muddy.

"Simple. I plugged my ears. My father taught me what to look for and what to fear." He held out small plugs that Muddy guessed were made of wax.

Lyra punched his chest. "Fool! He told us never to do so. You know how many have perished doing just that."

The leader stepped off the boat, carefully avoiding the water, obviously intrigued. She stood well over six feet tall. Muddy could only imagine her wingspan.

"I know you fear what the water will do to you," Luke said. "Just think, with these seeds, sailors from other lands will beach themselves for you and fish will hop from the surf when they hear your music." The teen was a good guide. He played her like a well-tuned violin.

Muddy finally took in what he saw before him. They were just like in Greek mythology, but not completely. Their beautiful eyes, silvery blue or green, stared at Luke and the others. About a dozen perched on the long ship. The apparent leader's long, straight hair hung in front of her womanly torso and tapered off to even longer legs. Yet, instead of human feet, five talons jutted delicately from her ankles. She reached out to Luke.

"Give, please, and I'll take you anywhere."

Luke retrieved the bag once more. "Only for a trip to the mountain. *All* the way there."

She cried out in a voice that sounded like a thousand song-birds dying at once. The others joined her. The cacophony dropped the band to their knees in pain. Muddy covered his ears, jamming his fingers in as far as he could manage.

"You know we can't do that," the leader hissed in song. "The Tritons would kill us all." The others echoed her in sweet harmony.

"They can kill you?" he taunted. "The great sirens?"

She slashed out with her left hand. It was attached to some-thing other than an arm. It was human as far as the forearm, yet the fingernails appeared to be retractable. A slender wing about twelve feet wide nearly knocked the teen down. Gorgeous feathers unfurled in a stunning pattern. The wings connected in the middle of her back.

"Give," she said. "Now, and I'll take you to the shore of the caverns. We'll take you to where the supposed gauntlet exists. You know that's our limit. It's anyone's limit, so don't tease me, boy."

At the end of the wing, beautiful, slender, human fingers beckoned to him with the longest nails Muddy had ever seen. Muddy had figured out the game Luke was playing and took his turn. "Look, they stole my brother and brought him to the Dark Muse." He gathered up his strength, ignored his anxiety. "We're going there, with or without your help. So, if you want these songs, which I've heard myself, take us to the cove of the gauntlet, like my friend here knows you can. If not, we'll find another boat. But these are killer songs. I'm sure there are others who will take them."

"Give," she repeated, but shrank back a bit. "Fine, but allow me to sample one as a matter of good faith." Muddy knew those nails and talons could shred them to pieces if she so wished. "We want the Tritons gone more than you do, so we agree to your terms. We're tired of singing only where they allow us to sing. We ache for the freedom of the olden days."

Was that sadness in her voice?

Luke reached into the bag and grabbed a seed. Before he tossed it to her, he spoke. He also nodded to the band, a signal to ready their instruments. "If you trick us or attempt to score an early meal, the entire bag goes overboard, as do all of us, and your meal sinks to the bottom, ruined."

Her eyes flashed an anger Muddy had never imagined in the worst horror movie villains. "But you'd be sealing your own fate as well, boy."

He shrugged. "So be it, but I have a feeling you won't dare lose a chance at these." He grabbed hold of Muddy's guitar and shoved the bag into the sound hole. "Now it's safe for the ride."

Muddy gave him a confused look then smiled. "You can't touch these instruments, can you?"

She didn't answer.

"I don't know why," Luke offered, whispering close, "but the legend has it that whoever carved those protected them with something. Something that no one here can touch. As long as you hold them tight, you'll stay alive."

He relaxed a little, breathing a deep, shaky breath. "Really?"

"Maybe."

The anxiety shook Muddy's bones again.

"Let's hop aboard and see what this boat can do."

He held his guitar tighter than his fear.

Once they were seated in the rear of the boat, they huddled together, and Poe asked, "What is this? Is it theirs?"

The ship ran roughly forty feet long and wide enough for the band to sit on dual rows of wood benches that stretched from bow to stern. A tall mast launched into the sky about midway, holding up a sail almost as wide as the ship was long.

Corey, the resident historian and *Jeopardy* freak, smiled at her. "Likely not. It seems like a Viking longship." He stood and peered over the edge, being careful not to step too close to the sirens that were rowing. "Why would they be in a longship? Norway's quite a way from here."

Muddy looked around, fingers tapping the boat's rim. "Shouldn't we be worried about where they're taking us?"

"Stop worrying, you," Otis said, doubling his buddy's rhythm. "These ladies seem to know where they're going. Never question a lady, especially one who might off us when they start singing."

Anxiety skittered up Muddy's spine again. They might not even make it to where Zack was, if his feelings were true.

"Anyway," Corey continued, "if you dorks knew anything about history, you'd know that the Vikings came down through Canada into America long before Columbus did. People found artifacts along the east coast a few years ago. Heck, they even found some as far south as the Carolinas."

"Okay, genius," Otis replied, "then, why don't we celebrate Erik the Red Day?"

Corey grinned. "Marketing. They'd have to change all the calendars."

"Well, since we're here," Muddy said, "we might as well find out how much they know about what we're doing."

The leader stood a safe distance away, but with one ear cocked. Her hearing must have been as keen as her voice because at that moment she turned toward the group and smiled.

"You really want to know the way to your goal? Maybe how to live through it?" Her voice purred liked the sweetest song-bird with just a tinge of venom.

Muddy stood, steadying himself in the swaying boat. "Please, that might do a ton of good, miss," he said, his voice confident.

He watched the smoke-like haze on the water around the boat, remembering Silver Eye's words about the inspiration for music.

"Of course," she replied, "anything to topple the Tritons and allow us to go back to the lives we once knew." Her smile turned crafty. "But everything has its price, right?" Her wings folded inwards. "Later. I promise it will be only a small favor in the grand design of things, especially to save your kin. But enough of that. You desire a map of clues and I have more than that. A story I hold, with bits that will keep you and your music alive forever. Just sit back and listen. Your lives depend upon your heeding every word."

Muddy leaned in close to Lyra. "Map? Clues?"

She patted his arm. "Soon. Listen now."

The others began to slink closer. As she spoke, her wings swayed with an eerie dance in time to her voice. Then it got *really* weird.

"If the deal is right, we can save your lives,
for journey is long, into the heart of evil we drive."

What? Muddy's head swiveled. The conversation spun first into stereo then into surround sound as more of the sirens sang around them, sounding as if one mind controlled them all.

"To the hive, where the evil one dwells,
the darkest one lives where the innocent one fell."

The hairs on Muddy's arms and neck rose. Something just wasn't right. He looked over at Poe who gave him that "we need to hear this" look. Still, her hands gripped the railing tightly.

"Follow the smoke, which lies along the waves,
maneuver the currents, row past whispering graves."

Many of the creatures flitted from floor to mast, from sail to bow, singing along in harmonies the band never heard before. Queen would have sacrificed a gold album to blend voices as sweet as these dangerous birds.

The leader swooped down and sung into Corey's ear.

"From the shores of where bones sing,
follow the ridge to the gauntlet ring."

Otis's head swayed to their beat, his fingers adding their own counterpoint. Two of them curled long toes on the wood on either side of him, drifting in, fading away.

"Find the key of earth to open every door,
for the wrong tone will drop you into mythical lore."

What's the key of earth? Muddy thought, becoming entranced. The others looked toward him for an explanation, but he shook his head, giving his best clueless expression. Music theory didn't come easy to him. Corey and Poe knew that stuff, but from their bemused looks, he'd guessed them to be as lost as he was. Otis kept to the rhythm, but he turned to the twins, their sibling guides, the only ones who knew the land.

Lyra pulled at Luke, but he just stared ahead through the smoke, his face set with a grim expression.

He knew something. What, Muddy didn't know, but it scared him something fierce. Still, they needed the clues.

Without Silver Eye, only the brother and sister knew more than they did, which didn't offer much comfort.

"But—" he began. Poe immediately shoved her hand over his mouth to shush him. His anxiety kicked in and he ached to run, to scream at them. Something! Why weren't those things doing anything?

> *"Without the key, you will fall,*
> *into a pit of discord, forever like babes, you'll bawl.*
> *They will rip from you, your soul,*
> *song removed, dying together, but not whole."*

His vision swam, doubled, but peace slid into his veins, battling for purchase with his anxiety.

> *"Seven trials await, each born of muses' breath,*
> *familiar to your world, yet played off brings death.*
> *Solve the puzzle of the room and play the next tone,*
> *out of tune, out of key, and your friends will find only bone."*

The fog appeared to break, or at least thin on the next wave. Luke scampered to the bow, but two harpies spun in front of him and unfurled their wings to block his view.

He attempted to scream, but their song drowned him out.

The leader stepped in front of Muddy and finished the tale.

> *"If you recall each lyric's melody or clue,*
> *the door into where you first began will cue.*
> *You'll step into the final realm, where a certain harmony will break,*
> *the hearts of Triton souls of which the darkened muse was made."*

Muddy tightened his grip on Poe. "I think the song's over."

The moment the siren finished, Corey and Muddy ran to help Luke battle for sight of what lie ahead of the haze. The others tried to flap them away and sing in their ears to subdue their efforts. The fingers of the trio in front of them lengthened into talons. Sharp ones. Their eyes focused into hawkish, hungry stares. Their mouths opened wide. Their teeth shrunk into smaller rows of jagged peaks. Muddy wouldn't have described them as beauties to begin with, but now their faces had morphed into something monstrous. The leader approached Muddy and the others.

"It's time for the payment!" she nearly squawked.

Muddy stood in front of Poe. "And what is that?" He asked, shaking.

"Nothing much, considering what we just offered you. All you need to do is follow our directions exactly and you will find your brother."

"How many have succeeded in getting through the gauntlet?"

The beak-like thing smiled. "You'll be the first, I assume. You have something the others didn't."

"Which is?"

"You have the determination to save a loved one, instead of striving for riches or fame. I assume those instruments you're carrying can do something quite amazing for you. That's a lot more than the last few who have ventured this far had in their possession."

Muddy held his guitar tight. "Did you lead them all the way, or did they perish on the boat?"

She laughed, a hideous sound. "Silly boy. You think you know us? From your folk tales? *Nightmares?*" She brushed her wing's edge against his throat. "You know nothing about our race. We scheme only to survive, to thrive, the same as anyone. Are we to be punished for that?"

Luke grasped hold of the oar he had pointed through the fog. "Tell them," he said. "Tell them your price, beast."

Otis screamed through the fog as it suddenly lifted. "I can see it. The shore! It's right there. It's—oh, no. *No.*"

The band pushed past the sirens as they pulled their wings back.

"What is that on the beach?" Poe strained to focus. "It looks like driftwood."

Corey finally spoke. "It's not driftwood. They're bones."

Chapter Thirty-One

"So that's your price," Muddy said, his anger rising. "You take your passengers all the way here, building up their confidence, their hopes, only to show them this? What kind of sick savages are you?"

The leader fluttered with a thump to the bow in front of them. The rage burning in her eyes almost forced them to turn away.

"You think we're savages?" she said, seething. "You think you're so high and mighty when you hunt for your food? How are you different than us? We need to feed as well."

Lyra spoke for the first time since she'd come aboard, her face green with seasickness. "You are killing people. We don't kill our own kind."

The creature smiled. "And neither do we. Now pay up."

Poe jumped in front of Muddy, getting in the siren's face. "How dare you sing to us your tales of how to beat the gauntlet and how to save Muddy's brother. Was it all for nothing? Just so you can eat us? I don't think so." She pulled back her arm to swing and, in a flash, a massive burst of feathers knocked her, along with the rest of them to the deck.

"All of you?" she cackled again. "No, no. Just one is our price. Just one, that's all we want. A mere pittance for our service."

Muddy looked toward the littered shore, white with bones. *How long had they been doing this? How many had paid the price?* He thought of his friends.

"Will you be like the others and choose for us? Or would you prefer us to pick for you?"

Otis brandished his sticks like weapons. With a shriek from

a pair of sirens, he jumped to his feet. "We're all getting off of this boat right now!" He turned toward the shore and it seemed to be at least a hundred yards. Easy to manage, even with a rip-tide, considering the current plight. If they judged it correctly, they'd be far enough away when the sirens took off, if the beasts were capable.

In an instant, while everyone focused on Otis, the smallest of the prey, Muddy heard a deep grunt. A painful grunt.

Corey.

A quartet of sirens had descended on the sax player, holding him down with little effort. The teen had rock hard muscles, but these birds made him look like a scarecrow. Then Muddy saw why. Each had a talon pressed into his flesh just outside a key artery. One on each side of his jugular pricked his skin and the others dug into pressure points under each arm and into his heart.

"Go!" His eyes bore into Muddy's and the intent was clear. "Get off the boat and flee these beasts before they change their minds."

Luke held up the seeds. "I'll toss them!"

"Go ahead," said the leader. "We're still getting what we want. You know you weren't going to hand those over, anyway. Tonight, we'll still feed. Will you still breathe?"

"Go!" Corey was frightened, but he wouldn't risk their lives for his own.

"Listen to him," said the leader. "You've earned the secrets that will likely save your brother. You must have known there would be some collateral damage. No one leaves the gauntlet unscathed. We're an honorable breed. Others here would skewer you for dinner and suck the marrow from your bones."

Corey's eyes went wide at her words but remained calm. The big guy had witnessed much more than many kids his age had.

"We'll bring you to shore. Just leave us our fare. We did our part."

Poe, who had been sitting silently, left the safety of the bench. "You. Lied."

"We never do," replied the siren. "It's impossible for our species to do so."

"You never said you'd kill one of us for the information!"

The sharp smile cut the sea air. "And you never asked. I believe that's *your* fault, dear.

"Prepare him."

The ship bounced over the cresting waves as it neared the shoreline. The rest of the band and siblings held tightly to the rails as the creatures held fast to their positions. Muddy realized that if he were to attempt a rescue, the creatures would slash them all to ribbons, meaty ribbons, turning a snack into a buffet. Five bodies against an octet of half-bird, half-woman beasts equaled no contest. He would have to think fast, unless someone else had a plan.

"You'll thank me for this one day," she said. "You'll be accomplishing something no other human, no other musician has ever done, along with saving your family."

"You are nothing but beasts!" Muddy shouted. "Trading one life for another is murder."

Why wasn't anyone else jumping in and helping him? There had to be some way to bribe or trick these creatures, wasn't there?

"We'll bring you the Dark Muse himself," he said, immediately realizing how idiotic he sounded.

She cackled above him. "Of *course* you will. He will easily allow you to bring him back through the gauntlet and to our boat where he knows what will befall him, won't he? And I thought you were a smart one."

"Well, that's a first. I've never heard that claim from someone."

From behind him one of the highest notes he had ever heard sounded, tearing into his ears. Soprano range but thick in tone, it rose to a crescendo that threatened to shatter his ear drums. It then fell, rose again and began a fierce aural dance over his head. Others joined the song but in pained, discordant harmony. Someone pulled at his shirt from behind and he nearly tumbled over the edge of the boat.

His eyes caught sight of the song's source. Poe way out on the bow, holding onto the rope descending from the mast with arms outstretched. Her mouth hung wide open and her throat vibrated in a sultry song that pierced their strength, leaving them all weak-kneed on the deck. Her head tossed back and forth in a snake charmer's slow dance, almost like her effect on the grass. The others lay close to him, helpless, but smiling.

His bewildered look must have cued Lyra, who eased her head toward the beasts holding Corey. They had released him, hands and talons pinned to their ears in agony, obviously trying to block out Poe's attack. He skittered away from them and moved toward the band, safe, aside from a few shallow cuts. The leader fought it hard, flapping her wings in defiance, yet her head swung from the song. She wouldn't give up that easily. Her eyes burned at them using their own weapon against her and her sisters. Her mouth opened, attempting to form words, but it failed as she crumpled to one knee. Soon, all the sirens lay on the deck, writhing in confusion and pain as the band eased to where Poe stood. With one hand, she beckoned them. Muddy didn't know what to make of the gesture until Luke pointed toward the water.

"Jump," he mouthed, his voice swallowed in the volume.

Are you kidding? They'd never make it the couple hundred feet in rough surf before the creatures caught up with them. Then there was the beach run all the way to the cave.

Poe turned to them and nodded. *No!* They never would. *She* might not, but the others had begun to recover and were crawling to the edge of the longship.

"I'm not leaving you!" he yelled. Then someone pushed him, and his world turned upside down. He tumbled end over end for a long moment before splashing into the sea. Silence flooded into his ears, blocking out everything else, but he remembered to hold his breath. His dad had told him that drowning was the worst way to die. He only needed to hear that once.

Splashes erupted around him as he tried to find the surface. Light beamed down from above and he clawed for it. Muddy felt bubbles pushing themselves from his lips, but the waves held him down.

Up. Up. Fight! His lungs burned as he pinwheeled his arms. One hand broke the surface, then the other. He kicked his legs through the churning water. The current pulled at him, but he couldn't let Poe down. Next to his brother and his dad, she was the only other person he would die for without hesitation.

"Poe!" he cried as his face felt the ocean air. He sucked in a lungful of the cold, salty, lovely, air but it burned his insides as he coughed out seawater.

A wave knocked him under, and he instinctively kicked downwards. With both hands and feet, he broke through the water again to suck down air. Wiping away the salt, he squinted through the dimming light around him for the shore. The current must have dragged him out a bit more, but he could still see the shore. Now, about two hundred feet away, he knew he would have to swim to where the swells grew big enough to break, then ride a wave onto the beach without drowning or being smashed onto the rocks. He swung both arms into the cool water and began his quest for the perfect ride. After wading through a trio of breakers that failed to carry him, he noticed a massive one swelling up right in front of the ship. Three dark shapes rose and fell with it as it approached him.

No! Muddy cried inside. *Not before everyone is safe.*

Get to the shore first, and then find a way to get Corey and Poe back alive. He cursed himself for sounding selfish, but deep within he knew that to do anything else was pure suicide. His only skill lay with that guitar and now it hung on his back, soaked in sea water, probably ruined. His muscles wouldn't even get him back to the ship. He would hit bottom with lungs full of water.

He turned back to try to catch sight of Poe on the ship, but the waves pushed him too far. He prayed she had jumped soon after the rest were in the water.

While he was feeling sorry for himself, that wave began to break. A ribbon of white foam curled at the top and he knew he would either take it to the shore, or to his grave. He thrust his arms straight out in front and kicked his legs as hard as he could. A thousand pounds of ocean slammed into him and pushed. Hard.

Like a leaf in a storm gutter, he became a victim of the current. Water bubbled all around him while he struggled to keep his head above it all, to keep sight of the beach. He was able to see until the undertow sucked his arms down and flipped him over. He banged against the sand and rocky shore, over and over, head, then knees, then his back, until it threw him onto the soft water's edge.

Am I broken? Air failed to enter his sore lungs. He felt only pain but rolled his body onto all fours. The current had only knocked the wind out of him. His voice sounded odd when he inhaled, squeaky, but he tried again. This time, a little breath filled part of him. Another inhale filled more. A few more times and he finally breathed normally.

"Muddy," someone cried. "You okay?"

He *was* okay. He *was* alive. The wave didn't kill him. He willed his body to function, sensing nerves in his fingers and toes reawaken. He pushed himself to stand on rubbery legs and turned to face the voice.

Otis and Luke turned him over to face the lifeless forms of Poe and Corey, unmoving lumps upon the sand behind him.

He fell to the sand and his world went black.

Chapter Thirty-One

Hands pulled at him, shaking him back to reality. Now he truly felt broken.

"No," Muddy wheezed, feeling his chest contract. "No. No. No." Each time he tried to scream his lungs betrayed him.

She couldn't be gone. He grieved over Corey too, but he'd promised Poe that he would always be there to protect *her*.

Don't leave me now, please.

He dove into the sand between them, tears welling up in his eyes, blurring his view of the bodies. He ached for his guitar. That would fix it. The guitar had power. Silver Eye told him so. He'd *seen* it himself.

It lay in the surf, yards away. He raced over and picked it up. It felt as heavy as the metal he grew up listening to, and he couldn't sling it across his shoulders.

Water. Dump it. Now.

He flipped it over and the seawater oozed out. His arms ached with exhaustion as he shook out the insides. Clumps of sand tumbled out onto his sopping feet. The bag of seeds that would become songs. His fingers clamored for a thick power chord to shake his buddies to life, but the sand felt melded to the strings, glued to the fretboard.

He swatted at the caked strings with both hands, hearing someone yelling at him, someone bellowing or growling behind him. What was there? The sirens? Of course. They would follow the crew onto shore to finish the others off for a dessert.

"Muddy!" someone screamed.

He turned and threw the guitar into the surf.

"Muddy!"

Otis flapped his thin arms like an angry crane. He pointed at the ground.

Corey was on all fours, hacking up what seemed to be most of the beach.

How?

Luke sat atop Poe and pumped her chest, his mouth on hers. Muddy burned with a pang of jealousy before he realized that the boy was performing CPR. Why didn't he think of that?

He didn't know the procedure, that's why. This guy, who had his lips pressed to hers, knew exactly what to do. *What is wrong with me?* Her life was all that mattered. Period.

He dropped to his knees by the teen, wishing he could help. The blond boy pressed rhythmically on Poe's chest, hoping to dislodge the water. Lyra and Corey joined him. Out of nowhere, thunder sounded, and time stopped.

They all shook, and Muddy fell backwards into an oncoming wave then turned.

There he stood. Otis. With a mallet of driftwood held in one hand like a club, he swung it down. Again and again he struck the mass of bones from so many creatures and humans. The booming vibrated the group nearly off the ground.

Next to them, someone coughed. To Muddy, it was the most beautiful sound ever. He saw Poe spit out a stream of water over a foot in the air. She coughed again.

Alive! Muddy screamed inside to no one at all, except his heart.

He crawled over and cradled her head in his arms. "Let it out," he wheezed between tears.

She opened her eyes and gazed up at him. It was something he had not gotten used to yet, but prayed he would have a chance to after this was over. She *saw* him. What did she see? The special ed dweeb the rest of his schoolmates saw or what he'd hoped she saw in her blindness, who he truly was within?

"What happened?" Her voice croaked with remnants of seawater.

"You," he answered. "You saved us. That's all that matters."

"Guys," Corey said, looking like he just crawled out of a grave, "I'm just as happy, but I think we should get moving. Now."

They turned and saw that their pursuers had yet to give up.

Chapter Thirty-Two

The sirens flew toward the band. Fast. With wingspans wider than the mouth of the cave behind them, at least six sirens jetted, each appearing to target a particular individual. Muddy locked eyes with the one drawing a bead on him and froze. He shot a glance behind him and saw an opening in the side of the mountain.

A cave?

Protection.

How big it was and how much protection it would yield was unknown. Still, it wasn't as though they had a choice. It would provide some shelter, but these beasts could still hunt them down inside. They made a mad dash to the entrance, about a hundred feet away. Their attackers were right behind, moving slow and vicious, with a practiced purpose.

He and Corey ran the distance, making it safely inside. They scanned the interior, taking in the deep purplish walls splashing shades in all directions, forming an oblong, slimmer than a football field, only a few first downs long. They crept to the ceiling, the height of the amp stacks at a rock concert with just as few footholds.

The rest of them tumbled inside, finding themselves standing within a solid room. No doors, no openings save for the one they entered. Then realization crept over them. The cave would become their crypt. As the others joined them, Muddy's fear grew into a physical being. "They *did* lie," he said.

"I guess they'll be eating in today?" Otis never stopped joking, but this time, his voice shook just a hair.

"Look for cover!" Muddy yelled over the din of the beating wings approaching. But where?

Poe and the twins raced toward the back of the cave on the right side, feeling for a corner where none existed. Corey and Otis stood tall at the entrance, appearing to protect their brave little troupe in vain.

Where do I go? Muddy thought, panicking. *Do I try to hide her or give up my life with my friends? Which is braver, and which might allow her to live longer?*

His mind raced as he pondered how to spend his last few moments. Surely, Otis and Corey knew the futility of the situation. No way out meant no way out. By nightfall, their bones would be indistinguishable from those carpeting the beach.

Then Otis did something Muddy would never forget or understand. He turned to the opening, raised his sticks and muttered a few choice words. The diminutive drummer ran right *at* the winged creatures.

Muddy and Corey screamed at him to return, but the teen kept going, drum and sticks in hand.

"It's suicide!" Muddy cried, hands clenching, wishing for a weapon.

The sax player stood still, frozen in place. "If the little guy wants to go out with a bang, let him. At least he's doing it on his terms. It's better than a disease killing you."

"Is it?" Muddy couldn't just let one of his best friends die for him. Could he?

"We'll likely be joining him, but I don't plan on giving those harpies fast food, either. They're going to *earn* this meal."

As Otis dove through the massive pile of bones, under the bones themselves, they realized both had been wrong.

"What the heck?" Corey shook his head. "He can't be hiding. After all he's been through, he's hiding—while we're in here waiting to be shredded?"

Muddy turned back to the trio still attempting to find a way out that didn't exist. "He's not afraid. He wouldn't. Just couldn't." His friend faced death every day. It just didn't make sense.

The sirens either lost sight of him or simply didn't care to pick through the mess when they had a captive meal fifty feet in front of them.

Thoughts of dying churned though Muddy's mind and suddenly he realized he would soon reunite with his mom. *Maybe it wouldn't hurt much,* he mused as he kicked a flat, ocean-smoothed rock.

Rocks? He picked it up and realized hundreds surrounded them and amidst the bones. Corey noticed what his band mate was up to and shrugged. "It couldn't hurt, could it?"

Neither of the boys were athletes, but Muddy figured that Corey had a much better arm and aim. As the sirens neared the entrance, they slowed and formed a half-circle before them, sniffing out their prey, finalizing their attack.

"Ah, geez," Corey said.

People dealt with impending death in different ways. Muddy remembered his mom reading every book and cooking every recipe she could before cancer took her. He remembered asking why and then mentally kicking himself after he spoke the words.

"So, I'll have more to talk about with all those dead authors and chefs in the afterlife," she'd quipped.

His buddy suddenly didn't seem like the joking type. They looked at each other and Muddy knew their faces said plenty.

Let's go out fighting like the Jets against the entire NFL hall of fame roster.

Corey wound up and launched a baseball-sized rock. It sailed upwards and hit the closest siren smack dab in the face. She dove and crashed on the rocks.

Both cried in triumph and gathered more rocks.

The siren raised her bloody head. *Just dazed,* Muddy thought. She shook off the pain and took to the air again, angered.

The others spread further apart and prepared to dive. They would sacrifice one or two for a good meal, especially with these odds.

. Muddy had been in a good brawl before, but not with friends nearby needing protection.

But Muddy was not going out without a fight. He and Corey

called Luke to join in the fight. He hesitated before leaving his twin. Right behind him rushed the girls. *Idiot*, he chided himself. Muddy thought. Of course, they could take care of themselves. Lyra was tougher than him and Poe's new sight probably gave her better targeting. Each gathered rocks of varying sizes and began a full assault on the winged beasts. One by one, the rocks hit their targets, more connecting than missing. Still, hardly any sirens dropped out of the sky. Those who did got right back up, even if some flew broken and bloodied.

Death was practically visible and near to Muddy, just like his mother saw hers coming. It calmed him. If he'd had time to ponder it, he might have been amused, or more frightened.

The sirens wailed and sang the song that would hypnotize their prey and gain the easy meal. They began to land and hit the shoreline in formation. With measured jumps, they advanced on the teens like hungry checker pieces. Just like on a game board, the teens had nowhere to go. They could only back into the cave, but that only allowed another few yards of retreat.

Just maybe there was a tunnel, and they might find if they searched hard enough. Heck, maybe they could even dig one.

"Retreat!" Muddy called, feeling like a coward.

They raced back into the cave and began feeling the walls for something—*anything*. Yet they found nothing. No doors, no secret passages. Nothing.

The howling hit the entrance of the cave. They were here to feed, and the only escape was death. Muddy wondered if he could end it quickly but knew their beaks and claws would finish him before he could try.

He stepped to the edge and looked at his approaching executioners. They now numbered about a dozen, hovering at the entrance, awaiting the call from the lead hunter. He wondered briefly if they'd ever had to truly fight for a meal. Not that this would be much of a battle, despite the group's intentions. His mind fought the siren song they now began to sing, knowing his group couldn't resist long.

Maybe falling under their trance would save them from suffering.

His mind raced with phantom sensations of pain. His nerves

previewed the tearing of flesh, the separation of skin from bone and watching them devour him while he was still conscious.

Mom, here I come. I love you. Dad, sorry I was too caught up with my adventure to say goodbye. He felt like the loser so many said he was.

He stood in front of Poe. Maybe somehow, they would be satiated after eating him and Corey. Maybe they could use her voice to help them. Maybe...

What was taking them so long! Just get it over with already.

Thunder burst through the cavern as he began his death prayer. It was if the heavens above broke in an avalanche of sound. Like an AC/DC concert with amps jacked to eleven. Like every drum set and amplifier in the world blasted all at once.

Every siren dropped to the ground, screaming in pain from the noise.

Then the bass drums began.

Another rumble sounded right before them. A roll of earthquake-like proportions hit, and Muddy forced himself to look.

Rocks,—no, *boulders* rained down on them. Not on them, but on the sirens. Falling on *all* of them. *What the heck?*

"Otis!" Luke and Muddy yelled as they caught a glimpse of the drummer standing amidst the cover of bones under which he had hid. He *wasn't* a coward. Muddy berated himself for even considering that Otis's sense of self-preservation had kicked in. Had he been thinking straight, maybe he would've done the same. Probably not.

The drummer stood taller than he possibly could and pinwheeled his arms. With each mallet strike, another peal of storm assaulted their ears and the rock wall above the entrance. The mountain in which they hid crumbled from above. Not all of it, just the outside crust, but still, it was enough to drop car-sized boulders on the predators. One by one the rocks tumbled and crushed the sirens. Many didn't even have time to scream. The sounds of their bodies crunching under stone sounded sickening, and Muddy felt sorrow—for a moment—until he remembered they had been seconds away from chowing down on the entire band like human buffalo wings.

Otis stood there, clamoring away while his drum solo literally brought down the house. When he realized he had saved
his friends, he cracked one of his *Otis* smiles and started to say
something. And then he disappeared.

A curtain of stones caused them to dive for cover. The avalanche managed to quiet their friend. Muddy would've grinned
if his best friend hadn't just died in front of his eyes.

A rain of smaller boulders brought down the last sirens, but along
with it a curtain of stone that quickly built up a wall between the
drummer and his buddies. They were trapped inside the cave;
safe but trapped and separated from the friend who'd just saved
their butts.

No one could manage a word. Was Otis buried as well? The
drumming halted just as suddenly as it began. He probably lay
in a grave of rock, a way he would prefer to die but still, just *gone*.

Maybe he'd managed to scurry backwards as the avalanche
happened, Muddy hoped. Maybe he stood there on the beach,
alive. Trapped away from us and safe for the moment, but only
until the remainder of the sirens came for their revenge.

Poe wasn't the first to cry. Corey was.

"He sacrificed himself. Why? He might have been able to
bring down the house from inside, not out there with them."

Muddy attempted to speak but couldn't. His friend was
dead, just moments before he'd resigned himself to death.

"He didn't have to give his life for us," Poe whimpered. "We
could've done something."

"No," Corey rebutted, "we couldn't. It was over. Done. We
were toast. We were caught off guard and he was the only one
who thought to use Silver Eye's training, just like Poe did on the
ship. He saved us. He knew what the consequences might be,
but we don't know if his death is definite."

Muddy prayed his friend was right.

"What now?" He found his voice. "Do we die in here? There's
no exit." He still felt like a wuss and hated himself for it. Despite
the new powers he had and all this travel to find Zack, what had
he accomplished? Nothing. As usual, he was the lesser brother,
the weakest of the family.

"We dig," Corey said giving an order in a gruff tone of voice.

They would dig. For what, Muddy had no idea. Maybe to find that Otis had killed all the creatures, and that they would be able to use the boat to find another route inside the mountain.

Corey looked at his friend. He cocked an ear to the rocks.

They both heard it. Scratching. From the other side. From outside the wall of rocks.

Was it a siren still alive, trying to get to them?

"I'll kill you!" Muddy screamed. "I swear I'll tear each feather from your freakin' wings and shove them down your beak."

The digging stopped. Something coughed.

"That's not cool at all. Not very friendly of you. Figured your diva guitar self would show eventually." More coughing broke up the sentence.

"Holy—" Corey turned to Muddy.

"*Otis?*"

"Who else would it be, dorkus? Justin Bieber?"

"Hey, diva!" Corey yelled, slapping Muddy on the arm, his happiness spilling over as tears of joy. "Dig!"

Rock by rock, they worked. They pulled and dragged them all away. One by one, they removed the barrier and prayed their work wouldn't cause another cave-in. Within a half-hour they found success. Poe screamed when she saw a bony hand reaching through the debris and they pulled the drummer through a tiny but welcomed opening.

Chapter Thirty-Three

Soon after they pulled Otis from the rubble, Muddy realized his condition. His brittle bones were broken all over.

They lay him on the cavern floor and let him rest.

"I'm fine," he said, coughing up dust and blood. "Really, it's only a flesh wound."

But he wasn't. Every visible inch of his body had turned purple and red in bruises, contusions, and fractures. Blood covered his Rush t-shirt and cargo shorts.

They wouldn't give up on him, not when he saved them. They never gave up on each other. In a world where they couldn't count on much, they counted on each other. Screw what the world thought.

Besides, that world wasn't anywhere near where they were now.

Poe began her song, hovering above him, a lullaby-like tune they had never heard before. Corey joined in with a vocal melody on his sax-type thing. They performed a duet in a sweet harmony, lines weaving between each other.

Suddenly, Otis' eyes glazed over in pain. "Stop it!" It was hurting him.

But Muddy understood their intention. He picked up his guitar.

Lyra and Luke simply stood there, smiling

She sang. Harder. They played. Louder.

Each note was somehow healing Otis. Musical surgery. Did they know that they were doing it? How would they know? Yet as he stared at the group, he knew that they did know, somehow. It just felt…right.

Musical magic. Harry freaking Potter with rock and roll.

An hour later, the drummer slept, his bruises visibly fading.

Muddy hugged Poe. Before he had a chance to ask the question, she spoke. "You weren't the only one who Silver Eye gave secrets to. He figured this song might come in handy. We're lucky Otis wasn't in worse condition."

Muddy just grinned and wondered if every guy got to feel that way at least once in life.

Otis awoke soon afterwards, joking and asking why the heck they hadn't found the way out of this hole yet.

"There has to be a way. The slaves who worked for the Tritons weren't dumb," Lyra said. "They wouldn't have sacrificed themselves for something they hated with all their being. There must be a way inside."

"What's that?" Poe asked, feeling along the wall with Luke. They stood against the far side, digging their fingers into a carving. It contained no words or pictographs that they could see. Then again, Poe didn't normally operate under the land of the sighted. Muddy never knew what to expect from her. First, she'd healed Otis, and now this.

"There's something here. Maybe it's nothing."

Lyra jumped up. "Nothing here is *not* nothing. It's *something*. It is."

But how would they solve it? What could they do?

The music. It had always saved them and might one more time.

Corey shrugged. Sometimes, the answer existed in a jam. Sometimes the best songs, the ones that changed people's lives, began on a whim.

"Should we?"

Otis picked up his drum and knocked off a rim shot. "Like, you had to ask?"

"You sure you're up for this?" Muddy stood looking at the drummer, still astonished he wasn't boulder pizza.

"Drummers never die, dude."

"Oh, yeah? Ask Led Zeppelin, The Who, Def Leppard..."

"Hold on—that guy only lost an arm *and* got better because of it."

Corey, Muddy, Poe, and Otis began the jam in E, their favorite, and played without purpose, just pouring themselves into every note, hoping for something.

Each note lived, just like it did in the River. It lived. It grew. Then it took on a life of its own and found its purpose with the secret in the wall.

"I *told* you there was a way!" Lyra hugged her brother, and then Muddy.

Poe smiled, winking at him. "People usually do find a way to get what they want."

Dust broke all around them as the wall belched. They'd found the way of escape, an entry that opened into the bowels of the mountain. A door had eased open, a thick slab of rock that their song unlocked. Strangely, no one celebrated. Muddy figured that they realized the journey had only begun. It had been a long time since they'd lost a member of their group and that scared Muddy more than the task ahead.

The scrawling on the wall before them was minimal at best. Muddy expected a code in some strange language. Everything he read was code to him anyway with his dyslexia. How he could solve this puzzle was beyond him. Every class, every day, he had to fight just to keep up with the others. Even Poe whizzed through books in Braille when the school could afford them. What did he have? He had a father whom many worshipped as a writer; he was simply the stupid son. Even musically, he held a distant second place finish in his family.

"What does it say?" He turned to Lyra and Luke, hoping they could decipher what he couldn't. After all, this was their world, not his.

Otis had pushed his way to the front, eager to try his hand at deciphering the secrets Muddy couldn't. His bruises and cuts were already healing to the point they were nearly invisible. Maybe Poe's song kept working on him. It was either that or Otis's own drumming had affected his body chemistry. They had learned about how the body was affected by vibrations and music in class, but back then, Muddy never thought it could *actually* heal or save a life.

"I can't see squat. Just scribbling, that's all. It doesn't even look like a language to me," Otis said. His parents spoke several languages, learned from their travels and a vast background of studies. Some of it had to trickle down to their son. If he didn't recognize it, maybe it was just rambling symbols.

Lyra rubbed her hands over it where the barrier had come down. She cleared away debris and found more room to move. Most of the dust had settled and an oval opening stood before them. The band stepped through it and examined their new surroundings. Upon the wall on their left were more etchings none of them could decipher. On either side, lights illuminated the hall, not with fire from the tiki torches expected in every cheesy cave movie, but rather with splotches of blinding white material within the walls themselves. He recalled some cultures used paints that were phosphorescent. Whatever this was, whoever lined the walls, it lit up the room just enough for them to see what they needed to see.

"Guys, maybe this isn't our last day alive after all," Muddy said. He viewed the various shapes on wall and believed he knew what to do.

"Caves hold some interesting secrets, don't you think?" Luke smiled. "It's just simple minerals that the slaves used to find their way during the construction. You'd probably find it in your caves back home." He wiped the greasy surface with his hand, which now glowed almost as bright as the markings on the wall.

Muddy examined the indentations of people and creatures and objects in many formations. *So many options,* he thought. So many odd carvings all around him. There could be only one choice, the choice presented to him in the River dreams. He pressed his fingers into a carving on the cave wall that resembled a guitar and the world came down around them.

Chapter Thirty-Four

Behind them, a wall crashed to the cavern floor. The walls to the front and sides fell away into dust, leaving them blinded for the moment, choking at a foul-smelling substance. The cavern behind them was gone.

"What did you do?" Otis screamed. "We're going to die, I know it. We've used up enough lives this week."

Muddy's brain scattered in confusion, thinking his friend might be right. He'd simply dug his fingers into what looked like the one thing that had made him happy all these years and nearly crushed them as a result.

Lyra and Luke rushed forward when they could see again. "We're trapped, all right, but there are more messages."

"Great," Muddy replied. "Let me try again and land the killing blow." But he felt more confident than he sounded. And he realized how pathetic he sounded.

"There's gotta be a way," Poe said, echoing her words from before. "The booby trap wasn't designed to kill. It's a test. It's got to be."

"Muddy," Corey stepped in, "you've got to find us a way out of here. Silver Eye trusted you with the River. He *knew* you were the one with the skills."

Right, Muddy thought. He knew how to kill them all, how to lead them all to their demise. If Silver Eye wanted company, wherever he was, he was likely about to get some.

As he allowed himself another weak moment to brood, Poe walked up to each wall and hummed to herself. Not in song, but in thought. As she did so, she made sure to press each finger lightly over the symbols on the walls, avoiding a repeat of the disaster Muddy brought upon them.

She walked back and forth, touching this wall and that one.

What was she doing? Muddy wondered.

"When the wall fell, that wasn't all that happened. We also sank several feet into the mountain as well."

"Great," Muddy said. "Now, I've really buried us."

"Will you please shut up?" Corey snapped. "Enough of the *Sad Sack* stuff. Like you're the cause of all our problems here. Really."

Otis piped in, "Sorry for yelling at you, but seriously, this downbeat stuff, really not attractive, man."

"That would explain a lot," added Corey, focusing on the wall. "I thought it was just a tremor. It wasn't. The room essentially fell. That's why the cavern disappeared. It's still there, it's just above us. I have no clue how far down we are."

He walked to the far wall and pressed his fingers to the smooth, dark surface. His fingers searched out another few feet and found an edge. Then he discovered another few feet of black coolness. Another edge. He kept going. Each section of the wall was partitioned by an edge of some sort, but he didn't press hard. 1. 2. 3. 4. He counted as he circled the band and they greeted his actions with odd expressions.

"What are you doing?" Lyra finally asked.

"Sh-h-h…" Corey replied. "Come here and follow me with your fingers. Run them along the edges and tell me what you feel."

Without questioning, she did, trailing behind him as her fingers rubbed against the dark surface. As they completed the circle, she stopped then reversed course and rubbed with her other hand, walking counter-clockwise this time.

"It's this one," she said.

"What about it?" Muddy challenged her.

"It's warm. I don't know how or why, but it is," she said. "It *must* be the way."

The others felt the wall for themselves and agreed with her assumption.

Poe cocked her head at Corey. "How did you know?"

He shrugged. "I'm amazed I felt anything with these

calloused fingers, but I did. There are twelve different sections, just like there are to the western scale, from C to C and all the sharps and flats within it. All seemed the same and I thought it was my imagination, but Lyra felt it too. One of them was warm. That's got to be a sign, right?"

Poe's eyes lit up. "That means something's behind it. A path, maybe."

"Hopefully, not one that's on fire," Corey said. "That would explain the cool to warm factor."

"Geek," Poe said, punching him in the arm.

They agreed, even Luke, who hung back a little.

"Now what, genius?" Otis readied his sticks. "Should I bang something?"

"No!" said the group in unison. Due to the cave-ins they'd already faced, they didn't dare risk another.

"Lighten up, folks. Just kidding," he said, grinning ear to ear. "Someone's got to kill the tension."

"So how *do* we get through?" Poe asked, then answered her own question by placing both hands on the wall. "Twelve steps. It's got to be a specific note."

Otis jumped up and down. "I never forget what a woman tells me, even if she's a beast. An actual beast this time. Remember what they sang to us? The ones who had a 'crush' on us?" Muddy groaned at the joke, cringing at the image. "That's right. They told us the key of this place, how to find entry."

Corey looked at his friend as though he'd been hit too hard by those falling rocks. "Dude, what are you talking about?

"She said, 'The key of earth.' Remember now?"

"And what key is that? I only recall the keys of fire, air, and water."

The drummer smiled his sarcastic half-smile. "Good one, but the key of earth, ground, the lifeblood of most rock and blues songs. Which is it?"

Poe blinked. "*Duh.* And I've been hearing it since the walls collapsed before. Stand back. I think I've got this one."

Chapter Thirty-Five

She sung a beautiful note, an E, the most universal tone in all of rock and blues keys. She didn't belt it out, didn't whisper it. She simply sang it aloud while pressing against the wall, flexing her arms and voice against the stone until it moved.

The wall became a door before them and creaked inward.

They followed her through in awe.

"Oh, wow," she said, still in key. "Now, what?"

Once inside the door, they walked into in an antechamber. It shook and then sank the moment all of them stood in the center of it. "What gives?" Otis moaned, steadying himself. "How many of these trials do we have to go through?"

And why did it sink when they stood on it? Did that mean they were in the right room?

As the room came to a halt, they were faced by a dozen more walls, but this time, each was notated, a specific pitch etched into every one of them. A dozen carvings in silvery-white beckoned to them against pitch-black walls towering at least ten feet high.

E. F. F#. G. G#. A. Bb. B. C. C#. D. D#.

The twelve notes of the diatonic scale in the key of E.

"A dodecagon?" Corey drew incredulous looks from the group. "What? I actually studied in geometry." The others shook their heads but took in the odd-shaped room. "Things just keep getting stranger, but at least this one makes sense."

"I suddenly feel like I'm in a bad *Indiana Jones* movie," Otis said. "Are there snakes? I hate snakes."

They gathered close and mused together.

"What now? Muddy? Where do we start? E—the tonic note?

But then what? Is it a scale, a chord? What do we do?"

This time, instead of feeling overwhelmed with anxiety, Muddy simply looked into each person's eyes. "I think you know what we have to do."

He gauged their blank stares.

"Who made this trail? What would *they* do? Not the Tritons, who want music removed from the people, but the music *of* the people who created this. Those who would make it so that anyone with a hint of musical knowledge within their world could pass."

The others stood in silence.

"No," he continued. "Especially if they needed to get back in, or out. Or get their families or friends inside. All slaves— from the Egyptians, who made the pyramids, to those in medieval times, to the ones in our own country—all of them devised codes. I watched a video on something like this where musicians the world over relied on *one* scale to communicate across cultures. It didn't work for everyone, but it sure did where slaves and captives of war were concerned. The leaders, those who held the power and ignorance, figured that if it was music, it must be complicated and must be classical or ethnic in the nature. It's not. We've been playing this for years."

"Seriously?" Corey said. "It can't be that easy."

"It's gotta be," Muddy argued. "It's the only way."

Lyra pressed against the E door. "Well, I have no idea what you're talking about, but I hope you do."

"He does," Otis said. "He does. He's never let us down before, musically, and we came to kick some Triton butt. Let's go rock their world."

The drummer raised his sticks over his head and threw himself into the door with the "E" marking and it shattered into a million little pieces. "This *is* an *Indiana Jones* movie," he said, scrambling to his feet, brushing off the shale-like shards of rock.

"That likely means we're headed for death." Muddy, like the rest of them, gazed at the open expanse ahead of them and exhaled deeply.

Chapter Thirty-Six

Muddy took in the scene before him: a vast expanse of stone squares filled the floor. Every inch was covered with either a black or gray tile of about two square feet, plenty of room for a person to stand. Every square had a note etched upon it. Not the lettered note, but one on a staff. *Thankfully, it's a standard one,* he muttered to himself. At least he could read music just fine.

He gazed across the floor. It spanned at least a hundred feet, maybe more. He couldn't tell from where he stood but knew it would be a task to get to the door on the other side. Two doors awaited them on the opposite side.

More etching covered a slab on the floor. A clue?

Poe kneeled and read, her fingers brushing away years of dust. "'Walk this way, said the blind man. Walk this way and not that way if you wish to proceed.'"

Corey approached the edge and nearly took the first step. "Could it really be that simple?" He grinned as he checked the others' amused faces. Only the twins wore blank expressions.

Poe stood next to him. "Dude, most people or things who got to this point likely have never heard that song. It's a perfect trap."

"Let's go," he replied, shrugging in agreement. "Seems simple to me. We just step on the notes in the—" The tile marked E before him fell away. Corey steadied himself as Muddy reached out to help his friend from falling. He grabbed the bigger boy's hand, but it slipped from Muddy's grip.

Without a scream, Corey, suddenly fell *through* the floor and tumbled into space. Muddy saw a look of utter confusion tattooed itself onto each of his friends' faces.

Gone. Just like that. *Dead*, Muddy thought. *I should've stopped him, but I couldn't hold him. This was my gig.*

He felt as if he were watching a horror movie instead of seeing his friend tumbling into the darkness below.

Poe screamed in agony over Corey's fall. Tears streamed down her face. "I could see enough to watch him go over, but not enough to help." Her voice, beautiful at most times, sounded strangled by pain and wrung out of tune.

Muddy stared into the abyss, hoping that it wasn't a long fall. Nobody heard a thump or a scream. *Maybe, just maybe?* "It was his own fault just like it was ours. Maybe we're not meant to succeed."

Poe looked at him and slapped him–hard. "How dare you?"

He ached to shrink back but knew he had it coming. "I'm sorry."

"You're always sorry!" she yelled in his face. "Don't be! We're all here because we want to be. You didn't drag us here. That idiot stepped over the edge out of arrogant confidence. You didn't push him!"

But she did just that. She shoved him so that he backed right onto the black A—and it held. It wasn't supposed to be the E note. They'd just assumed that, due to their choice of doors.

"Oh, Edgar, I'm so sorry! I didn't mean—"

"I know," he said. "I stepped back, maybe more than you pushed. Maybe I wanted to step backwards. Put myself in the hands of fate."

"Shut. Up." She grabbed hold of his face and kissed him—quick—then pulled away and dropped her head. "You can't leave us. Not now."

He struggled to find the right words but couldn't.

Otis looked at the others, who couldn't find the right words, either. "Guys, your timing just plain sucks."

"This doesn't mean he's dead. Nothing here is what it seems," Muddy said. "We now search for two people." Something within told him that Corey still breathed. The River lived in him now, reached out to others. Somehow, he knew that if his friend died in the fall, he would feel it. And he didn't.

"Time to go?" Otis stepped onto the same A that Muddy did and felt it hold steady. "Ready to lead us, maestro?"

Muddy bowed his head. "For Corey."

He recalled the song, the main lick, the riff that everyone knew from the band from Boston. It played repeatedly in his head and sung to him. Sure, it was in the key of E, but began on an A note. He felt certain the others knew it, save for the twins, but he would make sure he held onto them tightly as they stepped from stone to stone.

"Listen," he called back as they lined up behind him, "one on a stone at a time. We don't know how much weight it can take." He looked down at his feet and saw why the tile Poe pushed him onto didn't fall. It had a pair of wings on it, the icon of the band whose song would either save or kill them. Why didn't he notice it before? *Because it was too simple.*

What supported it? Something solid or was it something he couldn't comprehend?

"Ready?" He felt like he was beginning a deadly game of hopscotch.

He jumped from the A to the A#, or Bb, depending on the musician's preference and found himself standing, alive. He found the B just two feet away and jumped again. Then to the E off to the side. Another problem arose as more tiles stood in his way. "But I finished the riff!" He hummed the famous line in his head.

"Maybe there's a repeat?" Otis called out to him, the abyss below causing his voice to echo in multiple pitches. "Remember the whole guitar line. Maybe you have to keep going."

Geez, just when I think I have it down.

Poe called to him. "Well, if it was only eight notes, people or 'things' could possibly jump it instead of figuring it out. Look on the bright side; you love this song! Keep going!"

He sucked it up and did what she said. He could do this. After sensing the pattern ahead, he jumped with a bit of confidence. He turned back to the group. "Are you watching where I step?"

"Yeah," Lyra replied. "I see the pattern. Too bad you don't have something to drop on each tile, just in case."

"Like bread crumbs!" Otis always tossed advice into the air. Most of it was bonkers, but this time, maybe not.

"Or guitar picks?" Lyra offered the plausible solution, but Muddy never carried more than three or four at a time.

"Don't think about it, just go, but be careful," Poe said. "It's a simple path once you can see it. Take your time. We'll follow. It's so simple even a bass player can do it!" How they could joke about this after Corey's fall, he didn't know. Stress did weird things to people.

Moments later, he found himself hopping across to safety. He gazed down and saw no tiles under his feet. "I made it!" he yelled to the band and the twins at the winged stone. "You can do it. Just go slow and take your time."

This was going to be easy now. It had to be. He did it and didn't screw it up. They wouldn't either.

And they didn't. From A to Bb to B to E, repeated with the lowered E, then over and over again, they jumped like a spastic caterpillar connected by faith. All made each jump, even Poe, who swore she could see just fine. Maybe in here she still could.

Just as it all was going well, everyone jumping, humming the song along to themselves, the stones reverberating the deep, rich tones of the song, it happened. They heard his call from below.

"Guys!"

Corey? *Really*?

"I'm down here!" called a voice. "I'm beat up, but I'm alive."

Relief drained coils of tension from Muddy's body as his friend's words echoed up to where he stood. They had been in such a rhythm that the disembodied voice shook them off beat and out of their solemn trance.

"Corey!" Otis cried and skidded to a halt on a B tile. "Is that you, big man?"

Muddy found his throat closing up with emotion. His friend had survived the fall.

"It's a long story, guys, but listen to me. Hurry or you don't get to hear it." Almost a minute passed before he spoke again. "Something's coming after me. Something big. Hungry. There are doors ahead of me, two, actually. Which one should I choose?"

"Run!" they cried in unison and a few seconds later, heard a door slam. Scratching sounds followed, but no scream. Had he made it? Muddy had to believe he that did. Had to.

At least Corey was still alive. The two-ton weight on his heart crumbled in half, but they still had to find him. Before whatever was chasing him did.

But the echoing of the door that slammed deep below them shook the walls of the abyss, which in turn rattled the floor.

It shook again. Then they heard something howl. Its deep cry reverberated in harmonics, hurting their ears. It was a low note, low enough the shake the tiles, but rich enough to drop them and knock off their inner balance. He then heard a new sound. Claws on rock.

A climbing sound.

"Run!" Muddy yelled. "It senses us! Run to the other side!"

They ran, but whatever was down there jumped and yowled again, this time aiming its voice higher.

Lyra screamed and grabbed hold of Poe, who tried to steady her. Muddy felt Poe's fingers just before both went over the edge. He heard a thump, twice, right below the tiles and then a sliding sound.

"Edgar!" Poe cried, "we're slipping somewhere. Find us!"

He didn't allow himself to be upset. They would be fine, just like Corey. They had to be.

The only way to save them was to get to the out of the room and find a way down.

After their voices trailed away, Muddy assumed they were safe for the moment and attempted to help Otis and Luke. The pair jumped together and nearly made it. Nearly.

Three steps away from the long ledge on which Muddy stood they heard the thing launched itself upwards again. It had been climbing something beneath the tiles, something in the abyss. This time, it must have been pretty angry that it missed out on Corey and the girls. Claws that dwarfed the sirens' own had reached over the top of the tile Luke and Otis were jumping onto and caught Luke's boot. The teen steadied himself, but his eyes went wide.

A face peered over the top of the stone and froze the three

of them. What Muddy saw would give him nightmares for the rest of his life. Eyes of prism-like colors and mouths—plural, opened and snapped in all directions. That explained the harmonic voices.

Luke looked at where Muddy stood then gazed downward.

Down? Muddy thought. *Are you kidding?* He grabbed hold of Otis, who was gripping his drum tight, saw what Luke saw and jumped off the stone. He heard the same shallow thumps, followed by a shifting sound. The thing howled in frustration again, likely because two more meals had tumbled away.

"Muddy!" he heard Otis call. "Run! We'll be fine, I think, if this path takes us out of here and not into that thing's supper dish." The voice faded as Otis spoke and now sounded far away. "Get through that door and do this job!"

He saw the face of the creature again, those eyes, flashing at him now like strobe lights at a middle school dance. Was it trying to hypnotize him, making him an easy dinner? He resisted and ran to the door, which turned out to be a pair instead. They stood in front of him, each clearly marked. Each note's letter was carved into a dark mirrored door in a font he never saw before.

One was G. The other was F#.

The lady or the tiger? Life or death?

Was it the blues scale or the formal major scale?

He ran toward the F# and nearly crashed through it before he realized something. Who built this trail and the tricks within it? It was meant to keep the Tritons from killing the slaves, just like the Egyptians, Babylonians, Mayans, etc. They had a way in and out but wanted to keep those who threatened them far from success.

Only a slave who knew the pure power of music to keep one's soul alive would choose what he did. He dove headlong, smashing through the G door, just like the E. Scattered shale or fine quartz covered him in his landing, but nothing followed him. He looked back and saw that another door slid into its place. He checked for cuts and bruises and found himself unscathed, physically.

Would the creature be able to follow? He prayed not and ran down a narrow pathway. Right into the mouth of his next task.

Chapter Thirty-Seven

Along dark tunnel with angular twists and turns stretched before the girls, reminding Poe of the mirror maze down at the Jersey shore. The memories it recalled rang bittersweet in her mind as the scene unfurled before her and Lyra. She swore she was dead when they fell from the walk "not that way" trial above her, before landing on the slick rockslide which propelled both down into the depths where only luminescent moss from the walls led the way.

"This way," Lyra had said, even though Poe knew she had never been there before. Both paused for a moment before continuing, listening for the beast in the darkness. "It did climb up to them, didn't it?"

Poe nodded. "It sure did. It's a good thing I brought good musicians. The guys will be okay up there. I know it."

They followed the curving crevice which served as a path from the base of the slide to the wide tunnel. Poe's vision held, even in the diminished light. She never explained to Muddy or the others what she did see or how she saw it, mostly because she didn't care. Sight was sight and clear outlines were a heck of a lot better than clouds and colorless blobs, which were all she could see since the accident with her father a decade ago. Too much of her school life pained her, hearing the jibes and mocks from the girls and the lewd comments from the guys who thought she was just as dumb as she was blind. She often cursed her parents for passing along their intelligence to her, even if emotions skipped her father completely. Her mother could have saved her from most of her hell but didn't. Intelligence failed to impress her ever since. Loyalty and friendship always would.

"Wow," her new friend exclaimed with a whistle. "What in the world?"

Part of Poe relaxed when she took in the ordeal before her. The other part recoiled in pure fright, scaring her almost as much as those nights when her dad went off the rails. "I don't know, but it reminds me of a song my grandfather used to play all the time in his band."

Lyra shook her head. "You mean, a song about swinging or revolving doors?"

"Something like that," Poe said. "I think the trick here is the colors."

"The clue is a red door? Girl, you're confusing me. I really wish we had music here."

"We do now. There are black doors too. Just look closely."

Lyra squinted into the tunnel at the full-sized, solid, hissing slabs. "I don't see it."

"It's okay. I'm used to looking into the blackness and making sense of it. Sometimes, that's all I see."

"Wait. Look past the gauntlet. Tell me what you see."

Poe strained her eyes, somewhat hurting from using them for the first time in several years. Past the countless doors, she saw what Lyra saw, an opening about a hundred or so feet away. She could clearly see the end to this trial and hopefully, one better than her previous outcome.

"Let's roll," said Lyra. "I think I've got this. Follow me." Before Poe could utter a word, the girl took off like a cat. Even though she was nimble, cautious even, Poe knew she was about to die.

"Stop!" she cried and reached out at the same time but was a hair too late. Her agony sung out in the tunnel in a tone just out of tune. Pain usually pushed such noises sharp.

Lyra had run smack dab, headfirst, into a door that hadn't been there just a moment ago.

As Poe stepped across the threshold of the first doorway, where the door wasn't, a whirring sound filled her ears and dread ran through her veins. "No!" she screamed, harmonizing somewhat with Lyra's voice. The red doors started to revolve, or opening and shutting, right as Poe began her sprint. *Just like the mirror maze down the shore*, she thought. She raced forward and pulled the falling form down with her to the ground, pulling away from the living doors.

Lyra lay dazed and covered with a red coat of her own; not painted black by a long shot. "Why did they open?"

Poe scanned her body, noting small cuts on Lyra's face, arms, and neck, each oozing blood, but nothing appeared life threatening. Then again, she was no doctor and there were so many slits in Lyra's flesh. She listened to the girl's ragged breath and attempted to decipher if the reason was pure fear coursing through her lungs or internal injuries. She prayed the former, but had no idea if she was right, given the way the door swung open then slammed into Lyra with such force. "You must have tripped something."

The girl regarded her with an amused look. "Really?"

Poe smiled. "Sorry. The obvious. Still, you asked, and I don't know any more than you do. Except—"

"Except what?" Lyra spat out something, flecked with blood.

"The song. I don't know how or why, but red is never good. Usually, the only thing running toward it is a bull."

"Thanks again," said Lyra. "You're making me feel pretty good here." She coughed again, dotting her white tunic.

"That's not what I meant." Poe thought of a red-light analogy, but there were no cars here. Not much would work, though she had an idea. Judging by the blood in the girl's spittle, the idea had to work fast. Otherwise, she might as well be another bass player.

"Can you stand?"

"I'll try. Somehow, I don't think I want to die here looking at all these doors swinging like they're waiting for a cat's tail to catch."

"Wait, you have cats here?"

Again, the amused smile. "Of course. We're allowed some pleasant things by the Tritons."

"Funny," Poe replied. "I just figured that if you did, they'd have three heads meowing in harmony or more teeth than a xylophone."

"Who says they don't?"

Poe helped the girl to her feet and prayed she never found out. "Now watch what happens. Look at the space to the left of the red door."

They focused on the spot next to what almost killed Lyra. Something shimmered slightly, like when the band used to sit on the front porch in the summer. The sun baked the street so much that the air above it appeared to waver like a video out of focus.

"There's something there."

Poe thought aloud. "Another door. A black one."

"Isn't black supposed to be bad luck too?" Lyra leaned on Poe as they stood before it.

"It all depends on your perspective. I love my clothes and most of them are black, so whatever."

They looked again past the first set of doors. Another red one stood. Was there another shimmering black one?

It came to her what to do. There was a way out, if it didn't destroy them in the process. She couldn't bear to think how Muddy would deal with her death.

Back to the Jersey Shore. Teens, kids, and parents paid a buck to maneuver through the maze for fun. She remembered sailing through it each time while every one of her friends slammed into the Plexiglas walls that faced the wild teens and children in every direction. She had felt her way, utilizing her lack of sight and her enhanced sense of perception to keep her from a broken nose, toes, or bruised self-esteem. While her friends took forever to navigate the false turns and dead ends, she simply breathed deep and felt her way, knowing that it was set up in a logical puzzle. It had to be. The designers couldn't make the maze too difficult. No one would ever emerge back into the New Jersey sun. All the while, DJs often played that Stones song since the doorways had wild colors and the way out was often bathed in black.

"Let's do this. We need to find Muddy's brother and get out of here."

She helped Lyra to her feet. "Can you make it?"

Once again, she received an odd look. Usually Poe had caught every bit of sarcasm and tossed it back in spades, but the sight she now wielded dulled her wit. Just a bit.

"You're kidding," the teen replied. "Why would you ask something dumb like that? If I don't move, I'll die. I don't know what it's like where you come from but dying kind of sucks here."

Poe felt the blush hit her face before she could stop it. Did Lyra mean the words in a harsh way, like they sounded, or was Lyra messing with her?

"Sorry," she managed. "I'm used to watching bad horror movies. The terrible dialogue sticks with you sometimes."

"Maybe if we survive this, you can take me to one of these movie things I keep hearing about," Lyra said. "I'm tired of visualizing everything without seeing them."

"Yeah, I get it." Of course she did. Too well, but the girl wouldn't know she was blind back home. "Are you able to travel between dimensions?" She stumbled a bit at the first of the blackness. "I mean, can you cross over?"

"If you guys can, there must be a way to bring a visitor."

But they all had the instruments. And a talent. "Sure. I'd love to have you over." *Just not* my *house*, she thought. The image of her father came storming back to her. He might hate Lyra and take it out on her, or even worse, like her.

Chapter Thirty-Eight

As they stepped over the threshold, the circus began. "Oh my," Poe exclaimed.

Red blazed into their eyes from all directions.

Every red door began to open and shut. Slam, rather, with the force that nearly killed Lyra. Though the path ahead was clear moments ago, the bright color blurred her vision, as if every opening gave birth to an inferno.

But where were the black doors? Were they still there?

"How are we going to do this?" Lyra's voice shook. She coughed again.

"I've got it," Poe said, though fear struck her from all sides. She recalled those bad nights at home when everything she did drew a fire of another sort. The kind that forced mom into a corner and ignited the man she hated to call father.

"You sure?"

Not really, but it sounded good. "Now, when I step, step with me. Same time, same speed."

Lyra rubbed her arm. "I think I know what you mean. If one of those doors hits my head, game over. Head over."

Poe counted, thinking of the flashing lights in the mirror maze, the timing she needed to sneak out when all hell broke loose at home. Timing was everything. Sometimes it saved your life, or parts of it, like jumping rope with razor wire.

"Go!"

As the red door slammed to their left, they bounded right, into the blackness so dark, all vision burned away. A hot wind hit their backs, but they stood in safety. Safely behind the door.

"That wasn't so bad," Lyra said, taking a deep breath. "If

that's all it takes, I might just live to die by the hands of the Tritons after all."

Nothing in Poe's life ever came that easy, except singing. "*That* wasn't bad. *This* will be. Look."

They peeked out of the corridor where they stood and saw another red door then another black door. And then another red on the opposite side. Two red doors swung with the safety of the black in the middle. One swung clockwise, the other slammed counter. If either hit them, their bodies would turn into flat cartoon characters in a heartbeat. "Okay, that's not so bad, is it?"

"Hope not. It's probably best not to overthink it," Poe said. "Ready?" Lyra nodded, and they stepped together just as the reds swung closed. They made it to the next safe zone. And froze. "Okay, this *is* bad."

The path became crystal clear as Poe studied her options. First, they passed one red deadly door. Then two. With each threshold, another joined the gauntlet, turning the scene into a blender they would have to run through. That is, if they held their timing in check.

It's like jumping through razors, Poe reminded herself. *Pretend it's just a game.*

"Can't we just sit here for a while and plan? Maybe there's a back door."

That was it. Why didn't she see it? *Because it would likely kill us both,* Poe thought to herself, though choosing not to speak it. "Ready?"

"No," Lyra said with labored breath. In the light reflecting off the doors, fresh blood appeared on her brow. "I need a minute."

"Oh, no," Poe said, dread raining down on her. A faint creaking sound ahead threw new fear into her. "Watch."

Ten feet separated them from the next black zone, which signaled safety in its invisibility. A quartet of doors awaited them.

"Are you worried about what we can't see on the way?"

"No," Poe said. But then again, she did wonder what lie on either side of the path they would run through. Was there a step, jump, hop, or free fall to the left, or right? Even on the straight path?

"Just watch," she said. All four doors creaked open slowly before slamming home into some unseen frame.

"That's all? We can time that, no problem."

Yeah, it was a problem, but not the big one. After the doors slammed shut, the creaking began again. In her mind, Poe counted 1, 2, 3, 4, 5, 6, 7, 8.

All four doors swung open the opposite way, right into the black where they had planned on running. If they made it to the black, the red would open right away and crush them with no room to spare. Poe hated revolving doors as it was, and this tossed the biggest monkey wrench into their situation. At least with normal doors, if you got stuck, you lived to tell about it.

"But," Lyra said, "that means there is no chance to get through there. We're squished!"

Poe inhaled. She didn't survive her home life this long just to die here at the random moving of some doors. "No." She took a deep breath. "Eight beats. That's two measures. We have plenty of time. We run, right into the closing doors and slide in between. We find the next opening, finish the count and run before they make us skinnier than one of those cover models that make me sick."

"What? We're not going to—"

"Just zip it and follow me. No excuses," Poe said as resolve bore into her heart. "You want to live, move with me and fast, step-for-step."

She pulled the injured girl through the quartet with only the breeze of the crimson door touching them—only to find a quintet. Beyond that, they encountered a sextet, a septet and finally, an octet—eight doors swinging in blender-like fashion.

They were going to die if they tried the octet. There was no way either could fit through before all the doors swung shut, even one at a time, especially if they weren't in sync.

But she would try anyway.

"You know," Lyra said, "whenever I wanted to skip out and listen to a musician visiting through the River, we always watched through the—"

"The window!" How did Poe miss that? With the path lined up so tight, the walkway seemed the only way to escape.

Neither one of them had thought about a side exit. Most of the Egyptians and Mayans, who built the pyramids, the non-martyrs anyway, always had a way to sidestep the pitfalls they built.

"But we have to find it first. Remember the misstep we took when we didn't walk *that* way?"

The fall still caused her body to ache. But sometimes, one just had to go for it and not worry about what could happen. Just live and aim for your goal. Even her father said that once, right before he'd smashed one of his cars while driving drunk then came home to take it out on both his wife and daughter.

"It's now or never."

"Where do we aim?" Lyra shook as she attempted to right herself.

"I have no idea, but if I'm right, we'll know before we die."

"Good to know. I'd hate to find out *after* it killed us."

They stepped off the path, and to their relief, didn't fall into a bottomless pit. A sturdy surface greeted their feet. "Ready?" Poe's smile matched Lyra's. "For the music they didn't want us to hear." For the freedom, and all that they took away.

Lyra followed Poe, taking each step one at a time, both trying not to let the flaring red of the doors blind their way. If there was a window, Poe shuddered to think what would happen if they missed it. Second by second, step by step they walked, each breath echoing the hammering rhythms of their hearts. Where was it?

A dozen more steps. Neither of them plunged to their death.

"There." Poe pointed just three feet ahead of them.

"Where?" Lyra couldn't see it.

Well, firsts do happen, Poe mused to herself. She could see the way when someone else couldn't? Mrs. Berg would be proud. "Give me your hand." She took the other girl's hand and felt for the rectangular opening in a wall that neither could see. Then she waved it around the sill where a hard material lined the escape route.

"How do we know what's on the other side?"

Poe went silent.

"That's what I figured."

Both felt their way and perched themselves on the sill. What would happen if it was another trap? She remembered her dad stumbling up the stairs in the middle of the night and she prayed she would die. That was before she'd realized one of the band would take her in for the night. Only her mother knew the truth. She'd confronted the man once and threatened him with the loss of a body part or two. But she wasn't a part of Poe's life any longer and never would be again. Even if, by chance, her mother did want to come back into her life again, Poe knew the woman would never stand up for her.

"Rely on yourself," her mother had said. *Thanks, Mom.* Maybe for once, the woman had a point that made sense.

She smiled at Lyra and pushed off.

Both of Poe's feet landed on solid ground. Ahead, a light and another door stood in her way, but somehow, she knew this phase of the fight was over.

"How did you learn to not care if you would be willing to die like that?" Lyra stared her down, amazed and admiring. She'd landed carefully, but in obvious pain.

"Try living where I live."

"You have jails too?"

Poe flinched. "If we did, I'd stay in my cell all day. It's my warden who scares me." As they walked through the exit to find their band mates, she wept and spilled her story for the first time in a long time. Nobody had heard her voice her scars since the band had broken wide open with all their baggage during one of their first practices.

Now, again, the tears flowed like pain.

Chapter Thirty-Nine

Corey landed in a world unknown to him; someplace he didn't think could exist inside a mountain. Then again, this wasn't Jersey anymore. He brushed himself off after tumbling head-first at the bottom of the slide, feeling lucky not to have incurred a concussion.

Where were the others? Would they be coming down before or after him? He thought of the monster that chased him and figured they'd taken a detour.

If one of them didn't make it, he'd never forgive himself. He always thought of himself as the big brother to the band. They trusted him and took him in when it seemed like both of his worlds eschewed him. His old stomping grounds didn't want him, and the suburbs, lower middle class as it was, still regarded him with a cautious eye.

The band had always been there. They treated him as an equal. When they heard him play his sax in class, they'd almost knighted him on the spot. Nobody, besides his parents, ever took him at face value before. His old neighborhood didn't, simply because he wouldn't play their game, especially after Iron took his cousin from him.

And here he stood, in a living metaphor for the jungle from where he came.

A howl bled from above. A vast tapestry of green and purple hung from the cavern's ceiling, woven into a living trap from the stalactites. Something squealed from the left. Another something echoed from the right.

If only he hadn't been so quick to step. And fall. Like a total idiot. Now something big and hungry hunted him down like he was a walking cheeseburger.

He'd assured the guys he would be okay. He always said that, even when he knew things wouldn't be all right. This was one of those times.

His parents named it The Jungle, not the townsfolk from the "better" side of town. Those people simply didn't refer to it at all. The kids and cops called it Iron, for the factories that once drove the town now sitting abandoned like sleeping leviathans waiting to swallow whole the rest of the neighborhood's soul. Cultures bled together like a soup so distasteful it choked many who stayed behind. Black, Hispanic, Indian, white, you name it—if you lived there, nobody thought much of you. The sense of community had died a long time ago and survival was the only motto that mattered.

Some people still got along, tried to hold onto something, but the gangs, drugs, and apathy strangled anything from blossoming.

That was why his family left. After a beating that nearly killed him and left his cousin dead, Corey's parents had abandoned their world and moved to the side of town where many people welcomed them with open arms. His parents, that was. He now wore the sign of pariah as teens from his school either feared him (the new neighborhood teens) or despised him and wouldn't mind him dead (the old gang). He suspected some of his friends were thankful he'd escaped, even though they would never dare say it in public.

Here, once again, he found himself in a jungle, but of a much different kind. "This would never be on Animal Planet," he said to whatever lurked in the green mess.

The sounds came from above, the sides, and below his feet ringing out in clanging melodies and off-key harmonies, threatening to bring on one of his legendary migraines. He couldn't allow that to happen. Down there, he was all alone.

He prayed the band was smart enough to stay far away from him.

Corey looked around, overwhelmed as his eyes swam out of

focus. A plethora of life sang to him, humming his death song. Greenery of the strangest kinds hung like a barbed wire blanket wrapped in poison and electricity over his head.

A path wound its way down the middle of the forest and he immediately thought of two things: Ray Bradbury's "A Sound of Thunder" and one of his favorite songs, "Jungleland." One took him away from Iron by nourishing his imagination and the other helped him deal with the hell in which he lived. That sax player in Springsteen's band helped guide him into a therapy of sorts, musical therapy, when he'd begged his parents for his own saxophone and told them he wanted to be the next Clarence Clemons. Now he needed both heroes to help him stay alive.

The stench filled his nostrils. A mixture of deep pine meshed with rainforest fleshed out with the rot of something long in decay.

"Why are you here?"

What? That voice—where did it come from? He whipped around, swinging his horn as though it were a bat. Was there someone hiding in the mass of trees and vines? The voice had emanated from the vines and flora overhead in a convoluted chorus, just out of sync with itself.

"Go home, boy. You aren't strong enough to pass. Death will be your last song."

"I didn't come this far to die in a demented terrarium," Corey said stubbornly to the air. "Who's there?"

"Who's there?" The phantom voice echoed his.

"Stop messing with me. It won't pan out well for you." He attempted to steady his voice, but it shook, at least to *his* ears.

"Does this feel like home, little man? We hope so, because it will be the last home you see. All of us plan a very, very long sleep for you. A forever bed would do you well and it's only steps away."

Each of the slow, lingering voices bounced off the walls in a pseudo-stereo effect, leaving him to decipher who, or what, said what from where.

Keep them talking and just keep moving.

The dark, spongy path led straight ahead. Straight ahead

was never a good thing, not without a solid plan and plenty of firepower, of which he had neither.

Except for his instrument.

He gazed down at it, the strange metal glinting off the phosphorescence of the leaves and glimpses of the bright wall behind him. The strangest sax he ever saw, he mused, keeping one eye on his surroundings.

He wondered what John Coltrane or Clemons would have done now. Those guys wouldn't turn tail and run, would they? Maybe one of those guys on the easy listening stations would, but not them. Satch, his music teacher, wouldn't either, and he grew up in Newark.

"Fight or flight," he said to whatever hung above him.

When they showed themselves, he knew both options were imperative if he were to survive.

Long, serpentine-like creatures poured from everywhere like streamers from Hade's New Year's party. From mere inches long to stretching a yard or so off the walls and ceiling, they reached out in waves toward him.

Each whispered, holding still, but many opened massive jaws, flashing fangs at him.

"Come lay with us and give us your song. You belong here."

A long, striped tendril with teeth wrapped around his left leg and tugged, its mouth turning upwards to his frightened gaze. The pressure pained him, but he froze, fearful to yank back in panic. Maybe that's what would trigger it to bite.

"They don't want you back home, do they?"

His head swiveled left and right, aware of the green and red creatures inching closer to him, the fetid odor of their bodies reaching into his sinuses.

Could they read his mind or was this just a mental trick they tried on everyone? Anyone who trespassed this way would be an outlaw or outcast attempting to flee to a better life. He pushed the familiar fears back and turned away with the instrument.

He swung the sax like a sword, slicing the creature clinging to his leg in half, then with a few sickening thuds, he crushed every sinuous thing that tried to bite him. They hung, broken from their branches or vines, some dead, some simply stunned.

Gotta move, he told himself, beating his way through the thick vines to find the path. Was it straight ahead? Too much debris hung over the path for him to see. "Keep going, be steady," he muttered. He sensed he'd be dead if he stopped moving. More and more of the vine-creatures lashed out as he crashed through the forest, some biting at him with quick strikes, others surprising him with sneak attacks.

At first, they numbered maybe a dozen or two, but the more he swung, the more emerged. His mind recalled the hydra, the monster that grew two heads for every one that Hercules cut off. Within a minute, they had surrounded him and bit at the metal in his hands. He dropped instinctively to the ground.

I'm as good as dead, he thought. *Just when we thought we would find acceptance, maybe show our world we could play with the best of them—here I am, snake chow .*

"Your music is our song now, *horn boy.*"

Horn boy? Something clicked. The switch flipped on inside of him. His weapon had greater potential than he'd realized. It was time for that power to emerge.

He licked his lips and thought of the song which probably inspired this gauntlet device. Maybe even "The Boss" himself had come here and fueled the fire without realizing it. It seemed as though every other great musician had been through the River.

Now or never, he hummed to himself.

He blew out a long G, a lower note in the sax-like thing's tenor tone. Both lungs emptied into the metal as his jaw tightened on the ivory mouthpiece. The note shook the living tapestries above and beside him. It also shook its taunting, hungry inhabitants. Each snake-thing quivered, hung in place and then retreated.

It was working!

He nearly screamed aloud, but instead watched as they recovered the moment he stopped the note. He sounded another one, a long Eb, a powerful somber note that shook some of them to the ground. Quickly, as they lay stunned, he ran forward and let loose. He recalled the best lines of his heroes and inhaled as much as humanly possible before blitzing the walls and ceilings with a rain of sweet tones.

"Why? Why are you doing this? We would help you live here."

He played harder.

"You're hurting us. Why? We only wanted your song. Why would you hurt music?"

Corey couldn't help but grin in victory, even though he still couldn't see the end of this trial. Maybe he *would* make it out alive. Poe and the others needed him to finish the mission.

Then the voices chilled him with what he knew couldn't be a ploy.

"We might die, but *he* won't. He'll be waiting for you. He always waits. He eats the song you play. He devours *all*."

"What the heck does that mean?" He let the sax fall away for a moment to cry out, knowing they wouldn't tell him anything, but fear burst through his veins, stronger than it did the night his family left the old neighborhood.

That night, over a year ago, the darkest, most soulless eyes watched him get into his father's car and mouth their final words to him. "You will never be free of here. We will find you and reward you for deserting the place where you belong."

But he didn't belong there, not with their guns and drugs and lost dreams.

And he certainly didn't belong where he was now. Others awaited him—others he belonged to and they to him.

He quickened his pace and played his heart out. He was going to make it. The tapestries slowed their movement, the snakes and worm-like things dropping, hanging silently as he sensed he was nearing the end of this nightmare.

And nearly ran right into *it*. It. Whatever the bowels of this world spit up through what could only be the sewer of this cavern.

"Clarence, don't fail me now." His voice came out in a hoarse whisper, but he forced himself to play on, blazing a fiery blues lick straight into the thing's maw.

Only to hear it laugh at him with fetid breath—and open wider.

The path through the dense forest turned into a dark walkway with a hardened surface.

With a quake, the thing turned a full rotation, twisting from its back to its belly to unveil a sight Corey knew he would wake up screaming at for weeks, if he survived.

Like an annoying mouse on a python's tail, it tossed him aside, preparing to deal with him another way. Maybe he jumped; it happened so fast his instincts took over. Images of that King Kong flick where the ape shook the crew off the log bridge into the nests of insects below whizzed through his mind. But then the log path completed its turn and what he saw caused him to vomit all over it.

Legs. Hundreds of them. Maybe more. All twitched, spasmed and grabbed at the air as they shook free from the ground beneath them. He wouldn't have to fall to enter that movie nightmare.

The creature's wordless voice shook the ground beneath its body as Corey feared staring at it eye to eyes. Its maw opened wide as eyes on stalks longer than his body focused and swung down at him. Over two humans tall, the segmented creature towered over him and breathed. A wave of decay from a meal it may have had ages ago wafted down at him, causing Corey to envision half-digested maggots burrowing through his hair.

He threw up again and the fluid sent the legs into a tizzy. They smelled food. Him.

He held his sax in front of him in defense but knew on too many levels that it wouldn't help one bit if he swung it. One errant step and myriad legs would pull him in, crushing him like a nut that the head would devour in one chew.

Finally, resolve forced him to meet the face that wasn't anything like any other he could imagine. At least six stalks now bore into him with pale, emotionless eyes. Corey wondered if it could really see. If it lived this far into the depths of this alter-earth it might be utterly blind, relying more on movement, but seriously, did it really matter?

Each stalk locked onto him as the mouth unfurled itself. He could only imagine the alien from the movie of the same name.

One set of jaws drooped low to allow another set to reach forward and drip something viscous onto the ground before him. The ground sizzled in its acidy odor.

"Give me your song."

The mouth rose up higher as the legs retracted and the segments contracted, causing it to lurch forward and upward, sensing its prey's futility.

A thought rumbled through his fear of a night, close to Halloween, late after his parents had fallen asleep. He'd watched the myth of the Saint of Ireland who'd lured the serpents away from the citizens who'd cowered in despair. The saint had used music to hypnotize them, to draw them out of the country.

Corey had one chance, one that would likely kill him, but the Accidentals didn't give up, especially when everyone— now everything—expected them to do just that. He smiled and winked at the behemoth, but still shook in fear.

"If I'm not going home in one piece, you're going to meet my good friend here you ugly spud." He inhaled, and the sax came alive in his mouth, becoming part of him. He felt like when he'd rehearsed with the band for the first time, the first time they played in front of an audience and another's solo became his own. But instead of burning notes into an inferno to annihilate the beast, he took the deepest of breaths and channeled the soloists who'd colored "Born To Run,

Dark Side of the Moon,

Kind of Blue" and those bootlegs of early Clemons when the song took a back seat to pure soul. He exhaled the notes. Each tone filled the cavern and embraced the beast. The sweet pitches developed and birthed new harmonics in slow vibrato.

At first, the millipede thing thrashed in anger, or terror. It needed its meal. The sounds disrupted its entire system and caused the legs to fail in their grasps at him. The eye stalks drooped in fatigue and the bulbs at each end glazed over. If they'd ever had sight, it was now fading. Still, animal instinct ruled his attacker.

Corey's blood coursed in jet streams as he felt fear and joy meld. *Slow,* he begged his lungs. *Slow down if you want to live.* He allowed more of the melody to fall out of him, echoing off the walls, deadening the living tapestries, and confusing the head of the monster.

Play, he told himself. *Kill the ugly thing*, even though he knew he only had to escape.

He played, easing out the sweetest of overtones in a D minor melodic scale, rising one step each phrase.

Then it happened. As suddenly as it rose, the head turned and sank back down into the path, the path that it was once again. Eyes and legs still swirled, but in a throe that might have signaled death. All those years living in Iron came back to Corey in an instant and he launched himself, vaulting over the legs then stepping right *onto* the head. He was careful to avoid the gaping maw. He'd expected it to open wide and suck him inside like Jonah into the whale.

But it didn't.

Instead, once he passed the head, he nearly cried at the sight of an opening just wide enough for him, or the creature, to wriggle through. The thing had been hiding it, hoping to have its prey eventually give in to broken hope. He tumbled past and crawled through the narrow, lava-formed tunnel on the other side of the monster. As he wriggled through the hole that something must have burrowed through, a pair of hands grabbed him and pulled him through.

He passed out when he saw who'd met him there.

Chapter Forty

Otis and Luke landed in a pile of limbs as the slide ended in a dead end.

"Ouch," Otis cried, even as the bigger teen took the brunt of the landing. "The last time I hit something like that, I was in intensive care for two months."

Luke brushed himself off. "I think this is what your people call the eye of the storm," he said.

Both boys looked across the flat, oval room and saw that the exit tunnel appeared to be more like the eye of a needle from across the cavern. Otis wondered if it existed a hundred or thousand feet away. It could be a way back to the others or a dead end. It also didn't look very big.

"Oh, no." Otis picked up his drum. "I knew I should've skipped that side of beef this morning."

Luke either missed the sarcasm or simply found the idea of impending death more compelling than a joke without meaning. He merely scanned the setting and looked worried when he found nothing to threaten them from reaching that tiny exit.

"At least it's an easy walk to a slow death. Maybe we can drum through it?"

Then the rain began, and their world turned to fire. Both teens hit the ground and covered their heads.

"Guess we'll be hot rockin' tonight," Otis said.

Luke stared, mouth gaping, but finally found his voice. "Better to burn out, don't they say?"

"Man, you don't know how right that sounds, but how wrong I think it'll feel."

As they watched the ceiling open its lava tubes and shoot

out balls of burning, flaming molten rock, Otis did something he hadn't done in over a year. He prayed as a tear met his eye.

To get this far only to fail the others, he thought. They'd lived for each other. Even though he was the only one with a tight family and everything a kid could want, his friends were what had sustained him through the tough times. They knew his pain and accepted him as he was, for however long he would be on the earth. Death would likely come soon enough for him. He could handle that, he hoped. He just hoped it wasn't before they'd saved Muddy's brother and accomplished something.

"Isn't that a person?" Luke pointed to a tall figure against the near wall, out of reach of the firestorm.

Otis felt his tears dripping onto his lips, causing an ear-to-ear grin to form. "Man," he cried, "I guess Tony Iommi came to this place once before. That's how we get across and hopefully live."

A giant suit of metal in the shape of a warrior wearing a helmet with slits for eyes rested against the wall as the room lit up like the Fourth of July, Hades-style.

Luke didn't get it, *yet.* "But isn't that just a man-suit? A model of a warrior? It has no weapons and it looks old."

"Exactly."

"What is that thing made of, anyway? Could it fight the fire?"

Again, Otis grinned. "Of course it can. It's solid iron, man."

"What do we do with it, wear it?"

Otis had already found a latch on the side of the armor and was working its spring. "If this can actually fit us and help us walk, we might be able to get to the other side."

"Like the chicken?"

"So, you've heard that joke?" Otis felt like ribbing Luke, but even he had his limits. "Many times, even the chicken met a truck before he found his home."

They both felt for the many latches and found that they existed only on the outside. But there was another, a smaller one, behind it. "Maybe we can both wear them?"

"Buddy," the smaller teen said, "unless this thing is made of aluminum foil, I doubt I'd be able to take more than a couple of steps in it before dropping." He tried lifting it and couldn't. His muscles couldn't handle the job. Drums gave him power in this world, but not complete strength. It didn't take much to humble him anymore.

Luke recoiled. "But then you'd be burned alive!"

"Not if you walked with your arms protecting me. Some things aren't that hard to figure. Those fireballs are hitting the cavern at a certain angle, but not every angle. If you walk to the exit in one direction, off center as it may be, we'll get there unscathed. Well, at least I will."

"You'd do that? Take that chance?"

Otis sat down as he opened the boots of the iron suit, the one for Luke. "Buddy, you haven't heard much about my plight. Sure, I've got the women. Sure, I've got the friends and the music. But there are a few things that I don't have and one of them is time."

Luke stepped into the leg as several molten balls bounced off the floor and careened into the far wall, bursting into red flames. One of them could easily ricochet into them if a stray rock diverted it. Otis wondered briefly how quickly one of them would die if just one fireball struck. There wasn't any water to put out the fire and even with his healing powers in this River-led world, he doubted anyone could survive a direct impact.

"What do you mean?"

Otis found that fighting back the tears became easier each time he told the tale, but now that he had a purpose, a legacy to fight for, another creased his eye.

"I was born with a death sentence. Mom didn't expect me to last a year. The doctors predicted five. When we went to the genetic experts, they told us that if I graduated grade school, it would be a miracle."

"But how?" Luke stood still as the other teen locked him up latch by latch. Now he had both legs and his lower torso snapped into place.

"Is it comfortable?" Otis had to keep Luke on his heels if this was going to work.

The boy grimaced. "It feels like wearing a metal coffin, but if it means I don't become a human bonfire, I guess I have no choice."

"Then shut your yap and let me do this." He wanted, no, he *needed* to help save his friends. "I've had my nose broken by a pen tossed at my face. My arm fractured when I slipped out of a desk. A leg snapped by trying to run to first base."

"What's first base?"

As Otis snapped Luke into the upper torso, he smiled. "Something you deal with on a first date. Maybe I'll hook you up with a friend one day and you'll find out."

Otis wondered if he'd ever get to kiss a girl, one who liked him for himself, not because he was a novelty. He would never tell anyone that in the band, even Poe. She'd understand, but he couldn't do it without breaking down.

"Then what's second? How many are there?"

"Too many for my taste."

"But you seem so strong here." The bigger boy wriggled into place as Otis lifted the helmet for a sizing.

"It's the drum. Maybe the River's effect on us. But, take me back home and my bones are like tissue paper. Every day is a crap shoot."

Luke's eyes regarded him with confusion. "Then stay here. Live like there's a million tomorrows." The boy beamed. "We have girls here too. The others, the musicians, they seem to think our girls are okay."

A big grin stretched Otis' face to the point of near pain. "You're tempting a poor boy who is about to live one of the greatest lyrics in history. Tempting. But it's not real and it's not me."

"What's real? Is it where you were born or where you find yourself? Somehow, I think your mother and father would want what's best for you."

Otis slammed the iron face shut on Luke. "Ow! I can't see right." The drummer turned the mask until the boy claimed his vision was clear.

"It's not about what they want. It's my life."

"Will you think about it?" The voice sounded tinny and much farther away. The boy in the iron suit took a cautionary step, then another. Both seemed balanced, but unnatural. "Will you at least consider staying? We need someone who lives the music like you do."

Otis just shook his head. It was too much to consider when you already had your death date carved in your head and couldn't foresee life past your own senior prom.

"Let's make Ozzy proud."

And they began the journey through the fire.

Chapter Forty

Both watched the rain of fireballs streak across the cavern, shot from tubes by some active magma strain deep within the mountain.

Otis thought, *if this thing ever blew...*

One softball-sized blaze buzzed his head, searing a curl of hair. Even though it passed in a blur, the heat caused his skin to tighten in pain. "First time I've ever had a cave burn," he shouted to the boy in the iron mask. The smell of burnt hair turned his nose, reminding him of a barbeque gone wrong.

Luke began to walk, one heavy step after another. Otis hurried in front of him, judging the trajectory of the deadly balls with his own steps. The clang of the metal joints reminded Otis of the Renaissance Faire in New York, where knights jousted, and swordplay thrilled the crowds. He wished he was there now, walking through the shady, cool paths with his family, sucking down an Italian ice, surrounded by ladies clad in medieval attire.

Instead, he felt sweat run off him in streams that did nothing to lower the temperature. "You okay in there?"

Another clang as Luke fought to keep his footing. Otis knew that if the boy fell, there would be no rising. Otis didn't have the strength to help and with the weight of the suit and barrage of lava balls, he would be a sitting duck. A cooked one, too.

"No sweat," the other replied, but his breathing already sounding labored.

A basketball-sized flame struck him dead center in the chest. He staggered but held his ground. "Get. Under. Me. Now." Pain sounded in his voice.

Otis looked around for protection. None showed itself. Across the cavern, no shelter was present. As open as a football field with opponents that put the hardest hitting Giants and Jets to shame, the area stood barren and deadly.

He recalled the film he saw in history class about World War I and trench warfare. Soldiers on both sides waited in deep ditches that ran miles in either direction. They shook in fear, awaiting the whistle or siren that screamed at them to leave the relative safety of the trench and venture into the open grave-yard where protection existed only in hopes and prayers. When they left their safe haven, the young soldiers found countless bullet-riddled bodies where the only barriers existed in the form of razor wire.

He and Luke had even less to block incoming death. Should he stand behind or under Luke? Did it even matter? Logic told him Luke was probably right; the greatest safety from a mass of molten rock obliterating him would be under the armored suit, but he didn't wish to be a coward. He wanted to be in the suit, to be the hero for once.

Not happening this time, he thought as he looked up at the suit that likely inspired the song. Never could he have fit in there and walk. If Luke moved steadily, they should be fine. If the suit didn't melt. The teen held his arms up, forming a protective barrier as Otis huddled beneath.

Another fireball slammed the iron with a metallic clash. This time, it bounced off the teen's head. A glob of rock stuck to the helmet and sizzled.

Otis looked around for a stick to strike it off, but the cavern floor was barren save for more rocks. He grabbed one and yelled at his comrade.

"Lean down!"

No reply.

"Bend down!" he screamed, noticing that the rock still burned at the helmet. It stuck like crazy glue to the surface. It likely wouldn't burn through, but the temperature must have been several hundred degrees.

Just as Luke appeared to listen to him, turning his head and gazing through the fine slits, another shot struck the metal in the upper thigh, a few inches from Otis' head. The heat bowled him over, partly from surprise but also from the wave that threw furnace temperatures into his face, burning his skin. It probably wasn't much, but a bad sunburn hurt like no other. Otis imagined how it would feel if any of the liquid rock or flame touched his flesh.

It wouldn't be like the movies, he thought, where it just sloughed off like pudding, or would it? He'd faced some horrible pain in his life from broken and shattered bones and torn muscles, but he knew this pain would beat all other. He looked to the other side where the supposed exit was—a bunch of rocks, a hole in the wall that he hoped led to his friends.

How many more of these direct hits could Luke take? How many steps would it take until he reached the safe zone?

Luke moved his right leg, the one hit by the fireball. He seemed a little less determined and less in stride, but still he moved. His breathing flowed from the mouth hole in gasps, as though he had been sprinting at high altitudes.

The mess on his helmet dropped to the ground, sending up a quick shot of black smoke.

"I can't."

"What?" Otis barely heard him.

"Breathe," a small, shaken voice said. "Burning. Up."

He imagined the worst, how the teen looked under the mask, if his flesh bubbled like fried chicken. He would never touch Kentucky Fried Chicken again.

At least twenty feet remained until they would reach the far wall. Either they sped up or they would fry like Kentucky Fried's special blend.

More and more fire showered them, four then five big ones striking hard. Two barely missed Otis.

"Move!" He yelled, begging Luke to shake free of his stupor. The teen needed to move faster if they were to survive.

Just as he moved again, fate slapped their hopes to the ground.

The boy toppled over with a resounding thud. He likely never even saw the massive fireball that dropped him. He fell face first and nearly bounced off the floor. Otis knew it was over. There was only a slim chance he could even unlock the clasps and remove the mask. Even so, if Luke remained conscious, Otis could never move him to safety.

He pushed at the boy. He needed to turn him over and see if he still breathed.

Please don't hit me, he begged at the tubes from the cavern ceiling, though in his mind, he awaited the final blow. He wondered if he would even feel it, even see it, or if it would mercifully happen so fast that he only would see a flash of light before the blackness.

The iron suit barely budged. And it cooked, paining his fingers. He stripped off his shirt and wrapped it around both hands. He pushed and pushed. His skinny arms failed to turn Luke over. They felt weaker than ever. Some things never changed.

Two more balls hit, one to the left, one to the right.

A backbeat? *Whoa.*

Otis counted, first in his head, then by tapping on the iron suit.

One, two. One, two.

Bass, snare. Bass, snare.

He waited for more. It came. A higher pitched burst off to the left; a few seconds later one pitched to the right—just like cymbal crashes.

Why hadn't he noticed it before? It couldn't be this simple, could it? Deadly, but simple. Make the right moves and live. One wrong one and burn like that Def Leppard song.

At least, he thought, it wasn't as random as being pummeled by great balls of fire.

If his new friend wasn't in the process of being barbequed, he just might have smiled at the irony.

"Luke," he said. "If you can hear me, roll. Over." He pushed again. Nothing.

"Please."

He shoved with all his might—nothing.

Then a groan emerged from deep within.

"It's alive!"

Otis turned him slightly and took the opportunity, launching himself into the boy with a painful body block. As Luke's head turned, the latch for the helmet showed itself. Otis wrapped his hand in his shirt and flipped it open. The heat seared the material, but the latch popped wide. He wasted no time placing his small hands on either side and pulled. Hard.

With a sickening sound, akin to cutting open a turkey wrapped in foil, the helmet slid off.

Otis bit back a cry.

Luke's face was covered in blisters and his mouth dropped in pain.

"Kill me," whispered the twin.

Something in Otis snapped. "Seriously? What lame movie did you get that from? We don't play that game here. Get. Up!"

Wrapping his hands tighter, he unlatched the rest of the suit and helped the teen out of it. Most of Luke's flesh was reddened but not damaged much. Otis turned the boy's head, carefully, toward the exit. Neither paid much attention to the rain of fire around them. Until they moved, heat was the biggest worry.

"Think you can make twenty feet or so?"

Luke shook his head.

"Tough. We're going."

"But," Luke wheezed. "No. Protection."

Sometimes, the iron ain't in the suit, Otis heard his grandmother's voice reverberate in his head. *Sometimes, it's much deeper.*

Why hadn't he thought of that earlier? The old woman had always pointed him in the right direction. Without her advice, his parents might have given up on him years ago and listened to some idiot doctor who believed he had no chance to live this long.

Go, Grandma.

He stared at the path he formed in his head, punctuated by the rhythms he both saw and heard in his head. If only he could help Luke move in time with the rhythms. *If only.* The weight differential might be too much.

"Okay, farm boy. We move. Now. I pull, you move with me. Otherwise, we both cook.

"You want to fry, that's fine, but don't make me burn out

with you when I'm trying to keep your butt alive."

Luke half-stood, partially holding back from his injuries, but partially from not wanting to see Otis killed for helping him. Otis saw this as all-too-obvious and knew he just had to get the boy moving, not thinking about what might happen.

"If we don't get out, your sister might be dead as well."

"Nope," he replied. "She's smarter than me. She'll find a way."

Otis groaned in despair. Was this how he sounded when the pain kept him up at night, crying to his parents?

"Well, I'm not going to tell her you died a wuss. You want to, go ahead, but please get off your swollen, barbequed crack and do it so I can live for another hour or so."

Luke cried out as he pushed himself off the floor on knees covered in blisters and burns.

"Twenty feet?"

"Yep."

"Then what?"

Otis started into the dark of the exit. It looked almost too tight for a human to fit through.

"Don't rush me. I haven't thought that far ahead, yet. Just imagine you have rhythm and follow me. Please. I don't want to be something's fried chicken tonight. Not enough meat on me for anything. I'd be shorting them way too much. You, on the other hand—"

Another cry, but one with movement. "I'm coming."

Then they were off.

Otis waited for the fireball then pulled Luke along. The bass.

He waited for the snare then pulled again. Both flamers missed them by hairs but missed just the same. As long as they kept with it, they had a chance to make it to the crack in the wall.

Otis imagined being behind his drum set and holding the sticks in his hands. He controlled the beat. Without the steady beat, the song fell apart. The band would suck. Everyone would know it was him, his mistake. But, only one mistake was allowed here.

"No way am I screwing up this song," he said to himself.

A crash singed his hair, leaving another streak of charred hair behind. Other than that, they maneuvered the distance, only to find the opening in the exit as small as he feared; too small for Luke.

The teen began to cry, not for himself, but obviously for his sister and family. This must have been his first attempt at living, and he blew the deal.

Luke picked up a cooling piece of rock in one hand, not caring about the heat. He slammed it into the wall above the crack with a stream of words Otis could only imagine were curses in his village.

Another groan sounded, but not from the teen.

Otis put his ear to the wall. Seriously? "Hey. Hit it again."

"What?" Luke had nearly gone over the edge to looneyville.

"That rock ball in your hand. Hit the wall with it again. Now. Hard."

The boy did, and the groan repeated. Otis wondered why, and he spread his hands all over the surface, feeling for something. Anything. Nothing.

Then, there it was.

The simplest of symbols.

Lightning from the sky. Thunder usually followed. The carved bolt gave him the confidence he needed to try once more. He picked up his own cooled-off ball of rock and told Luke what to do.

After a four count, they hit either side of the crack, dead in the center of the drum cymbal. Again, one more time in the most basic of rhythms which created rock music.

Like magic from the corniest of movies, the wall cracked and crumbled, opening a foot wider and showed them freedom.

"It worked!" Luke dropped the ball and completely missed the wall of fire rushing at both from behind.

The opening must have triggered a back draft of some kind and within seconds, the cavern lit up like the Rockefeller tree on Christmas—doused in gasoline.

All Otis could think was that this must be how the people on Hiroshima felt right before the first atomic bomb hit. A massive heat fist sucked all the air from their lungs as it struck.

The firewall slammed both with a death hand and flung them straight through—right into the arms of the final test.

As Otis felt consciousness fading and air finding its way into his body, he couldn't believe his eyes. "I think we're gonna be okay," he said, right before the darkness took him.

Chapter Forty-One

Muddy fell through the glass-like opening and found himself in worse shape than a moment before. He looked around for his band mates. Just as he had feared, they were nowhere to be found. He called out for them, but only echoes answered him, along with the rush of the subterranean river in front of him.

Where did this come from? Did the ocean feed it or did the mountain bleed a deep spring?

His feet slipped on the stone ledge and he landed on his side with a painful thump. He moved each of his limbs, squeezed both hands and turned his ankles. Nothing was busted. Nobody saw his boneheaded move, but how he wished someone *was* there to laugh with or even at him. Before he arose, he pulled himself up to a sitting position and gasped at the scene in front of him.

The ledge jutted out only four feet. After that, only water and the steep sides of the river filled his view. No banks rose from the water, only a curve from the bottom that continued to the top of the tunnel where he stood. The diameter of the river tube couldn't have been more than twenty feet across.

He could swim his way out, but as Muddy watched the tumultuous flow he knew he wouldn't be doing much of anything except being flushed away at a high speed. He would likely drown before arriving wherever the river headed. What if the tunnel ended and the river continued under water? He imagined the burning of his lungs and the terror of getting trapped under water, knowing he was going to die.

But his friends were somewhere in this place and they were

here because he'd asked them to embark on this strange trip.

He examined the ledge and attempted to gauge the depth of the water beneath him. An odd luminescence emanated from the walls and ceiling, likely from molds and quartz, but it wasn't bright enough to help him see much under the surface.

He half-expected the ledge to retract, to close the wall behind him and force him into the water like in some *Indiana Jones* or *Star Wars* movie. But it didn't happen. However, he couldn't just sit here waiting for a hero. He was supposed to be Zack's hero. Poe's hero. He couldn't do squat to save his mother so could he even handle this? His only other choice lay in ruin behind him and even Steven Tyler would never tell him to *walk that way*.

He lay down flat and reached into the water, feeling for the bottom. His hands found nothing but water. Cold chills raced up his arm in goose bumps as he fished around, hoping nothing bit them off. Could he chance it? It wasn't like he had a choice.

Then he saw it. A lightened piece of wood peeked out from under the ledge.

He stared at it for a moment before grabbing hold of the corner and sliding it out.

Mark Twain might be laughing his butt off, or trembling in fear, if he saw what Muddy had discovered.

An old-fashioned raft.

And here was the mighty river.

Muddy climbed onto the makeshift raft and found it sturdy enough to stand on, but still he sat, feeling safer that way. It stretched about eight feet long by six feet wide and the wood looked to be old, very old, but was coated with some sort of lacquer or wax that would keep it from becoming waterlogged. Two oars lay strapped to either side. He took hold of one and placed the other by his feet. If he waited any longer, the dread might overwhelm him, so he pushed off. Immediately the current pulled him along. Even before he got his bearings, he felt the rhythm of the water pulling him to an uncertain destination as the music began to flow in his head.

More like Finn, he decided, than Sawyer, but Rush wrote it their way. More likely, he had the brains and skills of

Huckleberry, along with the bad luck. Still, the adventurous streak in him had turned up to high since that first night at the crossroads. Someone must have known where the river went; was this part of *the* River? Somehow, he doubted it, but still didn't want to fall in and find out for sure.

Soon the raft steadied enough in the unseen current for him to stand and survey his surroundings. Things wavered in the light against the walls and the ceilings but didn't appear to be interested in him. *Thank God for that,* he mused. Maybe all he'd have to worry about was whatever lay at the end of this tunnel.

Surely, the slaves who built it had an end in mind, some kind of escape route to rid themselves of the Tritons—or did they? No, no one would be that blind to their cause. Then he remembered some of his history class and the recent elections in the world, and prayed he was wrong here.

The river flowed and curved this way and that without incident or forks in the path. He barely steered at all, just mostly pushing off the walls when he got too close. Nothing but water flowed before his eyes.

Muddy began singing the song, hearing the guitars, bass, and drums in his head. He was thankful no one was here to hear his voice. He loved guitar and could dabble in backup, but there was a reason he never sang lead.

Today, there was no one around to hear. Otis loved the song more, but the main guitar riff was too cool for him not to like. And that nasty bass line, if only they could find someone to play it—consistently.

Thump.

The raft must have hit a rock or stalagmite, maybe a piece of debris. Regardless, it was only a bump.

He barely shifted his stance, but steadied his guitar, just in case. It looked like a tree stump in the middle of the river, about thirty yards ahead. Just a stump, or rock.

Keep rowing. Keep steering.

Another appeared on the left side about ten yards past the first one.

Now that he was closer, he got a better look and wished he hadn't.

Chapter Forty-Two

The stump sank about a foot. The good news.

Then it rose up again and broke open. Not-so-good-news.

How did it break open? Muddy wondered, fingers whitening on the wooden oars. If they hadn't slipped into the rings on either side of the raft, he'd be floating without a paddle—and this wasn't a creek.

The stump appeared dark, yet opaque. Muddy remembered seeing a man-of-war once at the Jersey shore after a bad storm. It looked monstrous, but kind of see-through. Those jelly-bags didn't have mouths, though. What broke open on these things were definitely mouths. Wide open jaws, seemingly without hinges.

Another image came to mind. That movie his dad showed him from the 1980s. *Alien.* It had plagued him with nightmares that took a week to wear off. He wondered if he would live to suffer through another bad dream.

The oar swung in his hand and wavered as he pushed away from the wall toward the middle, leaving a stump with a brutal maw waiting for him to venture too close. Both mouths tilted in his direction as he passed and showed an internal view of teeth—layers, rows, and more layers of silvery teeth. The mouths managed to open even wider as if attempting to scream or beg him to row over to them.

He looked for eyes and saw none, thankfully. He guessed none were needed down here. The vibrations of passing prey triggered them and they held open their mouths until something fed them. It also reminded him of some other things from the Jersey shore—the ones with two legs on that reality show.

He glanced off the right wall, something he had failed to see at first, and the raft bounced up a little, but it jumped too much for simply hitting into smooth rock. He jammed the oar down as hard as he could. It stuck. The river didn't care, however, and continued to push him along. The raft turned. He was no longer pointed forward and couldn't see where he was going, if he was going anywhere.

He wasn't.

The oar came apart and as he pushed off the cold rock with bare hands, he looked down to check the damage. The man-o-war stump had chewed the wide end of the oar to splinters within seconds. Muddy watched the creature inhale it all as the teeth shredded the wood quicker than a piranha hopped up on energy drinks. Then it was gone. A roar he felt more than heard burst forth from somewhere around him. Not the one with the oar in the mouth. The other two had disappeared, so where had it come from?

He straightened the raft and paddled on with a single oar.

Just ahead, the monsters in the water made the movie *Alien* seem like a cakewalk. At least in *Alien*, there was only one of them.

One by one, they arose from the water. Left side, right side, and center, they emerged, obviously sensing he would be smart enough to avoid the walls.

Muddy's mouth hung open. How could he avoid all of them? The current didn't propel the raft fast enough to zip through their territory before they could converge on him. Could they move from where they rose? Were they grounded to the bottom? Just how deep *did* the river go? He didn't wish to find out but realized if even one of them overturned the raft, he wouldn't last long enough to find out.

It hit him like a bass drum when he was thinking of how to paddle through them. It has been about the music all along—why quit now? The old two-four beat that made rock music *rock*, came to him in a flash. Ten feet before the next creature, he rowed left, narrowly avoiding it. Another popped up to the right. Muddy kept the beat, felt the rhythm.

He rowed and pushed, the snare to the left's bass, the backbone to most rock songs since The Beatles hit the American shore. The beat struck long before in hidden roadhouses down south, far from the public eye, blazed by the bluesmen and women who laid the tracks for all to follow.

He could do this.

He rowed left, they arose on the left. He rowed right, they met him there.

Keep the boom-snap, boom-snap of the rhythm, he thought, *and I'll make it.*

For a few minutes, he did just that. Then something else happened. They caught on. They learned the beat. They adjusted.

How the…?

They arose before he could row away, and one cracked its head under the front edge of the raft, shattering two planks without effort. Cold water flowed across his feet and colder blood shocked his system.

Now what?

The two-four, left-right rowing worked, but some of them had learned, proving a little intelligence existed within those jaws.

Out of nowhere, a voice sang in his head. *Remember where you are. What you are. What this river sings to you.*

Silver Eye?

The words repeated. Then—*you must get to the Dark Muse. You can't allow him to win.*

Another stump smashed the middle of the raft. Its head burst through, nearly between Muddy's legs. He jumped back a step and swung the oar as hard as he could.

Home run! The oar connected with the stump thing and broke.

Both disappeared instantly. He was left without a paddle, but he recalled what his dad always said when he was trying to meet a deadline.

All that remained was his guitar; the one that really wasn't anything like what he'd ever played before, but Silver Eye had given him the instrument and that meant something to him.

The old man died because of them and Muddy would be both a fool and a coward if he failed the mission now.

Remember what this river sings to you.

The song. He'd been singing it all along, but what was different about it? He'd passed the first test by handling the steps, the right notes. How would the slaves build in a fail-safe here?

One more stump-creature crushed a plank on the right side. The raft tipped a bit with the water rushing over the side. Muddy shifted to ease the weight. Another waited on the left side for him and nearly caught his sneaker with razor teeth. If they broke another plank, the raft would likely disintegrate and pitch him into their hunger.

How many rows of teeth?

He wished he was as smart as Tom Sawyer was in that book, or song. Wait—that was it, the clue. Most of the song had worked just like it was meant to work, but the end, the solo, break part changed to something most people, most musicians couldn't handle playing.

Could he?

He counted in his head, first. He needed to—it was the only way to time the song right. Another creature hit the raft and broke up more wood.

Quickly! Remember the song, came the voice again.

Forget the counting, he thought. *It's the song.* He remembered a few musicians who played in odd tempo songs. They sometimes said, "It's a feel thing." They didn't count; they knew it would kill the passion of the song. They let it breathe through them. Just like this band did. Like he would.

He hoped these things hated his playing. His rowing couldn't help him anymore.

He unslung the odd wood and steel instrument. He'd never let this guitar, this gift from his mentor become sullied by the filthy water. Yet he really felt like shoving it down one of their throats.

Muddy felt the inspiration from Silver Eye encourage him and although it felt odd not touching the water, it seemed right. He would do this without an oar, without steering. Sort of. He aimed the guitar at the first creature and played.

The "A" he plucked shot out at the thing ahead of him. Though he couldn't see it, he felt it fly like a bolt of electric directly at the open mouth. It shrieked as the note struck it and sank it.

Did it die? Muddy wondered for a moment then realized he didn't care. He wouldn't be returning this way. He struck out the next note in the pattern, to the right this time. Again, a direct hit. The creature howled and sank out of sight, but the next ones lined up in the order they expected him to turn.

Left, right. Left, right.

They anticipated the primal beat. Muddy smiled. As they sank one by one, the waves they created pushed him left and right, so he didn't even have to steer.

It was both a good thing and a bad thing, he mused, knocking out the F# to the left, the current and swell leading the way. He readied the next note and struck to the right. The next three lined up so close together on the left that there was no way he could nail all of them without one gnashing its teeth into him.

Just as he'd planned it.

The middle and end sections of the song had changed to 7/8 time, an odd meter that most bands hadn't touched, at least the popular ones. The one who wrote this song did and thanks to Otis' fetish for cool drummers, Muddy bought into them and fell for one of the few bands that didn't follow the normal rock and roll way. The time change meant that the usual downbeat, upbeat, one-two-three-four count was shortened. Otis had taught him to imagine walking eight steps then subtract one, ending on the left foot only to begin again on the same foot, but without losing time. It lost just one step, which, in music, often killed the heartbeat rhythm that fans loved. But the great bands made it work somehow. Still, most didn't follow and couldn't tap their feet to it.

Just like Muddy wished.

One and two and three and four. Then again. One half-beat missing that threw off so much and left the listener hanging. Perfect for strong musicians to send a strong message.

The three things on the left never saw it coming.

He aimed and shot sharp tones to the left. Then to the right, and when the left one rose, he shot to the right once more, keeping him on track, away from the line of predators. The vibrations the guitar threw out knocked these primitive beings for a loop. They stood fooled and like he hoped, rooted to their spots.

More lined up, in the same pattern, the same rock pattern. Once more, he played the three-and-a-half-beat rhythm and careened safely through without any creatures touching the battered raft. If he kept it up, safety had to be around the corner. Hopefully.

For the next minute or so, he played his heart out and though several of those things almost caught on and learned, he avoided the maws and teeth. Just in time for him to hit the end of the tunnel that had emerged without warning. The wall appeared out of nowhere and with the swift current, he slammed into it at full speed.

It knocked him out completely.

He didn't even manage a cry before blackness claimed him. As he faded, he felt his body being pulled under. *This was what it was like to drown,* he thought. *Mom couldn't be far away now.*

Chapter Forty-Three

In the dark, Muddy saw her. His mother, six months removed from the cancer, and his father and Zack. His father coped by diving into his books; Muddy had his music and Zack. Well, Zack swam deep with his drugs, music, girls, and anything else that would hide him from the pain.

Muddy was in the water but drowning in it. Until this happened, he'd never believed in what would happen after death. He believed his mother went to a better place, even Heaven as many of his family and friends said, but still, he didn't believe in it for himself. Maybe it happened for only those who were pure or had suffered enough. Now he was there and feared he would never see his father again.

Or Poe.

He could handle the rest as they would live happy lives, but he knew Poe had so little to look forward to, other than the band. Even though they all tried to protect her, he wanted to be the *one*. Her savior, even though he knew she'd saved him lately and was likely the strongest of the group.

He opened his eyes and saw nothing but black. Maybe there wasn't anything there after all. Maybe he didn't deserve anything.

Edgar.

Someone called to him.

Mom? I'm coming home. Even in death, that felt cheesy to say. But he meant it.

Edgar.

Yet, it didn't sound like his mother. Then who in the world was it?

He still floated towards it.

You must finish the journey. Finish the songs. Do what needs to be done.

Who?

Finish it the right way. Save him. Finish it.

Confusion rang through his being, whatever that was now, as he continued to float.

Edgar?

Another voice. Female. Was it his mom taking him away? A sudden pain leapt into his chest and tore into his heart.

Edgar!

Fire burned in his lungs as he breathed; first water then cold, pure air.

Chapter Forty-Four

"You're back."

Muddy forced his eyes open and knew he was alive. He wasn't sure if he should be happy or depressed that life still held him, though. Pain reminded him of life. His mother had shown him that no matter how much she tried to hide it, life was pain.

Until he looked into *her* eyes and realized it didn't hurt completely. "Poe?" He choked out more liquid. It tasted and smelled like a mixture of toilet water and the beach. "No. You're not dead too. Please tell me that."

Someone laughed.

"You moron," Poe cried in her typical dry humor. "Neither of us is dead, but we came pretty close. Can you sit up?"

He hacked up more water and looked around. He saw Otis, Corey, Lyra, Poe, and a body leaning against the wall he assumed was Luke.

"Is he dead?"

Lyra turned away. "No," she said, "but he needs help. He won't make it without medicine." He noticed the teen's face wasn't in great shape.

"Then let's go," Muddy said. He stumbled and fell as his legs remembered how to move. His gaze took in the cavernous room with massive amphitheater, a beach area where the River must have drained out, and beyond that, a lake with black water. Walls shot up in all directions, higher than he could see. An eye of light winked at him from somewhere near a ceiling that he couldn't make out just yet.

All around him lay busted up shacks. Buildings, maybe. He

thought he noticed more across the lake, planks and boards lying in odd positions, seemingly standing in the middle of darkness. "What's the deal here?"

Corey held up his shoulders, steadying him. "Look at you, fresh from the other side and ready to fight one more time."

"Isn't that what we're here for?" Still he felt woozy. Maybe he would until his brain and lungs had enough oxygen.

"Don't you want to know what happened to you?" Otis stood on his other side.

No, he didn't. None of it seemed real and it scared him that he'd almost died, especially since he didn't see his mom there.

But Poe turned him to the back wall where Luke sat. An opening like a drain hung about a story high. Water flowed from it in a steady stream.

"Remember Action Water Park?" Otis asked, laughing. "That place where the water slides are almost as deadly as the Jersey roads? Buddy, we were exploring this place and suddenly you came shooting out of there like a turn on turbo flush. It's a good thing the water was nearby. You skidded like a flat rock on a lake."

Corey still held him. "Yeah, otherwise, just like that park, you might have lost half your skin sliding over that beach."

He gazed downward. Sharp rocks and rough, hot sand covered the area leading to the lake. Wow.

"Lucky for me, too," the sax player said. "I was nearly something's lunch when little drummer boy and Luke pulled me out of the frying pan."

Otis chuckled. "Buddy, don't ever use that line again. You have no idea."

"What about you?" Muddy almost hugged Poe. "Where'd you wind up?"

She sighed. "Let's just say I won't be putting any Rolling Stones on Spotify for a few months."

"Or The Doors?" Otis elbowed her, making her wince.

Muddy turned back to the wall. "Is he okay?" He pointed at the male twin.

Otis' expression changed. "He nearly gave his life for me. We need to get him out of here, but he won't budge until we finish this."

"Then let's do it," Muddy replied. "It's not like we can leave. Not yet, anyway."

He gazed up at the eye of the cavern. "Has anyone figured this one out yet?"

They shook their heads then looked around the shore. This was nothing but a dark cavern, the biggest one yet. The lake stretched out from the shore into—nothing. When Muddy squinted, he could see an opening hundreds of feet high and out of reach. A vast wall with handholds existed for those with mountaineering skills. They had none. Besides, the climb would be brutal with an injured Luke.

"How?" He gauged the depth of the lake and the height of the opening.

Poe shrugged. "Maybe there's another way.

"You've seen these rooms. Those slaves were pretty smart."

They all seemed to be thinking the same thing.

"If they built all of this to help the Tritons, but also to build in a failsafe so that someone, like us, could sneak in and stop them, then they wouldn't be so dumb as to not take care of themselves. Would they?"

Poe spoke, her voice unsteady. "No, they wouldn't."

"What do you mean?" Corey asked, looking around.

"Hey!" Otis yelled. "Across the lake, I think I see something. It's a bunch of rocks. They lead upwards. I wonder..."

They all looked, except for Poe. True enough, starting halfway across the lake, blending in with the black water was a massive pile of boulders. They *could* climb. That couldn't be hard, could it?

A hissing sound emanated behind them, above them, beyond them.

"Sounds like steam," Muddy said.

"Anyone notice that you shot out of a river, but there's not much water in here?" Corey gazed at the lake. "Oh, no."

Lyra looked up, staring just below the eye. "Well, that explains the smoke we see sometimes over the mountain."

From several large openings below the eye-like opening high above, something now flowed. When it hit the lake, water turned to steam on contact.

"I'm tired of magma," Otis groaned. Luke echoed his pain behind the group.

"What?" Muddy was confused. "Magma? Like lava? Why?"

"I'll tell you some other time," he replied wearily, "when we're not going to be buried by melting rock."

Muddy looked at the cascade of black rocks. "Still, that looks like the way out. The lava isn't flowing over all of it. But, what's with the leftover shacks?" He pointed further along the shore, far from where he burst from the river.

Luke now stood. "I've heard," he breathed, obviously in pain, "that the slaves taken by the Tritons were the brightest we had in the city. Some were strong, but all of them were smart. But where did they go once they built this place? They had to live somewhere."

"Well, this isn't exactly the Hamptons," Otis said.

"Why are the buildings all busted up?" Muddy asked, looking around at the condition of the structures that might have once housed the slaves and wondering why Poe had been so quiet. He noticed her staring into the distance along the far shore. "Did they rebel?"

"Maybe because the Tritons didn't need them anymore," she said.

Luke continued. "One or two who supposedly escaped, according to my grandfather. He said something about a spell. The slaves said that the Tritons never needed replacement workers."

"What about when they died? With all those—things—in there, some had to die. And it had to take forever to construct. Some *had* to die."

"They did," Poe spoke again, her voice going flat.

"How do you know?

"Because they're still here—and obviously not thrilled we're here." Her hand shook as she pointed in a direction across the lake.

Muddy saw what she did. "Maybe just the opposite. Maybe they *are* thrilled we're here. Maybe we're lunch."

She turned to the band. "Now would be a good time to run."

Chapter Forty-Five

If there ever was such a thing as zombies, Muddy now believed. Whether or not that was what they were, didn't matter. About a hundred or so of the living dead emerged from the darkness of the far shores, all looking like they hadn't eaten in decades.

Lyra stood, stunned. "The slaves never did die," she said, her voice thin. "How did they survive all these years?"

Luke grabbed hold of his sister. "They didn't."

Forget the shambling, rambling creatures of the movies, Muddy thought. "Run," he said, "into the lake. Get to the rocks."

"But they're going to be flooded with lava and hot rocks in minutes," Lyra said.

"Great," Corey said. "Cooked or eaten sushi-style. What a way to go."

"Either way sucks," Otis said. "Isn't there another way?"

"Nope," Muddy said, thinking of what he'd learned when he was in the River. He had to finish this journey. Looking at Poe, he knew he had to make sure he returned with her. "We're going to do some building of our own. Everyone grab some wood and run like zombies are after us."

Corey chuckled, just for a second, before bolting for the other side with an armful of planks from the broken houses.

"Seriously? Zombies?" Otis kept looking back as he watched them gain ground. They were only a hundred yards off, if that, and running like the New York Jets—when they were good. "They're just so passé."

Muddy grabbed a few pieces of sturdy wood. "Tell *them* that. I think they believe they're still the 'in' thing."

Poe stopped at the base of the rocks, touching one and

pulling back her hand in pain. "It's already hot! Please tell me what you're planning."

For the first time in months, he smiled a confident smile. "Trust me. This goes all the way to—"

The horde hit the water in a cacophony of violent splashes. The first few rocks weren't too hot yet. The magma had streamed off to the left and right, thankfully. Much of it wouldn't hit their direct path until they reached close to the summit, if they lived that long.

All of them, even Luke, scrambled over the two-, three-, and four-foot high boulders. Luke's injuries didn't appear life-threatening to Muddy, but then again, neither had his mother's. It's what happened on the inside that mattered and after hearing what Otis said about the searing suit, he mused that some of the teen's organs could be steamed like a clam, ready to burst open and kill him if they weren't already in that state.

Once they'd climbed about twenty feet, they stopped to catch their breath and examine who'd chased them. Muddy felt sweat pouring into his eyes, dizzying his vision. Poe seemed to be affected as well.

Muddy, Poe, and Otis were avid fans of horror films, but hated zombies. Other than what Romero did with his *Living Dead* series and *The Walking Dead* show, they felt most shows had missed the boat. Zombies were a metaphor for society, Poe often said, about how people who followed others blindly, such as politicians, traditions, sports teams, and music. "Group think," she'd called it, and if she said it, the band knew she had researched it thoroughly.

Did this bunch below them blindly follow the Tritons? Did they believe in what they were told? Or did they just wish to save themselves or their families?

They numbered at least a hundred. At least the ones that he could see.

But were they really the undead or just slaves under some terrible spell? Muddy couldn't wait to find out. Yet if they retained some of their humanity, maybe beating the Tritons would cure them.

Slender bodies with an alabaster sheen on light gray flesh

clamored together, looking downright famished. Were they alive or just animated by some power of their keepers? They didn't shamble like the undead in the movies. They moved with purpose and strength. Their eyes stared up at Muddy with a hunger that appeared anything but lifeless. He imagined them slaving over all the rooms, all the booby traps the band had survived. Was it a labor of love, fear, or did they secretly hope for someone to enter their maze and defeat their makers? He wondered if it even mattered to them now. Maybe they thought no more. Maybe their souls had left them and all they wished for was for someone to feed them. He had a feeling he would never know.

One began to climb.

"Oh, no," Corey said. "Move. Now."

Otis was the first to scramble upwards to the next big rock. "Is this what they mean by the dead will rise?"

"Will you shut up!" Corey had little patience left for his buddy, but everyone knew it was stress talking.

Two more pale figures jumped on the rocks and began their ascent.

Someone screamed.

Muddy looked up and saw Lyra blowing on her hands. "It's too hot!" Her hands were red and obviously pained.

"Now we use the planks."

"Muddy?" Poe grabbed his arm. "It's just a song. You don't think you can honestly build this, do you?"

"What else can we do?" His voice came out stronger than he'd intended and immediately he regretted it. "What do I do? All I have left is the music."

"And us."

Of course, the band.

He turned to her and froze.

She wore an expression he couldn't understand. Then suddenly she leaned in and planted a kiss on the corner of his mouth. Just where he could be utterly confused. *Was that a kiss? Or just a peck?*

She smiled as she pulled away. "Maybe when we get back home, we could grab a movie."

His heart leaped with joy, but he didn't know how much he should read into it.

"Just—not a horror one, okay?"

One of the zombies below howled in a strained, dry-lunged voice.

Muddy really hated zombies. If he never read another book or saw another movie with them in it, he might die a happy guy. Well, not just yet.

"Grab the boards!" he yelled at Corey and Lyra. Each of them had taken a couple from the piles at the bottom. The sturdy ones, he hoped. He helped place the first one on the rock in front of them.

Otis looked at him with a curious grin. "We all going to stand on that one?" At about four feet long and about a foot wide, it would be tough.

"Shut your face and put down yours—right there."

They did, forming the second one. Corey nodded, got the gist of it and grabbed another of his. He laid it right on top of the rock above the others, jammed in the space between. All were careful not to touch the burning stones directly.

Muddy hoped it would hold their weight. He had no idea how long those houses below had been there or how much damage the heat had inflicted on the wood. He really hoped termites didn't live in caves. When he gazed up at the shining eye and saw it was still at least a hundred or so feet away, he felt his resolve waver but knew they could pull off his plan.

The good thing? The rocks appeared to become smaller as they climbed. There were fewer boulders, more stepping-size stones.

The bad? Another river had picked up steam. The magma river. It was about fifty feet away now and as he watched, he gauged it to be about thirty seconds away from them by the way it snaked downwards, mostly around the rocks, not *over* them. He hoped the planks would hold long enough for them to build a new step.

"Muddy!" Otis yelled. "Are you that much of a Led Zeppelin dork?"

He smiled at his friend. "Yes. Yes, I am."

"I thought these were stairs, but I couldn't bring myself to say it."

It truly was a stairway, but to where, Muddy didn't know. Somehow, he doubted it led to the place that band sang about.

"Let's move!"

They climbed on top of the first one and it held two planks without any problem. Each stood on that one before pulling up to the next without incident. Corey and Muddy took turns helping to lay down the subsequent planks.

"Hey," Muddy called to Lyra and Poe. "Can you grab the one we just left?"

"Remove the stair?" They looked at each other. "Why?"

He simply pointed upward. "It's a long way to the top."

Otis sang the rest of the line. "Wrong song, but nice try."

"And I do want to rock and roll some zombie butt," Poe said, reaching behind her. Without removing each one they used, they would have needed well over a hundred planks, far more than they could carry. They built it, stair by stair, but the zombies climbed steadily behind them, the lava creeping down from above.

It was working, but one misstep and they'd be burned to a crisp or eaten—or both.

"Build!" Muddy felt like a slave driver, maybe like the ones these zombies had once, but at this point, he didn't care. It was fight or die. He stepped up three sturdy stairs, each lodged or balanced just enough on the hot rocks. Corey went first to help pull up the others. Muddy brought up the rear and helped Lyra pick up the wood. His fingers began to heat up big time underneath the planks as the rocks all around began to steam.

"No more!"

Who was that? Muddy looked up to see Luke stumbling on a stair in a wounded dance, struggling to get away from the embrace of Poe and Otis. "No more fire!"

His sister rushed to him and helped him up the last stair. "Sh-h-h... There won't be any more fire. I promise. You'll be okay."

Muddy doubted she truly believed that, but she had little choice. Family came first.

Poe grabbed hold of Luke and whispered in his ear. Maybe it was piece of a song. It caused his eyes to focus through the blisters surrounding them. He nodded to her and leaned down to grab a board.

Muddy thought, *that girl has power over every guy*. He smiled, wondering if he'd ever get a *real* kiss from her. He picked up the last two stairs, both smoking. Suddenly, a gray-white hand clasped bony fingers onto his. A strong one. He didn't scream. He couldn't scare the others. "Hurry," was all he managed to say in a hoarse whisper. Another hand reached over the top and pulled at his foot. A harsh stench invaded his nostrils. Now he felt the need to let loose. "Corey!"

More hands yanked at him, pulling him off balance. He looked down, fifty feet or more over the steaming rocks to the shallow lake below. The writhing bodies flowed much deeper. If he fell beneath their surface, their current would do much more than drown him.

"Corey!"

More hands grabbed at him, this time from above. He howled again.

"Gotcha, big guy," said the sax man. "We got ya."

Muddy pulled loose from the mottled hands that tried to pull him down and skittered up to the next stair, right before a board swung before his eyes and with a sickening thump, hit the zombie in the lead. It toppled backward, sinking into the sea of gray.

Dominoes? Muddy hoped they would all fall backwards, but it only knocked over a trio of them. Still, it was enough for him and Corey to catch up to the others.

"Faster!" someone cried. The clunk of the boards hitting together nearly drowned out the howling from below.

A stair was lowered, and they climbed two more steps. Corey brought up the rear, ready to swing again. He pulled up two more planks and passed them on. Muddy held one in his hand as it crumbled. Underneath, it was totally black. Burned. Another body blocked his view. It held a solid slab of wood.

Reddened hands swung at the horde.

Luke?

Muddy wished Poe could sing another song for Luke. One that would heal *her,* so she'd never hurt again. If she could sing just a few notes for the twin, to rescue him from the experience of whatever he'd encountered, maybe she could help herself. If not, he'd still be there for her.

The lava stream had turned their way and sped up. There were only about ten more steps and they'd reach the eye. A ledge jutted out from the opening and sloped down. Underneath, magma flowed from a trio of holes.

How could they pass over those without getting burned?

"Muddy!" Poe called to him. The lava stream had cut them off from the next stair by a good three feet. Steam rose up and blinded him.

Could they jump it? Would the steam burn them too much?

He counted the boards the group had in their possession. Most were still in decent shape.

"Muddy!" Corey yelled from two stairs below. Multiple hands had him in their grasp.

Lyra and Poe jumped down each with a board in their hands and began swinging away. One by one, the zombie things fell away. It took a few hits before they relinquished their hold. Muddy noticed that some looked past the group and into the eye. Could they be desperate to escape, too? Or did they just want the lot of them to join their legion?

The girls swung at the zombies until Corey was free enough to join the batting practice. As hard as they swung, the more they knocked off the tower of bodies, the more the zombies came, as steady as the lava. Fear skittered along Muddy's arms and down his back. Had it come to this, to escape drowning—twice—only to die this way? He couldn't bear the thought that his friends could die and yet it seemed they might all perish from fire or gnashing teeth.

From above, Otis called. "Boss, you ready?"

What? Boss? "Otis?" Confusion washed over him. "What are you talking about? We're dying here."

"Not yet, bud!" The slam of wood against rock with the hiss

of steam called out to his ears. "Now get your butts up here and fast! Hurry!"

Corey, Lyra, and Muddy turned tail and moved fast, climbing the remaining stairs to where Otis stood, smiling.

He had laid each plank across the gap, two layers deep. They just barely covered the flow of liquid rock. Solid, but the fire riding the magma was already touching them.

"Move. This wood will be ash in about a minute."

Thank you, Muddy mouthed. His friend just nodded.

Lyra went first to help Luke across, followed by Poe and Otis. Muddy and Corey brought up the rear as fingers grabbed at their heels.

One zombie had Corey's shoe and was opening its mouth to clamp its jaw on his ankle when the board it gripped snapped in half. The thing tumbled into the stream and melted in seconds.

"My shoe!" Corey just stood there, looking at his sock. "It ate my shoe!"

Shock? He punched his friend in the arm then pulled at him. "I'll buy you a fresh new pair when we get home, maybe even one that matches this time. Now, move!" The big guy slipped what remained of the shoe back on his foot and continued upwards.

They caught up to the others and saw that the eye stood only a body's length above them. The lava waterfall aimed at them was an illusion. It burst from the three holes, all right, but once it had cleared the gap, a path showed itself to be safe for those who dared to come this far.

We made it! Muddy screamed inside. But the zombies pushed onwards. They knocked each other into the gap and stood on top of their own to get across.

"Lift!" Corey didn't need a second direction. All of them jumped to reach the upper edge of the ledge and began pulling themselves up onto it. The girls went first again, but Poe flashed a stake of wood, ready to protect and stab anything that might be up there waiting. Lyra pulled Luke and Otis onto the ledge.

Finally, Muddy and Corey jumped, and even though fire burned in the guitarist's biceps, he managed to pull himself up. He'd made it. Both of them did. They rolled onto the ledge proper and away from the probing hands. Oddly, many of the creatures had begun backing down. Maybe they simply realized they couldn't reach their prey or escape.

"Are we done?" Poe finally broke down. "This is worse than being at home," she cried. "It never ends."

Muddy took her in his own shaking arms and held her. "No, it's not that bad. We're all here. We've made it. Look."

Chapter Forty-Six

They peered into the eye and saw a sheer glass plate with a pictograph of the gauntlet they'd just passed etched into it in a massive circle. Had they gone in a circle? No way, it depicted ups-and-downs and the crazed subterranean floors where they began.

"Look," Corey said. He moved his hand over the map of places they'd passed, with the songs from Aerosmith, Rolling Stones, Black Sabbath, Springsteen, Rush, and now Led Zeppelin. Outside, the ring showed the ocean of the sirens with the Deep Purple song.

What in the world? Was this planned? How? Did the slaves know this would be the way in? Out? How did these songs happen to be picked— were they the most dangerous ones the workers could find?

"Wow," Otis mused. "Rock radio will never sound the same to me again."

Poe backed away. "Guys, I don't think I can sing any of these after today."

"Now what?" Lyra peered into the picture and although she had likely met the writers of the tunes inscribed on the wall, she acted like she didn't know what was coming next.

Suddenly, Muddy realized something. Someone or something had engineered this nightmare, knowing they'd keep going to save his brother. His mind went cold as he backed up.

"What are you doing?" He didn't even process who had said it. He barely heard the words.

He knew. They knew. They always knew. But, why? With

a deep breath, he steeled himself and launched forward at full throttle.

He dove straight through the map, hands and head first, sounding the final note of the blues scale of the deadly path they chose. The sheer surface exploded in near silence as he broke it into myriad pieces. That note reverberated throughout him, sending a shockwave through his bones that allowed a flow of energy back into him. He tumbled down a slight slope, or embankment, and rolled to a halt, feeling like he could take down anything in this world.

He heard his name called and someone else telling the others to come on, that it was safe—in *his* voice.

But his mouth already hung open. In silence.

Who spoke in his voice? He turned to warn the others, but knew they'd already heard his call. He sensed the others sliding down to meet him. It didn't matter much now. Nothing really did. Only finishing this job did; right here, right now, and not stopping until he led everyone out alive.

"We've been waiting," they said.

"It was a little tiring, watching you fight through all those trials, but you made it."

"Now you can play your last song for us."

He tried to say something, but fear smothered his voice.

"Death is by far the prettiest song we've ever heard," came one discordant voice.

"Always was," sounded another in dissonance.

"Always will be," finished the third.

"Welcome to the tower of the Dark Muse."

Chapter Forty-Seven

"Zack?"

"Hello, brother." But it wasn't Zack's voice. Not quite.

"Muddy," Poe said, "what's going on?" She and the others gathered next to him after emerging from the slide.

As his knees buckled, he found a steadier voice. "I'm not sure, but I think we have one more song to play. A good one, I hope."

The three voices sounded as one. "As your last should be."

So that's what they look like. No wonder they're called the Tritons.

Muddy nearly wet himself. Each of them stood about eight feet tall. Three arms sprung from their middle section—their abdomens? They stood on three legs, three *long* legs which had several joints, just like a spider. But that wasn't what frightened him the most. It was their heads.

A triangular-shaped skull topped each of their dwarfed bodies, not in proper proportion. They appeared almost hammerhead-like, not unlike the aliens in so many science fiction movies. Eyes, they had a few. How many, Muddy couldn't tell as they were segmented, almost like that of a fly or spider. Yet those creatures didn't have the human focus that these things did. Every single eye stared into Muddy and the others. An evilness he had never felt before burned into his mind, emanating from the orbs on those massive heads.

The band's saving grace was the lack of crushing jaws or razor teeth they had faced earlier in their mission. Each open mouth sported a toothless opening, resembling the beak of a hawk rather than a shark.

That scared him more than any zombie or mouth creature ever could. Corey, Poe and Otis trembled with him. The twins stood frozen in their spots, but Luke had clearly seen death on its way and needed more help—soon. Still, the teen refused to give in to the moment.

As Muddy took in the entire Triton from head to three feet, he found himself shaking, despite his hatred for them and what they'd put his brother and friends through. Head, eyes, blade-like arms with something within them he couldn't discern. Their legs were smooth, muscular, and gleaming. They appeared sleek and powerful. He imagined the speed and dexterity they had. Escape would be futile, even if they could find a route to escape. Getting in was a horror; getting out was an even bigger nightmare to consider, so he didn't. Hopefully, the twins would help there. Yet he didn't come this far to run away. Instead, he took in the scene around him and saw a palace of sorts.

Paintings or etchings lined the walls of the odd, geometric-shaped room. Muddy recalled the word Corey used to describe the room with twelve equal sides. This one had more, and each section was a different size. He attempted to count the number of sides, but confusion blurred his focus as the high walls surrounded them in a silvery hue. The floor beneath their feet was comprised of thousands of triangular tiles, every single one a polished black.

Many openings spread above the Tritons' heads and Muddy knew, somehow, that they were now at the apex of the mountain. Even though he couldn't discern any glass or other material, Muddy felt no breeze. There should be some incoming wind, but the thin tapestries strung from the ceiling hung stagnant. He recalled the immense height of the peak they saw when they were miles away. There had to be a way down; one that wouldn't kill them.

He mentally catalogued the items around him, just in case. Windows, tapestries, images, Tritons—everything mattered. He swore each pictograph depicted a song that spun on every radio station, from various styles, from composers of many eras, each of them idolized in some way.

Hendrix and Elvis hung on one wall. Buddy Holly and Mozart hung on another. Janis Joplin, Randy Rhoads, John Coltrane, Robert Johnson and others smiled down from the one behind them. On the right side, John Lennon, George Harrison, Bon Scott, and Paul McCartney gazed in awe from lifelike life cells that looked like something between a painting and photograph.

"Whoa," Otis said. "I thought you only dealt in dead dudes here."

"All gave their innermost magic for the betterment of the River and more."

The drummer and Muddy looked at each other. They heard Poe chuckle and turned to see her smile, despite their situation.

"Um..." He looked at the beings attempting to frighten them. "McCartney's still kicking. You do know that, right?"

The three turned to each other slightly. Whispers fluttered, and limbs flitted that denoted some communication. "We were told otherwise."

Poe stood there, leaning ahead of Muddy. "I think he's even still touring. You might want to check your facts before immortalizing someone."

A sound brought him back to lock eyes with the center being. Fear splashed over him colder than the River which nearly claimed him.

It demanded his attention. All of theirs. Now.

Chapter Forty-Eight

"We'll give you a choice."

"I don't think so. Heard that already today," Otis said, his voice breaking. "We came to take Zack home. That's our *only* choice."

"Where is he?" Muddy struggled to keep his voice steady.

The three Tritons laughed in tones, a chord that pained all of them. The tritone in western music was an odd note halfway up the twelve-step scale. It was the "blue" note in the scale of the same name and sounded right in perspective. Yet these things sounded in pitches outside what humans were used to hearing. Their out-of-tune sounds and harmonic overtones drove mental spikes into each of the band member's ears. Muddy watched the light fade from Poe's eyes right before his legs gave out. The band dropped to their knees and blacked out as one. Muddy regained consciousness moments later, realizing something crucial had occurred in that small amount of time.

"Go ahead," spoke the one in the middle. "We were hoping you would take him, but we're not sure if he still wants to leave us."

"What's the price?"

No answer.

"Tell us!"

"Give us your music and leave. Or leave her here with us." They pointed at Poe, but Muddy already knew what they wanted. "And you."

"No!" He would give his life for the band—his friends, his family, but would never give up Poe, even if he died with her.

"Why?" Poe cried. "What do you need him for? Us? You

have the greatest minds in history coming through here all the time. We're just kids."

"But you have something they couldn't give us," said the trio in an augmented triad that sung in microtones. "Yes, you have something else."

Muddy rushed them, not knowing what they meant.

The trio turned together and struck a chord he wished he'd never heard. He crumbled and felt blood drip from his ears as darkness swirled around him.

Groggy, he fought back. Not now. Not again. He couldn't fail the band or his brother. He regained consciousness seconds later, his friends surrounding him.

The group faced the Tritons in a semi-circle. Even without instruments, Muddy knew they all felt the power of the River flowing within them. The power of the deepest, darkest currents.

"We want my brother," he said boldly. "You can keep me."

They laughed once more in that painful chord and he fell to his knees again. "Take him, if you can."

They gestured upwards to the right where Zack now lived.

Chapter Forty-Nine

They looked at Muddy's brother—and gasped.

Zack hung in a prism-like machine with metallic strings holding him up. Each string entered him from a different place in his arms, his legs, his chest. Others entered near his heart, neck, and skull. They had turned him into a living human instrument.

The structure rose up over twelve feet off the floor and stretched out at least six feet on either side of his torso. He resembled a flimsy Ferris wheel, scaffolding, or clock bred with the inner organs of a piano.

Corey whistled. "Geez, they turned him into a musical machine version of DaVinci's 'Vitruvian Man.' The perfect proportion."

Otis looked at him incredulously. "Seriously? Zack's up there and you're giving another history lesson?"

The bigger teen shook his head. "No, dorkus It was meant to show how man is the perfect proportion in architecture. It depicted the measurements of the universe's ideal design for many things."

The smaller boy snorted. "If only he lived to see how low humans have sunk since his time. Perfection, my bony—"

"I know, but look!" He pointed at Zack's face.

Zack's eyes were open and pleading with Muddy as they met each other's gaze. They spoke to Muddy, clear in their intent.

Help me. Or kill me.

A strange music emanated from the machine.

"Look what you've done to him!" Poe began to cry. "Is he still alive?"

"Yes," they replied in a diminished chord that kept the band in pain and off-guard. "He's growing stronger, just like he'd hoped. Like we'd hoped he would."

"But he looks like he's dying! He's a prisoner in there. You're no better than Hitler or Dr. Frankenstein!"

Did they just smile?

"Only his body," they said. "The strings, the machine will keep his energy, his music, alive. For us. For *it*. Unless you wish to take his place."

One of them unfurled an arm and plucked a string from Zack's side. It rang in a pitch-perfect tone. The harmonics echoed off every wall and sounded beautiful.

The other two joined in and began to play the Zack instrument, beautiful music emanating from his being, hooked up to their palace. He screamed with each note, songs of pain, and they thrived on it. The silver wires jutting into his flesh vibrated in macabre music. Each stood on a side of Muddy's brother, with one directly underneath and limbs churning like conductors teasing out a melody and harmony that sounded both sweet and bitter as notes radiated from all parts of him. Zack's face contorted in agony with each stroke. The quintet writhed on the floor, the power of the song paralyzing them in pain. "Join your brother. All of us would enjoy it. All." They elicited a pure song from Zack, his very essence.

This is our future, Muddy thought. The Tritons planning on either killing them all or milking them dry, as they did to his brother.

Poe stared, incredulous. She looked beyond Zack. "They really did expect us."

Four new empty harnesses hung on the walls.

Chapter Fifty

Corey pushed himself up, in pain but also in determination as he rushed the machine and its operators. He was immediately dropped by a slash of their arms and a piercing wail that pained him and friends. The sax player rolled on the floor in agony. A thin wound opened up across his chest.

"What do you want?" Muddy cried. "Why us?"

"We have the brother and the muse is strong in him, like the others who came before him. He wanted to stay, to learn; a mistake, that curiosity of his. He is weak, even though the music in him is strong."

"We can mold him our way. The others, the ones whose songs built the trials you passed, they would never enter our world. Not the way this boy did or like you did."

Muddy felt his entire world unravel inside his mind.

"*You* showed us the strength that we truly need. You're the stronger ones."

"Stay and he can go."

The eyes of the Tritons bored into each of the band members. "You're still pure, not sullied in spirit like the others had become." They gazed up at the images on the wall.

"Not all of them got hooked on the bad stuff," Corey said. "Some had been in accidents."

"Yes," one said, "'accidents.'"

What? No freaking way. Muddy's mind continued to spiral.

"They all came to the River pure as a spider's silk, but many couldn't resist the pull and compensated when not swimming in it. There are things in there which can kill a soul."

Muddy recalled how he nearly drowned in it. How he almost wanted to do so and leave his pain behind, but that wasn't really him, was it? What had it done to the legends who had visited and not leaned on drugs? Was it the pull of the River, or something worse?

"You haven't been tainted. That is what we need here. We thought we had solved the puzzle with your brother, and we still might. His soul runs deeper than we have only seen once or twice before. Maybe you can help him hold onto it."

Muddy's mind swirled in indecision. Could they? Or would they die either way?

He couldn't help but stare at their faces. Something human shone through the insect exterior. Were they always like this?

The Tritons continued their song and the band collapsed again. How could they win? As the song from the Zack-thing grew in intensity, so did the vibrations. The floor shook and somehow Muddy knew it wasn't just the bass notes. The entire mountain shook with the song, almost as if something lived beneath it and was fed by the song.

Muddy looked to each of his friends and saw confusion mixed with fear.

Another voice suddenly entered Muddy's head.

Don't give in. Those who do, agonize within them for all eternity.

Silver Eye? But how? Why? He turned to Poe then the others and knew they'd heard it as well.

Remember how you hear a song on the radio and it always seems to play, every day, without fail? You'll become something worse, a recording of this place—of them. We, as people will be gone, but the music in us will live on.

Definitely not!

Remember what you have within you. Don't give in.

Muddy hung his head. "Okay, you win."

"What?" The others echoed each other.

"What are you doing?" Poe's voice screamed as she rushed him. A force, something unseen, stopped her from reaching him.

"We'll give you our song—I will—but they leave, all of them, with Zack."

More laughter. "This isn't some romance ballad, boy." The tone of its voice shook him.

"I'm not kidding," Muddy continued. "Take me and leave them behind."

"You're nothing by yourself," said the left one. "We need you as a whole."

The right one spoke his turn. "Yes, the music as a collective is sweeter than any one voice ever could be. Solo efforts never measure up to the collective. Think of even the greatest musicians."

Muddy prayed the others heard the same song in their heads that he did. "You said we had a choice!"

Their eyes almost twinkled in a smile. "Did we?"

The band stood like tombstones, resigned to whatever fate befell them, but Muddy doubted any were surprised by the lies. Silver Eye had trained them, but really, he only awoke in them what he knew would already be there, which was why he allowed them to cross over. Their song was strong.

"Okay, but he lives. Our father needs him."

The rest of the band nodded their assent. They knew.

"Come up to the stage before you begin," said the middle one. "We need to hear it, feel it, as it flows from you."

Muddy flashed a smile that would have made any rock star proud. "You asked for it."

They reached for their instruments and found them missing.

Chapter Fifty-One

"What the?" Otis cried. "Where's my drum?"
"My guitar!"
"My sax!"
Another laugh sounded in triplicate. "In time."
Muddy knew before they spoke.

What about Luke? He'd betrayed all of them, standing off to the side, limping away from the group. Muddy felt the dream, his hope for their lives, drop to the smooth floor and shatter.

"Why?" His sister cried, balling her fists. "Why have you turned your back on us? You've suffered through all of this with us. You almost died to get here. They *saved* you!"

He hung his head. "I still might perish," he answered in a little voice. "When you were knocked out, they promised me that our village would be free, that we could finally enjoy our lives. I only had to guide them here." He shrugged. "These guys were coming here anyway. It was a small price to pay for our people."

"You did well, boy," said the middle Triton. "You did well."

Lyra looked for something to beat him with, her brother or the Triton, as she glared at them. Either would do. "As long as these *things* are alive, we'll never be free. You know that!"

Otis rushed at him, ready to swing. "You saved me. I saved you. That means something, doesn't it?"

The boy said nothing. He refused to meet any of their stares.

Lyra turned to see the instruments locked up tight in a quartz box behind Zack's machine. "You've just signed their death warrants. You do know that, you miserable weasel." Her voice dripped with poison.

"I thought you'd understand. This isn't life. Where they're from," Luke said as he waved at the band, *"that's* life. This is nothing but a prison. We're already dead; they just haven't buried us yet."

He turned to the others. "I'm sorry. I wanted the best for my people and I thought the Tritons would make you sing forever, not kill you. Honest."

The band seethed, everyone refusing to look at him. All through their lives, betrayal had been at the forefront. Now, just when they felt they could count on these two people, one turned his back on the bond. Muddy felt a tear form. He'd failed them.

Muddy fell against the wall, blocking out the song that pained him. The gauntlet had been an elaborate set up to test them. If they died, it would have meant that they didn't have the music in them. End of story. Or were the Tritons lying just to throw them off? Had the Tritons really won, and this was just the final test?

"What's your game?" He yelled at them. "To have us join Zack? What then? Take over our world?"

The Tritons didn't even flinch. "No, we just want to bring music into this one and conquer one or two others for the *other*. It's a vast world, parallel to yours with many kingdoms, many mountains. We want more. We want to control all the music. We all do. It's what this place was built for; to help those who make the music, to harness it all."

"You keep saying 'them' and 'others.'" His head spun as he formulated the plan he prayed would work. "Who are *they*?"

Wait, he thought. *If they could travel to our world, they would have done so already. They can't cross over, not without Zack's power, but they might be able to soon.*

They ignored his question but answered another. "Haven't you figured it out, yet? You came even though the old man warned you of what you might find here. Your brother has become the darkest muse of them all. We just helped him realize it."

Muddy looked at his brother's eyes and saw little remaining of the boy he used to play baseball with and jam with, but still, something familiar existed. He needed to save Zack.

"Now listen and please, take your places." They gestured to the harnesses.

The song they played on Zack sounded like a mash-up of Bach and Mozart crossed with Def Leppard and Metallica. It was beautiful, complicated, but with the power of a thousand electric guitars though a wall of amplifiers. As the song intensified, Muddy felt it penetrate his bones.

His brother's expressed surpassed total agony. His mouth hung open in a silent scream.

"Think of your lives here," said the first. "No more pain from society. None. You would always fit in here. Your song would feed nations and bring them happiness."

One placed its spindly arm on Corey. "Boy, you came from nothing and moved into everything, but you still felt an emptiness nothing can fill. Until you came here."

Another placed one of its long arms on Poe's head. She recoiled in revulsion.

"You, dear," said the creature, its finger-things lifting her hair. "We have sensed from your first trip here, the pain you feel, the most of all in your group. A father should be a father, not a monster."

"So says a monster," she said with tears in her eyes. The music from Zack was killing their resolve.

"You can escape it all here and make scores of children smile in the way your parents couldn't."

The third hovered over Otis. "Son, you have nothing back home."

Although he writhed in pain, he turned his head to glare at their captors. "I have more than you ever will. I have my family and friends."

"They will stay with you until the end of your life, but you know it's not far off if you go back. Here you would never fade, never hurt again. Ever."

Lyra was next. She still tore her brother apart with the fire in her eyes as he sat next to the captive instruments. "Your people have never known freedom. Your village will be spared if you cooperate, but they'll be vaporized if your brother doesn't honor his agreement with us. We have no use for you, so please don't stand in our way."

Finally, they came to Muddy. "Your brother was always the golden child. You know that. Without your mother, your father and Zack have withered into themselves, leaving you, the child with needs they couldn't address, to be neglected."

He felt his fists curl, aching for the guitar. No. They wouldn't rattle him or cause him to sell out all that mattered to him.

"Here you will never be picked on, never be the low man. Alongside your brother, if you wish, you can rule the music and be adored by many worlds."

Again, the voice whispered in his head. *You know the truth. You came here for a reason, for a task you knew you could accomplish. Now save your brother, my son.*

His anger boiled over and he kicked his left leg high, right into the joint where the Triton's knee should've been. Yet it didn't flinch, and Muddy bounced off, falling.

But his assault did have the effect he wished.

Chapter Fifty-Two

A ll three turned to laugh at the teen on the floor.

Lyra winked at Muddy and attacked Luke—hurtling herself into him, sending him towards the windows. As they tussled on the precipice in front of the window, they rolled into the pedestal which contained the band's tools in the clear case. It shook and teetered.

"I tried!" Luke screamed, pushing her off him. "When Zack first came to the village, I warned him, told him to go back home if he wanted to live, but he didn't listen."

"Liar!"

"No," he said, pinning her as she still kicked into the pedestal. "The prophecy. We've been told all along that someone would come to set us free. To give us the music that we see the visitors come for, and leave with, as we are left with nothing, time and time again.

"Someone was coming. I knew it and they found me in the forest. It was either them or the village. I didn't know them!"

"But now you do!" She rolled him into the pedestal, toppling to the floor in a shattering crash. The instruments scattered across the black floor.

"That boy, Muddy's brother, he never had a chance. He was clouded, they said, and I saw it too. He wanted to accept their power. He wished for power, for answers and would die if he stayed his course." Lyra skittered out of the way as the band grabbed their instruments. "But these guys stayed their course and now you'll probably not survive because of it."

Luke crawled toward the window and shuddered. "I just wanted to save us."

"And kill these people? You knew you shouldn't trust these…things!"

He cried. "I didn't know! I did it for us."

Silver Eye's voice echoed again in their heads. *Now! Play the music that makes the earth move!*

Each slung the instrument he had given them and played the song that had been in their heads since the moment the old man's ghost sang it to them the previous night.

This is your song, the one you played the first time we crossed over. I just helped pull it from your souls.

"It worked once before," Muddy said, to both the band and to their mentor, thinking of the melody and rhythms they wrote for Poe to escape her father.

"Ready?" Poe cued the band.

They stood on the stage before Zack, facing off against him, just like they would back home in a Battle of the Bands. It was simple, except that this one might end in the snuffing out of someone's life.

"You can't!" The Tritons screamed at once. "We're offering you what you can never have back home. Stop now and you can still live."

"I'm through with threats," she said and nodded to Otis, who slammed his sticks into the edge of the rim on his drum to begin the song.

Muddy hoped that their instinct was dead on, the blues rock fire opus they planned to one day win the Battle of the Bands with back in their real world. He hoped its off-beat, up-tempo blues-rock would keep the creatures off guard just long enough to finish their mission. He churned out the earthy riff, something he'd come up with while listening to his buddies jamming as they waited for Poe to join them. Born of worry for her, it carried with it an emotional weight he doubted these Tritons had ever experienced. Otis laid down the groove under Muddy and Corey added a line that functioned as a bass before snaking into other lands.

Luke had passed on his chance to be the bassist here. Muddy didn't need him.

The song rocked, tearing into the fabric of who they were. It embodied the songs they'd survived that day.

As the creatures roiled in confusion and terror, something nobody was expecting, Lyra rose again and gestured for Corey to move toward her. In a smooth motion, after he finished his line, they threw themselves linebacker-style into the structure of the man-instrument on either side. It shook. Zack's eyes flittered open and his song halted in an instant.

As his music stopped, the others grew in volume. The rest of the band appeared to double their intensity and come to life as the Tritons slowed their movements.

The metal and wire structure wobbled back and forth, tipping more each way. The Zack-instrument in the middle struggled. Did the teen wish to get out to protect himself or to continue the song?

Muddy tried to keep himself in the song, pushing himself harder, but also wished to help his brother, hoping that thing confining him didn't crush him.

As if on cue, Lyra and Corey hit it again, harder and up a little higher. It rocked further, once, twice and on the third time, she reached onto the edge and jumped up on it.

It fell like a musical tree into the wall next to the window with a massive, discordant crash. The tones it emitted when it broke nearly halted the band, but Muddy and Otis were locked in tight. Poe was no longer of this dimension as she sung with sweet pain her lyrics and melody.

Corey stepped up and launched into his solo, giving birth to deep, rich tones that killed off the reverberations of the Zack-thing as the boy collapsed in the harness, still strung tight by the myriad strings embedded in his skin.

He lay still while the creatures gathered around him, inching further from the band.

The band became one again and turned up the heat on the Tritons as they simultaneously lost themselves in the music.

Somewhere in Muddy's mind, he understood Hendrix, Vaughan, Page, Lennon, and the others. The feel of the music was beyond intoxicating. Nothing he could imagine would ever match the intensity of the feeling, but many had tried. Some did it with more songs and playing. Others turned to booze and drugs, like Zack, adding pain to his equation.

Muddy hurt just as bad over their mom's death. Plus, he'd had to endure much more in school and his future didn't seem as bright as his dad's or his brother's, but he wouldn't let himself wallow. He was nowhere near the strength he wished to be, but the band helped a lot.

What happened next helped him even more.

Chapter Fifty-Three

The Tritons skittered around like roaches caught in the light. Without their song, they appeared lost and without protection. Up and down the walls and across the floor they ran, everywhere except where the music emanated. They screamed. "You can't destroy us!" Their dissonant voices displayed fear and anything but confidence. "If you destroy our bodies, true power will find you. Those who live below the River will know."

"What?" Muddy almost stopped until he realized they'd nearly killed his brother. It was a ruse. *Keep up the song,* a voice from within urged.

"We are only a conduit for those who lie beneath. They have always been here and always will."

As Poe sang the last note and appeared to glow with power, back-to-back with Corey as Otis performed his rock star ending, Muddy held tight onto his final chord and let it ring.

"What lies beneath? Beneath what?"

"The River. We have powers you can't imagine and live in places no beings like you could ever survive, because of them."

"It wasn't *you,*" Poe said. "It was the River who guided us. It wanted us to get here, to keep things pure." She stood up to their towering height as they still shook from the reverberations of the song. "*Not* by you. It was the *River.*"

As the trio cowered, they appeared to shrink a little and said, "The River is power, but it doesn't choose. It doesn't love or hate. Our father, who lives beneath it, does and we feel his desires now. He wants you to die."

Muddy suddenly remembered something about his father's name. He'd changed it long ago. Right after he'd sold his first book. Why? Had he come here too? Had he recited a poem or story at the crossroads for the door to open? He never knew his dad's real last name, but he kind of wondered if it mattered now. He was part of this place just like his father. The River was part of their family, as it was for so many others, but if something horrible did live beneath, they could never leave family behind.

"You can't just leave," said the trio. Were they regaining their strength so soon? "We won't—and *it* won't let you."

Lyra stood up with Luke, who looked like he had just realized he'd lost his puppy.

"You said you're part of the power," she stated, "of those who live beneath."

"What do you mean, girl?"

Lyra turned to Muddy, mouthing a goodbye before kissing Corey on the cheek and winking. "We'll meet again. I promise."

She threw herself at the Triton closest to her and hugged his three arms so he couldn't raise them or right himself. They both screamed as they tumbled out the window. Right before they fell, Muddy noticed a coil of something in her hand. Before he could cry out they were gone, but he knew she would survive, somehow.

The other two stumbled, weakened. Broken from the whole, their power lessened. The Accidental's song had worked.

Luke screamed for his sister in a howl that didn't sound human. He turned to the others and cried, "I'm sorry," to anyone who was listening. He powered his sturdy frame into the other two and in their awkward, weakened state, caused them to crash into each other and slam against the wall with him. Then, in one swift move, like a cowboy at an otherworldly rodeo, he wrapped them with a coppery wire. He pulled them both through the middle window behind Zack's device. With nary a sound, all three bodies fell out of the window to the rocky shores far below. Muddy noticed that Luke had the wire attached to himself like his sister did.

"Holy..." Otis mouthed. "What was that?" He ran to the window and looked down. "I can't even see the bottom. We must be over a thousand feet high."

"At least," Corey agreed, a tear forming in his eye. "She did promise, though, didn't she?"

Poe hugged him and whispered, "Of course she did. She's not a stupid girl."

Chapter Fifty-Four

Muddy rushed to his brother and unfastened the wires jutting into Zack's flesh. Most of them simply pierced him by less than an inch. After carefully pulling a few out, Zack's fist suddenly tightened around Muddy's. Zack turned his taut, pained face to the others and spoke the words that would haunt his brother for years.

"I *am* the Dark Muse," he said in a hoarse voice. "The *new* one, anyway. Don't you get it? I belong here. I belong to the River, to them. They made me." He gestured downwards with a shaky hand.

"How could you want that?" Muddy stuttered the words. "They're monsters. They only want to use you. Besides, they're gone."

"Not them," he said, shaking his head. "Not them. I'm talking about something much, much more than they ever could be."

"What?" Muddy pulled away at more of the strings.

Zack began to slip but fought his brother to remain in the harness. "I *can't* go home. They own me." His voice rang hoarse, but with spirit. "I can be someone here. I can be their power. These people don't have the music. They need someone to show them." His head bowed. "They make it all happen."

"What? Who are *they*?"

Instead of answering, Zack crumbled into near unconsciousness and became Muddy's brother once again.

"Do we take him back or not?" Otis leaned over him as they all helped remove the wires.

Muddy grabbed Zack by the shirt. "You've got to be kidding. After all this?"

Poe and Corey helped Muddy lay the teen flat on the floor as he slept.

"We have to," Poe said. "He's family."

"But he said he wanted to stay."

Muddy erupted again. "He was under their influence. It's like a drug, but worse. We need to get him back home."

They looked at each other and even Otis nodded. "I'm sorry, bro. I'm just worried about something else following behind us and ruining our world."

"What about Lyra?" Corey asked, looking at the window.

Otis laid his hand on the big teen's shoulder. "She promised to see us again."

"But she's not music, like we are. How can she?"

Poe looked at him. "I guess we'll have to visit. Maybe she'll come back with us if this place doesn't improve."

"Think she will?"

She smiled. "Someone's got a crush. Yeah, I think she would, if only to visit."

"Let's get out of here." Muddy stood up and turned to the others. "Zack needs to see a doctor or something."

"Is that smart?" Otis asked. "They might ask questions."

"He's my brother. I have no choice. Besides, it's not like anyone would believe him. They'd think his story was crazy."

Poe paled just a bit. "But what do we do about that *thing*? That thing we let in that ruined Emerson Street? People will be asking questions about that."

Muddy grinned as he propped up his brother, wrapping his arms around Zack's, the guitar underneath both. "Two things. One, we remember to lock the door tight this time. We just might be able to get back there *before* that happened. Those people will live this time. And two, we're The Accidentals. People might not think we're important yet—but they will, someday."

Chapter Fifty-Five

"How are we going to we transport him back home? The crossroads are too far for us to carry him. We'll never make it. Besides, how do we get out of here? I won't go back the way we came."

Muddy smiled as he remembered Silver Eye's words. "There are many crossroads, all over the world and beyond." He looked down at his feet and saw that the Triton's inner sanctum *was* a crossroads. The "X" forged in the center of their lair in deep, carved lines was likely designed to reach into other worlds, other dimensions, even if they didn't have their own music to get there. "Finally," he announced to the others, gathering them together, "we've got ourselves a simple task."

They returned to their world playing the same song that brought them there, the song that Silver Eye taught them, the same one that automatically locked the door behind them.

As they shimmered out of sight, Muddy wondered when they would experience anything like this again. He had a feeling it might be before they were ready for it.

This world had more dark secrets than they had time for; ones that now placed bullseyes on each of them and would likely come to collect sooner than later.

He hoped the music would be enough the next time.

Chapter Fifty-Six

They returned home via the crossroads, complete with Zack in tow. They were worried he wouldn't cross over if he wasn't playing, but the music in him was too strong. Muddy placed Zack's pick in his palm then closed his hand. It worked. All crossed over and no one drowned.

However, Zack's condition worsened upon arrival. His breathing became erratic and he kept muttering to himself about nightmarish things none of them could decipher. Poe dug up their cell phones from the pile of tires where she'd hidden them. Of course, the group didn't expect to need them after their first journey and doubted cell towers even existed there. She called 911 and Muddy's dad immediately.

The paramedics brought Zack to intensive care where he lay comatose with undiagnosed symptoms. Of course, most everyone suspected drugs. Toxicology tests confirmed some still lingered in his system. But nobody at the hospital knew the real reason and those who did know wouldn't tell.

When Muddy returned home with Zack, his father knew. That look in the man's eyes told him everything; the novelist hadn't been the only traveler in the family. They talked for the first time since his mother had died, really talked. He told Muddy why he had changed the family name and called him Muddy for once, instead of Edgar, the legal name he had given the teen.

During the week following their return from the world across the River, life happened in a quiet manner. Every one of them needed it. The cops had called in some specialists from the

Environmental Protection Agency to investigate the worm invasion; a block-long insect that suddenly appeared downtown and caused a media sensation, especially in New Jersey. People all over the area believed that pollution or radiation had caused the mutation. Others felt that offshore drilling and messing with the shorelines had disrupted the earth's crust and allowed a subterranean creature to crawl on land. It made the bully of a governor look like even more of an idiot clown, but people just laughed at him, as always. Obviously, Carter Hills had to deal with two invertebrates that week. Soon, the buzz would die off and life would go back to normal. Well, sort of; not for the band, anyway, or the Brooks family.

Muddy's prediction about getting there in time to save the people from the creature wasn't warranted. When Otis had attacked it, apparently the beast had regurgitated them. All were fine, uninjured, but aching to sue the town for the pollution that likely caused the event. Yet since nobody could find the creature, people would soon get back to their lives.

The other positive thing that happened was the postponement of the Battle of the Bands for a week. It provided a much-needed respite for the group to recuperate and recover mentally, as much as reality permitted, anyway.

Poe moved in with Otis's family, at least temporarily. She had undergone the most change. Even though her vision faded again, it *had* improved enough to see plenty of things that would help her in life. The power she had touched over there had lingered just enough to improve her life back home. Most importantly, she now saw she had no future if she remained home. Her father attempted to quell her rebellion, but a few concerned calls to social services got the police involved and that forced him to leave her alone. She would be fine, eventually.

Muddy hoped he had garnered enough strength to ask her out. He'd faced zombies, giant worms, egomaniac hammerhead-spider creatures, and saved his own brother from a force he never discovered. Yet asking this girl to accompany him to a silly dance frightened him more than all the above combined.

Otis's sense of humor mellowed a little, which frightened Muddy. He had become subdued, focused. No one could figure where his focus was, but it worried them all. Poe heard him mumbling in his sleep one night about living forever. She said she could make out words such as "Rhapsody," "Reaper," and "Revolution." He would then awaken smiling and at peace. When he rehearsed for the Battle of the Bands, he played like a machine, but one with a soul possessed by a mission.

The only one who didn't benefit from the return was Corey. He walked to school in silence, only providing one-word responses to questions or comments from his friends.

"She's alive," Poe offered, holding his arm. "She wouldn't end her life like that, not with her town in need. Not with you waiting."

Still, he was focused on something only he could see, possibly something he would never see again. They worried about both him and Otis crossing back over without the others. Corey lost another friend, perhaps reminding him of his cousin. Death never became easy. When he played, a mournful tone filled the air, adding a midnight tinge to whatever song the band played. Muddy hoped it would help him recover.

Maybe one day, they would find Lyra once again.

They all struggled with the loss of Silver Eye, none more than Muddy. He couldn't get the image of the bluesman drifting away from him when they were deep in the River. The guitarist knew it was absurd, but he knew in his heart the two would meet again.

Chapter Fifty-Seven

"They're gonna kill us."

"Relax," Otis said, "relax. We have this one in the bag. They can't touch us because we're tougher this time, don't you think?" Even his voice sounded different. More confident.

Muddy stroked the first note of the song, the same one that helped them escape from the Triton's lair.

"Still," the drummer said, ready to hit the first rhythm. "A set of all covers is safe. I think we *deserve* safe for a week or two, don't you?"

All nodded except Corey, who simply gripped his sax as if it were alive. They knew he needed that right then, at least until they crossed back over—if they ever did.

His friends smiled, probably agreeing with him. This was the battle they had been waiting for. The only real competition would be Bentley's band—again. They had a set of all covers, plus one original, just like The Accidentals. They also had the support of over half of the school.

For once, Muddy and the band didn't care. They wanted only to play their best. They knew they belonged. Nobody could ever take that away from them.

Now, as they stared out into the throngs of smiling faces, they played through the song, almost as sweet as in the Triton's main chamber. Muddy struck gold on the solo, as did Corey, and actual cheers erupted from parts of the auditorium. As the coda rolled though the song, bringing their thrill to an end, Muddy felt his gut tighten. Something wasn't right. It wouldn't be for a while.

The song ended and a new one began. Muddy figured that Bentley's band would still win, but things had changed. Everyone in the band had changed or found their strengths, their true selves that had been struggling to emerge since before the crossroads. The applause drowned out the other sounds, the ones from outside the school.

Muddy gripped his guitar tighter. His smile grew despite the apprehension gnawing at him. His mother always said that while his father had the stories, the imagination, her Edgar had the intuition that would take him far in life. His cell buzzed in his jeans and he ignored it. He knew that whatever it was, he would be finding out soon, anyway.

The band had agreed to launch into their final song, a cover of a Guns N' Roses tune, but they hadn't decided which one yet. "Paradise City" and "Sweet Child O' Mine" were two of Poe's favorites to sing.

Suddenly, the doors to the auditorium burst open—*off the hinges* open. People scattered everywhere, and the power blew. Moments later, as the generators kicked in and the lights came back on, the band and most everyone in the audience turned to the source of the explosion.

Muddy's brother, the Dark Muse, stood at the entrance.

Chapter Fifty-Eight

Muddy didn't need to look at his phone now; he was sure it had been his father, calling to warn him.

The boy Muddy stared at had changed. The coma had been a part of that. The attachment to that machine drawing the music from him had let something in, something from deep down in that other place. Something that lived beneath the River.

"Hello, Muddy."

"Hello, Zack." He looked much older, weathered, than the brother Muddy knew just a week ago. He wore a leather coat that covered much of his body, especially his face. The rest of the world disappeared as Muddy took in the scene and what it might mean to him.

"Thanks for bringing me where I should be."

The knot touched his heart as he mouthed the words his brother now spoke. The auditorium's lights went out and a darkness the world had never known lit up the room.

"They knew you would."

"They always knew."

For the briefest moment, Zack's eyes changed. "Help me," he pleaded, before clouding over again.

Muddy grabbed hold of his guitar. The song would not remain the same.

Somewhere in the distance, he heard the sound of a harmonica.

This time, his song would win.

About the Author

David Simms lives in the Shenandoah Valley of Virginia with his wife, son, and animals. He works as a teacher, counselor, music therapist, ghost tour guide, book reviewer, and occasional guitarist in the Slushpile band. He is the author of *Dark Muse* and *Fear The Reaper.*

Curious about other Crossroad Press books?
Stop by our site:
http://store.crossroadpress.com
We offer quality writing
in digital, audio, and print formats.